DUPLICITY

DUPLICITY

BOOK SEVEN IN THE ON THE RUN
INTERNATIONAL MYSTERIES

SARA ROSETT

DUPLICITY
Book Seven in the On the Run International Mysteries series
Published by McGuffin Ink
Copyright © 2020 by Sara Rosett
First Paperback Edition: April 2020
ISBN: 978-1-950054-23-7

❀ Created with Vellum

1

Zoe
April, Present day

Harrington Throckmorton's posh British tones came through Zoe's cell phone. "I'm preparing a parcel for you. If you want it, that is."

"Oh, I love getting packages in the mail." Zoe grabbed a notepad. "What would be in it?" Zoe hitched the barstool closer to her laptop on the kitchen island, which functioned as her desk during the day. Sticky notes, printouts, and files surrounded her computer.

"Paperwork," Harrington said. "I'm afraid you may find this case rather boring. It's filling in a gap in a painting's provenance."

Zoe had worked for Harrington for a couple of years now as a consultant and enjoyed hunting down lost valuables for his company, Throckmorton Enquiries. Besides locating missing items—usually of the pricey variety—Harrington's company also provided background research on valuables. A painting's worth could increase substantially if an unbroken chain of ownership could be tracked from the creation of the work to its present owner. Tracing provenance often involved tedious examination of sales invoices and auction catalog listings, but Zoe wasn't one to shy away from detail work. In the past she'd worked as a freelance copy editor and was accustomed to focusing on tiny details.

Zoe eyed the stack of thick file folders by her computer, her closed cases. The words, *I'm sorry, I can't take anything else on* were on the tip of her tongue. She'd been working like crazy. After months of trying to establish herself in the field of art recovery, she'd finally broken through. She'd moved from people thinking of her as Harrington's assistant to being a professional in her own right. For the last six months, she'd barely been able to keep up with the work. It was wonderful but stressful.

In the last week she'd actually managed to get everything cleared off her to-do list, and she'd been looking forward to having a little downtime before she and Jack left on a trip. But this was Harrington. He'd given her a start in this business. She hated to say no to him. And he hadn't sent anything her way in a while. She didn't want their business connection to peter out.

Harrington said, "Routine stuff. I know you've been rather busy lately. And you have your trip coming up as well. If you can't take it on, that's fine. I understand."

Zoe pushed aside the thought of turning Harrington down right away. She'd just get a few details. "When's the missing chunk?"

"Early nineteen twenties."

"Could be fun. Flappers and jazz." She should be able to handle simple provenance research in a day or so if everything went well.

"Yes, the original owner, Sebastian Blakely, was certainly involved with both." The name sounded familiar to Zoe, but she couldn't place it. Harrington continued, "It's two issues, really. The first is the original bill of sale has been lost, but the current owner assures me the artist's estate can provide evidence of the sale. The second issue is there's a gap—no, *gap* isn't the proper word. A better description would be that there's a second party who's disputing the estate's claim to having had sole possession of the painting since nineteen fourteen."

"Interesting."

"The potential buyer ran across a post on a rather obscure blog, which hinted the painting, *Woman in a White Fur*, wasn't actually in Blakely's possession during one specific time period." Paper rattled. "Nineteen twenty-three, to be exact. The Blakely estate maintains that they've been the sole owner since nineteen fourteen. They're ready to sell, and a buyer is interested. But then this blog surfaced."

"What does the post say happened?"

"Nothing specific, of course." Harrington sighed. "Only hints and innuendo. Full details to follow in a soon-to-be-published book."

"So it could be a publicity stunt. What's the book, and when does it come out?"

"It's called *Secrets and Privilege: Sebastian Blakely's Untold Story*. No publication date listed, only *coming soon*. Ava contacted the author, but no reply as of yet."

Zoe knew Harrington's assistant would keep at it until she

got an answer. "But the post specifically mentioned the painting that's for sale?"

"It did, but as you said, it could just be a gambit to attract media attention. *Woman in a White Fur* is one of the most well-known works of art from the Blakely collection. It's probably just an author trying to stir up some coverage for their book. I believe the term is *generate buzz*. Whatever the case, the end result is that it's made the potential buyer go wobbly."

"It has to be cleared up." Zoe put down her pen. "This doesn't sound boring at all. I'll see if I can get to it before we go out of town." She was getting quite good at provenance research. It shouldn't take her all that long to sort out the details.

"Wonderful."

"Looking forward to dinner with you next week."

"It will be lovely to see you and Jack. I'll have Ava send the parcel right away. It should get there before you depart."

Harrington was based in London, and Zoe and Jack were traveling there in a few days. Jack ran a firm that was all about security. He helped businesses protect everything from physical items to digital files. He had meetings with clients in London, one of them a referral from Harrington. After Jack's business appointments they were meeting Harrington for dinner, and then they were on vacation, a whole week of just the two of them.

They needed to get away. Jack had been just as swamped with work as Zoe had. Recently their *together* time seemed to consist of a few moments in the morning when they gulped down breakfast bars and coffee before Jack headed out to meet with clients and Zoe "commuted" to her desk at the kitchen island.

Her phone, which was on speaker, flashed with an incoming

call. Evelyn. Zoe sat up straight. "Harrington, I'm getting another call. I should take it. It's Evelyn at Salt Grass Gallery."

"Ah, your Canaletto and Picasso, perhaps."

"Maybe. There's been nothing about either painting for months. I'll let you know."

"Yes, do."

Zoe switched to the incoming call from Evelyn, telling herself not to get her hopes up about the missing paintings. More than likely, Evelyn was calling to set up lunch.

Zoe had been working hard to increase her network of contacts in the art world, both in Dallas and beyond the metroplex. She was getting to know antique dealers, museum curators, and prominent donors, as well as gallery owners like Evelyn. Some of her contacts were developing into friendships. She'd met with Evelyn a few times since the theft of the two paintings over six months ago. They'd been stolen from the Westoll, a small private museum that had discovered the missing paintings during an inventory of their items in storage. It was only in the last few months that the Westoll had discovered more items had disappeared, mostly coins, as the museum completed the inventory.

The museum was reluctant to hire Zoe—or anyone else—outright because that would mean admitting there was a problem, which could make board members and donors nervous. Ruby Wu, who was in charge of the paintings at the Westoll Museum, didn't have the authorization to hire Zoe officially, but she was keeping Zoe updated on any developments. Not that there had been anything lately to share.

Zoe had worked her local and international contacts in the art world, looking for the two paintings. One was from Picasso's Neoclassic period and depicted ladies at the seaside. The other was a Canaletto, an exquisitely detailed view of Venice's Grand

Canal. Despite all her searching, so far the only lead Zoe had was Evelyn at Salt Grass Gallery. A young man, who Evelyn described as resembling the artist Giacometti in his youth, had visited the gallery and asked if Evelyn was interested in Canaletto. The guy's manner had set off alarm bells, and Evelyn had called the police, who hadn't been able to track him down. Then she'd contacted Zoe.

He'd visited the gallery twice last September, which was now over six months ago, then disappeared. Except for a grainy photo of him taken from the gallery's security footage, they knew nothing about the young man. There hadn't been another blip of news or information about the theft in the intervening months.

The line transferred to Evelyn, who spoke in a muted tone. "Young Giacometti's here."

Zoe didn't need more than that. "I'm on my way."

She grabbed her messenger bag and dashed for her car. Even though it was eleven on Thursday morning, traffic clogged the roads. It took her thirty minutes to travel what should've taken ten. Salt Grass Gallery was in an exclusive area called Uptown, which was filled with galleries, trendy restaurants, and upscale boutiques. Zoe cruised down the block with the gallery but couldn't find an open parking slot.

As she passed the gallery, she caught a glimpse of Evelyn through the store's plate-glass window. If Evelyn's auburn hair hadn't been enough to identify her, her gallery outfit was unmistakable—a crisp white Oxford shirt tucked into wide-legged designer trousers. She was speaking to a man with puffy dark hair who was several inches shorter than her.

Zoe had looked up an image of the artist Giacometti months before, when Evelyn had first described her visitor as resembling him. In the few seconds she saw the young man as she drove by, Zoe had to admit the guy in the faded red T-shirt did seem to resemble the Swiss artist. Evelyn and the man were moving toward the door.

Zoe whipped the car around the block. As she turned back onto the street, she spotted a car backing out. She waited, her thumb tapping away on the steering wheel at a much faster beat than the metronome-like tick of her blinker. A double-parked delivery truck idling in front of her blocked her view of Salt Grass Gallery. Once the car had finally maneuvered out of the slot, Zoe slid into the space. She slammed out of the car and raced down the street, slowing her steps only before she crossed in front of the gallery's window with its display of Rococo paintings. If she sprinted into the gallery, she might spook the guy.

She pushed through the glass door and into the open room with white bamboo flooring, beige walls, and the faint scent of cinnamon. It was deserted. Zoe's messenger bag bumped against her hip as she headed for the door to the back room. "Evelyn?"

Evelyn emerged, her phone pressed to her ear.

"He's gone?" Zoe asked, already moving back to the entrance.

Evelyn tilted the phone away from her mouth. "I couldn't convince him to stay any longer."

Zoe gripped the door's sleek metal handle. "Did he mention the Canaletto or the Picasso?"

"He brought up the Canaletto again. I told him to bring a photo if he had something he was interested in selling, but then he seemed to change his mind."

"Which way did he go?"

"To the right." She pulled the phone back to her mouth. "Right, the Westoll theft . . . when will the officer in charge of the case be back? It's urgent—"

Zoe stepped outside and scanned the street. There wasn't

much foot traffic. It was mostly cars, cruising slowly as the drivers looked for open parking spaces. Down the block, Zoe spotted a short man with puffy hair wearing a faded red T-shirt and baggy shorts. He was getting into a black hatchback. Zoe raced back to her car.

By the time she got to the end of the block, the hatchback was already turning at the corner. Zoe would be the first to admit she was a tad on the impatient side. Her instinct was to close the gap between their cars, but Jack had taught her how to follow people on foot and in a vehicle. She pushed down her itch to stomp on the gas and stayed a few cars back, never letting the black car out of her sight. They left the swanky area behind and took the interstate on-ramp. She loosened her grip on the steering wheel. She felt more comfortable with the throng of vehicles camouflaging her on the freeway.

After a while the hatchback swerved into the exit lane. Had he realized he was being followed? Zoe shook off the worry. Why would he suspect a woman in a beat-up Jetta would be the least bit interested in him?

Once he was on the access road, he didn't speed away. The hatchback moved at a sedate pace and didn't make any sudden lane changes. Within a few turns, they'd entered a residential neighborhood, and Zoe dropped farther back. Without any cars between her and the black hatchback, she drifted along, hoping he wasn't paying too much attention to his rearview mirror.

Cracked sidewalks, unkept yards, and houses with trim that needed to be scraped and painted gave the neighborhood a scruffy down-on-its-luck air. The hatchback parked in front of a house midway down the block, a tan two-story. Its stucco was veined with cracks, and the mini-blinds covering the front windows tilted at crazy angles and were missing several slats.

Zoe coasted to the curb several houses back on the opposite

side of the street in the shade of a large cottonwood. When the guy in the faded red shirt climbed out of the hatchback, Zoe had her phone ready and snapped several pictures.

As he walked up the sidewalk and went inside, Zoe sent the pictures to Evelyn with a text. *Is this him?*

She replied instantly. *Yes.*

Zoe settled in to wait, pulling up the county tax assessor's website to find out who owned the house. She was in the middle of the search when her phone rang with a call from Evelyn, who said, "I'm so glad you managed to follow him."

"I'm in a neighborhood in the Twin Oaks area. He just went inside a house. I'll wait here and see what happens. Were you able to talk to the police?"

"I had to leave a message for the investigating officer. I have a feeling it might be days before I get a call back."

"I'm sure they'll call you . . . eventually." Police departments were spread thin and property crime wasn't as urgent as other investigations. Zoe slid down a few inches. "Oh, he's back."

"What's he doing?"

"He's changed clothes. He's wearing a white T-shirt and pants along with a baseball cap." His hair puffed out below the cap, which had a logo on it, but it was too far away for Zoe to be able to read the lettering. "He's getting back in his car. I'll call you and let you know what happens."

The hatchback pulled away from the curb, revealing a *For Rent* sign in the front yard.

Zoe clicked another picture, this time of the sign, then crept along behind the black car as it left the neighborhood.

Once on the main road, he headed for the interstate again. He drove for about thirty minutes. Zoe was eyeing her gas gauge, which had dipped below a quarter tank, when he exited and turned into a neighborhood of sprawling houses. Plantings of bright annuals edged perfectly trimmed lawns.

Zoe slowed to a crawl, then parked a few houses back when the hatchback stopped in front of a Mediterranean-style house with a red tile roof. Several other cars along with a pickup and a scruffy white van were parked in front of the house. Young Giacometti joined four other men dressed in white shirts and pants who were gathered around the open doors of the van. They removed paint, rollers, and several ladders. Young Giacometti swung a roll of plastic sheeting onto one shoulder, grabbed the handle of a five-gallon paint can, and walked up the curving, brick-lined driveway along with the other men.

Zoe jotted down the address, then watched the house for thirty minutes. Some of the men went back and forth to the truck, carrying tape, rollers, and a small radio back to the house. Eventually, the movement stopped. Zoe waited another fifteen minutes, then pulled up the image with the rent sign. An online search showed the house had three bedrooms, three baths, and an attached two-car garage.

Zoe called the number on the sign for the listing agent, Julia Lessing.

"Hi Julia," Zoe said. "I just drove by the house for rent on Hyacinth Drive. I think it would be perfect for us."

"Great." She sounded distracted.

"The only problem is that I'm on a tight schedule. I flew into town to look for a place to live. I've been at it all week, and I have to leave tomorrow. I can't believe I didn't find your house until the last moment."

Julia's voice changed, becoming more intent. "You're leaving town tomorrow, you said?"

"That's right."

"Well, there's still plenty of time."

"Oh, good. If you could get me in this afternoon, I'd love to look around."

"I'll need to coordinate with the current renters, but I'm sure we can work something out."

Twenty minutes later, Julia called back. "How about two o'clock this afternoon?"

"Perfect."

J ulia Lessing was in her forties and had a quick smile, a firm handshake, and a steady stream of questions. By the time she'd removed the lockbox and opened the front door to the rental, she'd already asked Zoe if she was working with another real estate agent, how many properties Zoe had seen, and what Zoe was looking for in a rental.

Julia pushed open the door and called, "Hello?" When no one answered, she stepped back and motioned for Zoe to go first. "I always like to make sure no one's home in case there was a misunderstanding about the time. We don't want to scare anyone."

Before Julia could ask another question, Zoe wedged in a question of her own as she crossed the tiled entry. "The people who live here now, why are they moving?"

Julia closed the front door. "You'll see when we look at the bedrooms that it's two roommates who've rented the house. I believe one of them got a new job, which has forced them to move."

The inside of the house was better kept than the exterior.

The walls were freshly painted, and the sudsy scent of carpet shampoo permeated the air. Zoe had hoped that once she was inside, she'd be able to pick up some tidbit of information that could help her find out more about the man who'd visited Evelyn's gallery, but there wasn't much to see as she scanned the open-plan layout.

A large television dominated the living room, and a mass of game controllers was strewn across an L-shaped couch. A table in pale wood that would seat four looked too small for the spacious dining room beyond the glossy white cabinetry of the kitchen. All the walls were bare, and the only decorative touches were two floor lamps on either end of the couch.

The stark white walls and lack of any décor gave the house a temporary feeling. Either the people who lived here were only alighting for a short time, or they'd already packed most of their belongings. But no moving boxes were stacked in the corners. Zoe hadn't really expected to see the Venice landscape or Picasso's swimmers hanging on the wall, especially since the house was being shown to renters, but stranger things had happened.

Zoe already knew the paintings weren't in the garage. She'd arrived early and peered through the garage door's small square windows. She'd actually been relieved to *not* see the canvases in the garage—the heat and humidity in a space without climate control would have been terrible for the artwork. Thankfully, the garage had been empty, except for a mountain bike, a wheeled ice chest, and an old television.

Zoe moved into the living room. "The Dallas traffic can be a killer. Are they moving across town?" She wanted to get as much information as possible about the current residents, especially if Young Giacometti was the resident who had a new job.

"No, moving out of state. Florida, I think."

"Great," Zoe murmured under her breath, but she didn't

push for more details. It would look odd to be too interested in the personal lives of the current renters. Zoe went to the kitchen, where a stack of mail rested on the counter.

"Gas oven," Julia pointed out as she ran her hand over the appliance's stainless-steel finish. "The refrigerator stays, by the way. Do you have your own?"

"What?" Zoe looked up from the letter she'd been peering at, trying to decipher the name of the addressee without making it too obvious that she was staring.

"A refrigerator," Julia repeated. "Do you have one of your own?"

"Oh. Yes. Yes, we do."

"Then you could put yours in the garage."

"Right. We could." Zoe took out her phone. "I think I'll take a few pictures. It'll help me remember everything."

"Good idea."

Zoe snapped a picture of the kitchen as Julia said, "This neighborhood is a great location. Just minutes from the interstate. What do you do?"

"I work from home."

"Do you like it?"

"It's wonderful. No commute." Zoe took a couple of pictures of the dining room and living room but didn't move away from the stack of mail.

"What sort of work do you do?"

"Freelance consultant. The drapes stay?" Zoe motioned to the windows in the dining room. She wanted to get off the subject of herself.

"Yes. Have you—" Julia's phone rang.

Zoe fanned out the mail and snapped a picture of it while Julia checked her phone. Zoe managed to read the name on one envelope, *Bobby R. Greer*, but didn't catch the full name on another bill, only the last name of Lomax. Buoyed up with the thought that she at least had names, Zoe set about looking for any other telltale traces that might indicate where the people were moving, but the impersonality of the rooms defeated her.

Using her cover as a prospective tenant, Zoe opened the pantry and the coat closet. Since she was inside, she might as well look in every storage area big enough to hold either the full-size paintings or the rolled canvases. Zoe hoped the paintings were still stretched across their frames, but thieves sometimes removed the canvases from their frames and rolled up the artwork to make it easier to transport. The smallest, the Canaletto, was two feet wide, so it would be obvious if it was stashed in a closet, even if it was rolled up. But no large paintings or suspicious rolls of canvas were tucked away. The coat closet only had a few lightweight jackets, and the pantry was equally disappointing. It was empty except for rows and rows of canned tuna. "Someone's laid on a supply of tuna that could outlast the apocalypse."

Julia put away her phone. "I'm sorry. What was that?"

"Nothing important. The master is here on the main floor?"

"Yes, this way." The room was messy, with the sheets and comforter in a tangle and empty Styrofoam cups from fast-food restaurants scattered around the nightstand and desk. Julia frowned at the mess and quickly steered Zoe to the walk-in closet. It contained nothing more exciting than T-shirts, jeans, and a few button-down shirts, so Zoe assumed the man who was working on the painting crew had the room upstairs.

On the way out of the room, Zoe dropped her keys and managed to kick them under the edge of the bed. She got a quick glimpse under the dust ruffle. No canvases were hidden away under the mattress, only a battered laptop and some file folders.

"What do you think so far?" Julia asked at the foot of the stairs.

Guilt pricked at Zoe. She'd pulled the woman away from her work—it was no small thing to navigate through Dallas traffic—and Zoe had talked her way into the house with a bogus story. She didn't want to get Julia's hopes up any higher than they already were. "It's nice, but it's just my husband and myself. Now that I'm seeing the inside, I don't think we actually need this much space."

"Oh? No kids?"

"No."

"But there might be kids down the road?"

Zoe laughed. "No plans for that right now." Zoe loved the only toddler in her life, Nicolas, who was the son of her best friend, Helen. Zoe enjoyed playing trucks with Nicolas and listening to his laugh when she told him made-up stories about silly dragons and plucky gnomes, but she was content right now with her status as an honorary aunt.

One corner of Julia's mouth quirked down, and she turned to the front door. "Well, if it's too big, you probably don't want to see the upstairs."

The prick of guilt morphed into a stab, but Zoe said, "No, I'm here. I should see the whole place. I might change my mind later." Since she was inside, Zoe didn't want to give up before she'd checked every possible space for the paintings. She climbed the stairs, leaving Julia no choice but to follow her up.

Julia said, "Two bedrooms up here, and two full baths on the second story, which is quite a nice feature."

Zoe murmured an agreement as she scanned the first bedroom. The person who lived upstairs was neater than the roommate. The bed was made, and the bureau's surface was clear. A few packing boxes stood in a corner. A Marlins baseball hat was hooked on one corner of the headboard. Zoe was happy to see it was a platform bed so she didn't have to use any ploys to look under it. The closet contained casual shirts and jeans along with several white shirts and pants. The label on one of the shirts read *Bobby*. So at least she'd sorted out the painter's name.

After a glance around a fairly spacious bathroom with only a toothbrush on display, they went down the hall. The third bedroom was completely empty. Zoe opened the closet. It held only a discarded curtain rod. She squashed her sigh of disappointment. A closet in an unused room would have been a perfect place to hide the paintings. The only place left was the attic, and she sincerely hoped the paintings weren't up there. If they were, they'd be ruined. She was trying to formulate a reason for looking in the attic when Julia pushed open a door in the hallway and turned on a light. "This is the third bath. So handy to have it upstairs. Your guests could each have their own bath."

"Yes, that would be nice." The narrow bath had a small vanity and toilet on one side of the room, with a tub and slender linen closet opposite. Keeping up her cover as a thorough inspector of a potential property, Zoe checked the cabinet—no rolled canvases.

She peeked behind the shower curtain and caught her breath. A beautiful scene of Venice greeted her, a busy morning on the Grand Canal. From the tiny brushstrokes that created the sun glinting on the choppy water to the expression of the woman holding a basket at the side of the canal, it was obvious it was a masterpiece.

Zoe's heart, which had fluttered at the initial sight, plummeted. The paintings had been stored in a bathtub! But then she calmed down as she looked closer. The edges of the canvases were pristine. No water had soaked into the artwork. Another canvas, one that was taller and narrower, stood behind the scene of Venice.

Zoe used a fingernail to pull the Canaletto forward and rose up on her tiptoes to peer down at the other painting that was propped against the tile wall. Sinuous figures of women bathers filled the canvas. They were poised on rocks with the ocean in the background. One limber woman tilted sideways, shaking out her wet hair. Her wavy curls seemed to mirror the undulations of the waves behind her.

From behind Zoe, Julia said, "Goodness. What an unusual place to store prints. The tenant must have stuck them in here to get them out of the way during the showing. They're not water-damaged, are they?"

"No, they look fabulous, but they're not prints." Zoe took her phone out of her messenger bag. "They're paintings—stolen paintings."

3

Jack opened the pizza box with a flourish and held it out to Zoe. "Celebrated art recovery specialists get first choice."

"Thanks. I'm starving." The warm cheese stretched out into thin strings of delicious goodness as Zoe pulled the slice of Margherita away from the box. They were perched on bar stools at the kitchen island, the pizza between them. Zoe had spent the last five hours answering questions, first from the police and then from Special Agent Dirk Sorkensov from the FBI. When she'd pulled into the driveway at their house, she'd been thrilled to see Jack paying the pizza delivery guy at the front door.

Jack had worked late too. Working late was the new normal for both of them lately. Jack still wore a dress shirt, but his sleeves were rolled up. He'd also loosened his tie and undone the top button on his shirt. "So the paintings are real?"

Zoe had only had time to call Jack and share the briefest details with him earlier. "Yes—well, the back of the canvases have the right inventory stickers and markings, which means Ruby is pretty confident that they're authentic. She's lining up experts to examine them." The back of a painting was often the first place authenticators checked. If a painting didn't have the correct markings on the back, it was a clear giveaway that it was a fake. "Ruby's ecstatic."

Jack picked up his own slice of pizza. "I'll bet."

"I don't think you understand. She was over the moon. She said she's naming her firstborn after me."

"That's—"

"Excessive? Yes, I told her I won't hold her to it. Poor thing. She was so relieved when I called her and told her I'd found the paintings that I think she nearly passed out. She's been afraid she'd be fired at any moment ever since the paintings went missing. That's a lot of stress, considering they've been missing over six months."

"So what happened?" Jack lifted the pizza box, looking for a napkin. "How did the painter guy—Bobby, wasn't it?—get the Picasso?"

Zoe tore off several paper towels and handed them to Jack. "And a Canaletto. Bobby Greer is his name. He worked on a crew that painted the walls when the Westoll remodeled. After I answered all Sorkensov's questions, he filled me in on what had happened. Remember I told you that the Westoll was also missing lots of smaller items like coins? It turns out that a security guard had been taking them during his rounds at night. He'd rearranged the displays so it didn't look as if anything was missing. If the Westoll hadn't done the inventory, they'd probably never have noticed either the paintings or the coins were missing. Bobby was working late, finishing the painting job, and saw the security guard take a coin. Once he'd seen that . . ."

"He knew security wasn't up to par and he could bribe the guard." Jack wiped the corner of his mouth with the paper towel. "No matter what bells and whistles you install, the weakest point is usually personnel."

"When Bobby realized he was caught, he was happy to sell out the guard."

Jack folded the pizza slice in half length-wise, Italian style, to make it easier to manage. "I wonder why Bobby took two paintings. That's very different from coins."

"Apparently they were the biggest paintings he could still fit in his car. He figured the bigger canvases would be worth more." A warm dollop of cheese oozed over the edge of her pizza. Zoe plucked it up and popped it into her mouth.

"Not a well-thought-out plan," Jack said.

"It was a terrible plan. The Canaletto and Picasso were recognizable and listed in the databases of lost and stolen art. An internet search would show they were stolen. Bobby couldn't take them to an art dealer unless he knew the dealer was crooked and wouldn't report him."

"He didn't have a fence?"

"Nope. Since he didn't know any crooked dealers, he was stuck with the paintings while he tried to figure out how to sell them. He'd looked up their value online and knew they were worth over a million, so he didn't destroy them—thank goodness."

"So he just put them in the extra bathroom. That's what I'd do—toss them in the tub. Best place for them."

"Playing the long game wasn't his forte," Zoe said. "I guess he decided to make overtures at Salt Grass Gallery in the hope that Evelyn wasn't aboveboard."

Jack took a sip of his beer. "The strangest thing to me is that he left them in the tub when the house was for rent. Any potential tenant could have spotted them."

"Oh, but the house wasn't supposed to be shown. Julia fudged a little. The agreement was that the tenants would have at least a day's notice to prepare the house for a showing. It had just come on the market—I was the first person to see it—and Julia was anxious to get me inside, so she ignored that condition. She let me in when she realized the house was empty."

"What was she going to do if somebody was actually home?"

"Probably make some excuse and ask if we could take a quick look since we were there."

Jack balled up his paper towel. "What about the roommate? He didn't notice the paintings?"

"Apparently the roommate rarely went upstairs. He didn't even know they were there."

As Zoe closed the empty pizza box, Jack said, "So we're not using Julia Lessing as a listing agent if we decide to sell our house."

"I doubt she'd take us on as clients. She was a tad upset with me when I insisted on calling the police." Zoe had felt bad about deceiving the real estate agent, but the blast of Julia's rage directed at her when she'd insisted on calling the police had cleared away a good portion of Zoe's remorse.

Jack leaned back and lifted his beer. "Well, congratulations. You found them. Good job not giving up." The skin crinkled around his silver-blue eyes as he smiled.

"Thanks." Zoe clicked her glass against his bottle.

Jack tilted his head. "You don't seem thrilled."

Zoe pushed the pizza box away. "I thought I'd be ecstatic like Ruby. But honestly, it's a bit of a letdown."

"What do you mean?"

"Well—I know this sounds a bit silly—but Bobby Greer was so *stupid*." The pace of her words quickened as she worked out what was bothering her. "He picked the paintings on a whim. He had no plan—no way to sell them. And then he hid them in his house, practically in plain sight."

"Not all criminals can be masterminds. Some are just—well, dumb."

"I suppose so."

"And whether the thief was an imbecile or not, the fact remains that neither of those paintings would have been found if you hadn't followed Greer to his house, figured out a way to get in there, and searched the place. You, Zoe Hunter Andrews, saw to it that two beautiful pieces of art will be back in a museum. That's something to be proud of." He kissed her quickly on the mouth and picked up the pizza box. "Allow me to do the dishes. Then I suggest we call it a night. I have a breakfast meeting tomorrow."

Zoe caught his tie and drew him toward her. "Then we'd better get you to bed right away."

His phone rang. "Let me check . . ." He slipped his phone out of his pocket. The corner of his mouth quirked down. "I better take this. It's a new client."

Zoe's nose wrinkled. "The Bauer account?"

"Yeah."

Zoe sighed and released his tie. "You have to take it." Zoe reached for the pizza box.

"I'll try to keep it short."

"Good luck with that," Zoe muttered to herself. The last few times Bauer Enterprises had called, Jack had been on the phone for hours.

Jack's voice faded as he climbed the stairs two at time. "Let me take a look. Yes, I understand why you'd be worried . . . of course I'll check . . ."

Zoe dumped the box in the recycling bin. "And that's why we need a vacation."

The doorbell rang. Nicolas dropped the toy car, scrambled to his feet, and ran down the hall, his chunky legs pumping.

Zoe followed him and opened the front door for Helen, who swept Nicolas up in her arms. "How's my little man?"

Nicolas buried his face in her shoulder for a moment, then wiggled. "Down. Cars."

Helen set him on his feet, and he zipped back to the living room. "How was he? Was he good?"

"Perfect, as always."

"*Always* perfect is overstating it, I think. He's only perfect for Aunt Zoe."

"That's one of the perks of being the babysitter, not the mom. How was the appointment? You look fantastic."

"Thanks. It's amazing what a few hours at the salon can do." They'd been walking down the hall, but Helen stopped short as they entered the living room. "Oh my." Toy cars, blocks, and all the pillows in the house were strewn across the floor.

Nicolas crawled out from between two propped-up couch cushions that had a sheet draped over them. "Fort, Mommy."

"I see that."

"Don't worry. It's not that bad," Zoe said. "It'll only take a few minutes to put the cushions and pillows back. Do you have time for a glass of ice tea before you have to go?"

"Sure." Helen followed Zoe to the kitchen, where she pulled out a barstool and nodded at a stack of *Smart Travel* guidebooks. "What's this? Are you copyediting for *Smart Travel* again?"

"Hardly. Jack's making plans." Zoe poured two glasses of tea and handed one to Helen.

"Oh, that's right. Your trip." Helen tapped her forehead through her freshly highlighted bangs. "Mommy brain."

"Jack's got a huge itinerary planned for Amsterdam—all sorts of stuff from tulips to museums."

"Laid out in a timetable?" Helen asked with a smile.

"Close, but not quite." Zoe ran her finger around the rim of her glass. "Jack hasn't been able to go on many vacations. His family was a little strapped for cash when he was young."

"But back when he was—um—working for the State Department, didn't he see all sorts of amazing places in Europe?"

"Yes, but he was working. That's not the same as being a tourist."

"I guess so."

"It's not. He never had time to do much sightseeing when he was working. He wants to do all the touristy things."

"When are you leaving?"

"Tomorrow."

"And you said you'd babysit for me today? Shouldn't you be packing?"

Zoe waved off Helen's concern with her glass of tea. "It's practically done. I just have to throw a few more things in the suitcase and find my passport."

Helen pressed a hand to her chest. "That makes me anxious for you. If I didn't know where my passport was and I was leaving in"—she looked at her watch—"less than twenty-four hours, I'd be in a panic."

"It's somewhere in the bedroom. I'll find it."

Helen shook her head. "I'm sure you will." She tilted her head toward the guidebooks. "So, where are you going?"

"Amsterdam first for a few days, then . . ." Zoe shrugged. "We'll see."

Helen blinked. "What?"

"We're going to play it by ear. Barcelona, Athens, Prague, and Vienna are all on the short list. It depends on where the weather is the nicest and who has the best ticket prices."

"That's a lengthy short list."

"I don't want to box us in. Jack's planning the first leg of the trip—the Amsterdam portion—and then it's my turn for the second leg."

"And you have no idea where you'll go during your part of the trip?"

"Nope."

"That's a very Zoe plan." Helen smiled. "I can picture your itinerary." She waved her hand as if she were reading a line of text off a sign. "Itinerary: get lost in Europe."

"That's about it."

"It would drive me crazy, but a package tour wouldn't be your thing. You've always liked to do things the unconventional way. I'm sure you'll have a wonderful time. Oh! I have something for you." She twisted around and retrieved her enormous designer purse that she'd hooked on the back of the barstool. "Here you are." She pulled out a flat square package.

"Oh, fun." Zoe ripped the paper away. Helen had clipped that morning's newspaper article with the headline *Stolen Art Recovered* and framed it. "This is so nice. And you highlighted my name in the story," Zoe said with a laugh.

"It's quite a coup," Helen said. "You need to celebrate that accomplishment."

"Thank you. I love it." Zoe ran her hand along the sleek frame. "I'll find the perfect place to hang it when we get back from Europe." Seeing the newspaper article in that morning's paper had gone a long way toward easing the sense of letdown Zoe had felt the day before.

Helen cocked her head and listened for a moment. "You hear that?"

"No."

"Exactly. It's *too* quiet." Helen downed the rest of her tea. "I'd better see what Nicolas is doing, then I do have to go. It's nearly nap time."

Nicolas had rearranged the pillows into a mound and was running his toy cars down it. Helen said it was time to go, and after several protests from Nicolas, they returned the living room to its normal state. As Helen gathered up the diaper bag and her purse, Nicolas gave Zoe a goodbye hug, wrapping his plump arms around her neck. He smelled of a mixture of baby powder and sticky little boy. Zoe squeezed him tight. "Next time you come over, we'll make sugar cookies."

He drew back, his face serious. "Sprinkles?"

"Of course, with sprinkles. Lots and lots of sprinkles."

As Helen and Nicolas crossed the porch, Helen said to Nicolas, "Look, Aunt Zoe has a package. Do you want to get it for her?"

Nicolas pounced on the thick envelope like it was Christmas morning. He toddled back to Zoe.

"Thank you, Nicolas. What a big helper you are. Oh, good. It's from Harrington—the nineteen twenties job."

4

Zoe put the empty ice tea glasses in the sink and moved the *Smart Travel* guides out of the way before she opened the envelope from Harrington, which contained a thick file. She spread the contents of it across the island—stacks of photographs, a family tree, legal paperwork, printouts from the blog that mentioned the painting, and photocopies of what must have been several fragile tissue-like pages, because the color copies showed the pages were yellowed with age.

Harrington had sent her an email with a summary of the case, so she knew the basics and had done a little poking around online that morning while Nicolas had played with his toy cars. She'd skimmed several articles about the artist, Tamara de Lempicka. Zoe had also read up on the original purchaser, photographer and art collector Sebastian Blakely. After skimming through a few of the internet search results, she'd realized why the name Blakely had sounded familiar when Harrington had mentioned it. Sebastian Blakely was a celebrity photographer. She'd run across a special about him online. He'd begun his career photographing his sister and other members of high society in the nineteen twenties, then he'd gone on to photograph the royal family, presidents, and Hollywood stars.

Zoe started with the high-resolution photographs of the painting she'd be researching, *Woman in a White Fur*. It depicted a woman in a purple evening dress with a white fur stole draped around her shoulders. A glimpse of a handrail and banister in the background showed the woman was moving down a staircase, the rich fabric of her dress seeming to swish with her steps. Although it was painted early in Tamara de Lempicka's career, it had her signature glamorous style and polished luminescence. The bright jewel tone of the dress contrasted with the paleness of the woman's skin and the fur. Zoe liked the combination of glamour and confidence that de Lempicka's women radiated. The woman in the purple dress was making an entrance. Every eye was on her—and that's the way she liked it.

Tamara de Lempicka's paintings didn't often come up for auction because they were usually snapped up through private sales, which was the case with *Woman in a White Fur*. The owner wanted to sell it and had put it on display in a London gallery. A buyer wanted it, but they had one stipulation. The process would move forward only if the painting had a complete provenance.

The thick stack of photos of the painting included images of the back of the canvas as well as a close-up of the artist's signature. The only marking on the back of the painting was a small metal tab affixed to the upper right-hand corner of the frame with "TDL-14-Paris," which was probably the artist's initials, year of purchase, and location of purchase. Zoe would need to check to see if the other paintings in Blakely's collection had been categorized with the same notations. The lack of other markings on the back of the canvas seemed to indicate a single owner.

Zoe skimmed the details about the painting. An oil on canvas, it was on the small side, thirteen and three-quarters inches by ten and a half. It was inscribed in the bottom right-hand corner with "de Lempicka." The current owner was Rosalind Kingwood. Zoe shuffled papers until she found Harrington's notes about the provenance.

Woman in a White Fur was painted in nineteen fourteen. Sebastian Blakely purchased it directly from Tamara de Lempicka. Harrington noted that the family owned two de Lempicka paintings and was selling *Woman in a White Fur* to fund repairs to one of their estates, Archly Manor.

Zoe turned to a printout from the troublesome blog Harrington had mentioned. Harrington's capable assistant Ava had added a sticky note with the information that the entire website had been deleted, but she'd accessed the post through a digital internet archive site. She flicked through the pages. Some of the posts were about Amsterdam—cycling around the city, restaurants to visit, which museums visitors should tour.

Ava had flagged one post about the Rijksmuseum. It listed the most famous pieces and reviewed the museum restaurant. Near the end, the author, Mallory Tredmont, wrote:

I've always felt at home in museums—probably because I was fortunate enough to grow up surrounded by art. Beautiful paintings and stunning photographs are part of my heritage. I've been working on a project related to that legacy, and I'll soon have exciting news to share with you about my upcoming book, Secrets and Privilege: Sebastian Blakely's Untold Story.

Everyone knows Blakely as a world-famous photographer, but he had another interest. He was also an art collector. I've discovered something truly shocking about one of his pieces of art, a painting that's now owned by one of Blakely's descendants. Even though I'm dying to tell you more, I can't say too much about it yet. Just know that no one will ever look at the painting Woman in a White Fur *the same way again.*

My news will set the art world buzzing. It's a story of a gorgeous painting, a swindler of the first order, and the mysterious disappearance of a priceless canvas from the Blakely collection in nineteen twenty-three. I can't say too much now, but there's more —much *more—to come.*

Ava's neat handwriting filled the bottom margin of the page. *Unfortunately, there's nothing else in the internet archive site about Blakely. The blogger didn't write any more posts about him. The site shut down a month after this blog post went up.*

"Well, that's not good," Zoe murmured. She could certainly understand why the post could put the brakes on a potential deal. The blogger had all but said the painting had been stolen, not to mention the coy reference to a swindler, which could mean she had info that the painting was a fake. That news—no matter how unreliable the source—combined with the detail about Blakely buying the painting directly from the artist would make most savvy buyers pause.

The art world had been rocked several times by con artists who'd "discovered" paintings from private family collections. With each scam, the con artists needed a story to sell the paintings to art dealers, a reason why the paintings didn't have paper trails of ownership, so they created fictional histories for their paintings. It was usually the story of an avid collector—a canny person who saw the value in Impressionist or Abstract art when everyone else turned up their nose. The astute and long-sighted art lover bought pieces directly from the artists and kept them in his or her private collection. In reality, the paintings were as fake as their made-up provenance.

The notion that a painting might have been in a private collection for generations wasn't unheard of, but many art brokers, gallery owners, and collectors had been swept up in the excitement of snagging a rare painting before the competition heard about it, and they overlooked the lack of provenance. That wasn't the case with the potential buyer for *Woman in a White Fur*. Harrington's notes indicated that if provenance could be established, the interested party would move on to scientific tests on the painting and the accompanying provenance paperwork to determine authenticity, which meant the buyer was a cautious person, not one to be duped or hurried along in the heat of the moment. Zoe shuffled papers, looking for the buyer's name, but it wasn't listed, which meant he or she wanted to remain anonymous. Of course Harrington knew who it was, but he hadn't mentioned the buyer's name in his notes.

Zoe read through Harrington's notes on the bill of sale. The Blakely estate had no paper record of the original purchase. The invoice had been destroyed when Blakely's London office had caught fire after one of the Zeppelin air raids during World War I.

Next, she turned to an envelope containing several black and white photographs along with a few articles cut from newspapers and magazines. Zoe studied a photo of Sebastian Blakely. It wasn't a small snapshot, but a full eight-by-ten that showed a slim man dressed in a double-breasted suit leaning against a wall with his arms crossed. His hair was slicked back from his bony face, which was in profile as he looked at *Woman in a White Fur*. The cavernous room where the painting hung had ornate wood trim and huge Oriental rugs spaced along the floor. A handwritten note on the back of the photograph read, "Self-portrait. 9 June, 1924."

Zoe leafed through the rest of the photos, which were a mix

of casual snapshots and posed images. A parade of different
people appeared in the photos, but one thing stayed the same—
the painting *Woman in a White Fur*. It provided an unchanging
background for the Blakely family and guests. Most of the
photos had the date written on the back, but even if they didn't,
it would have been easy to discern the passage of time as the
hemlines rose through the twenties. Then in the thirties, the
skirts lengthened and frivolous ruffles and beads disappeared.
Zoe lined up the photos in order of the dates written on the
back. She began with the earliest dated image, the self-portrait
of Blakely. When she was finished, she had a photographic timeline of not only the changes in fashion, but also chronological
evidence that the painting had hung in Hawthorne House from
nineteen twenty-four through the thirties.

Zoe flipped back to the page that listed Harrington's notes on
the ownership of the painting. The family stated Sebastian
Blakely had acquired *Woman in a White Fur* in nineteen fourteen
and hung it at a country manor in Warwickshire called
Hawthorne House, one of the homes his family owned. In nineteen forty-five, Blakely had gifted it to his niece, Rose, on the
occasion of her marriage. Zoe paged through the stack to the
family tree and traced the painting's transfer from one genera-
tion to another. Rose's daughter had married in nineteen eighty
and received *Woman in a White Fur* on her wedding day. The
chain of gifting the painting to the newly wed had continued.
The painting had been passed on to Rose's granddaughter,
Rosalind, the current owner, when she married.

Reams of legal documents held together with a thick clip
detailed the transfer of the painting from one family member to
another. After skimming through the legalese, Zoe was glad to
see the paragraphs related to *Woman in a White Fur* were fairly

straightforward. Harrington had already sent the documents to his legal team for them to review.

The last set of papers was an inventory of the Blakely collection, dated nineteen fourteen. She skimmed the handwritten list until she found the entry for *Woman in a White Fur*. The notation beside it matched the photo of the tag on the back of the painting, and the rest of Blakely's paintings had been inventoried with the same pattern referencing the artist, year, and location of purchase. "Excellent," Zoe murmured as she jotted a note.

Zoe skimmed over the photos and paperwork, her pen tapping away on the island as she thought. It wasn't quite the open-and-shut case she'd thought, but she could still wrap it up fairly quickly. The inventory along with the photographs and snapshots provided evidence that the painting was in Blakely's possession and had hung in Hawthorne House from nineteen twenty-four through the thirties, then legal documents traced the painting from after the Second World War to the present. Zoe needed to get a copy of the original bill of sale from the artist's estate to nail down proof that Blakely had acquired the painting at that time. And since the blog post brought into question what had happened in nineteen twenty-three, she needed to sort out the hints about what had transpired that year.

She typed up a quick email to the artist's estate, following up about the copy of the original bill of sale, then began to return the papers to the file. As Zoe tapped the edges of the pages of the inventory on the island to square them, a paper on the bottom of the stack fell away, a photocopy of a note. It had been stuck to the last page, and Zoe hadn't seen it.

The note was dated in November of nineteen twenty-three and had Sebastian Blakely's signature at the bottom. It opened with the salutation, "Dear Thea." Zoe consulted the family tree and worked out that Thea was Blakely's sister.

It was a chatty letter. The opening paragraphs were about a mutual friend who had asked after his "dear sister." Sebastian inquired after the health of his niece and nephew, then he mentioned the latest night club that had opened in London.

Zoe was about to tuck it into the folder, but then she went still as she read the last paragraph.

No need to worry about the situation at Hawthorne House. I'm sure these rumors you've heard are simply that—rumors. But to put your mind at ease, I've hired the ever-resourceful Olive Belgrave.

I'm sending her up to Hawthorne House to update the inventory of the paintings. The last one was done before the war. That shouldn't raise any suspicions with Frank.

After all, I sent that buffoon Corway to catalog the library last year —for all the good it did. Corway did nothing but drink my scotch and laze about the place. Thank heavens I had to run up there unexpectedly and was able to roust him out before he emptied the cellar.

I have no worries about Olive idling her time away. She's the industrious sort. She'll report back, and I'll let you know what she finds. If there's pilfering going on, I'll put a stop to it. Give my love to Paul and Rose.

Rumors and pilfering. Zoe didn't like the sound of that—and right at a critical point in the timeline.

Zoe went back and paged through each document in the file, looking for another reference to this Olive Belgrave. She finally found something mixed in with the legal paperwork—a copy of a letter on stationery and several typed pages that had been held together with a corroding paperclip from the looks of the rusty imprint left on the top corner.

She read the handwritten letter first.

Dear Sebastian,

I leave Monday morning for Warwickshire. I have your letter of authorization in hand and will let you know how the situation stands after I arrive. Thank you for entrusting me with the task of completing a new inventory of the paintings at Hawthorne House.

Sincerely,
Olive Belgrave

5

Olive

2 November, 1923

Olive Belgrave and Jasper Rimington stood in a London art gallery that buzzed with the low hum of conversation as people circulated through the small room. Most of the attendees seemed to be more interested in talking to each other than looking at the art—except for Jasper, who was staring intently at the display in front of them. It was a postcard reproduction of the *Mona Lisa,* but a mustache and goatee had been penciled on the famous face, and five capital letters had been typed across the bottom of the card.

Olive looked from Jasper and his concentrated gaze back to the postcard. She tilted her head, squinted, then gave up and turned to Jasper. "Is this really art? Or is it some sort of rag—an elaborate practical joke?"

Jasper pulled his gaze away from the postcard. "I take it you don't think I should purchase one of these fine examples of Dada art?"

"Do you *want* to purchase something here?"

"Wouldn't it be the perfect touch over the mantel in my lodgings?"

Olive had known Jasper too long to be taken in by his serious face. "Honestly, no. I can't imagine your taste would run to something like this." She looked at another piece of art, which was a gramophone turned upside down and bolted to the underside of a large shelf. The next display was made from ticket stubs that had been glued to a rough wooden board so that they formed the word "No!"

Olive paused in front of the mass of ticket stubs. "I'm sure your rooms are tastefully furnished." Not that she'd ever seen them. She might be a modern working girl making her own way in the world, but even the most forward-thinking young ladies did *not* visit gentlemen's rooms—that is, the well-bred young ladies didn't. But Olive knew Jasper was quite the connoisseur. He was partial to first editions and fine art. She couldn't imagine he'd add something like the postcard with scribbles to his collection.

His face broke into a grin. "I have a very nice Impressionist landscape above the fireplace. I have no intention of replacing it."

"Then why come here if you're not interested in buying any of this?"

"Because this is a rising trend. It's always good to keep an eye on what's en vogue."

The crowd was pressing in on them, and they moved on, allowing a new group of people to surge up and take their place. Olive scanned the art gallery again. "I'll confess, I don't see the beauty in this art. *Is* it even art?"

"Excellent question." Jasper's hands linked behind his back as they strolled into a less crowded part of the gallery. "Does art have to be beautiful?"

"I suppose not. Honestly, it's not something I've thought much about. I've been so busy looking for a new place to live that I don't have much time to contemplate such things." Olive waved a hand to indicate the gallery's displays. "What did you call this art?"

"Dadaism. Irreverent art created from ready-made items, which makes us ask questions about the art, the artist, and society."

"I suppose that's one way to describe it. Although I'd prefer a beautiful painting on my wall to bits of paper glued to a board."

A few moments later they stepped into the shock of the chilly November air, and Olive wrapped her scarf more tightly around her throat. Jasper placed his hat on his wavy golden hair. "I'm feeling a bit peckish. Would you like to join me at the Grill Room?"

"That sounds wonderful."

Jasper extended his arm. Olive hooked her hand around his elbow, and they set off, heads down as they leaned into a blast of wind.

After they'd finished their porterhouse steaks, Olive sipped her coffee, replete and satisfied. Since moving to London and earning her own income, she'd had many days where her meals consisted of tea and a single bun. A steak was a feast, something to be savored. "Delicious. Thank you for lunch, Jasper."

"It was the least I could do after dragging you off to look at something you're clearly not interested in."

"I wouldn't say I wasn't interested. I did find it . . . strange, but it was appropriate timing. I've picked up an assignment that centers on art. At least now I'll know not to throw away a post-card with a sketch on it—it might be art."

"Or gramophones attached to the underside of shelves," Jasper said. "What's the new job?"

"I'm off to Hawthorne House. Sebastian's asked me to inventory his paintings. It will fill the gap before I visit Gigi." Olive put down her empty coffee cup. "That sounds terrible—am I on the cusp of becoming one of those hangers-on, a permanent house-guest shuffling from one friend to another?"

"I have no worries about you on that count. You're not a sponger. Any luck on new lodgings?"

Olive's boardinghouse was closing, and she had to find new rooms. "Yes. After running all over the city, I think I've found something that's not horribly overpriced or already taken. It's a tiny basement flat."

"Good. I hope it works out. And how is our favorite parrot faring?"

Olive had unexpectedly come into possession of a parrot during her last case. "Fortunately, my landlady is quite taken with Mr. Quigley. She's agreed to keep an eye on him for me while I'm away."

The waiter appeared at Jasper's side, offering more coffee.

"None for me," Olive said.

Jasper shook his head and asked for the bill, then turned back to Olive. "I thought Sebastian was in town, not at Hawthorne House."

"Oh, he's in town. He's sending me to Hawthorne House unannounced."

"Why?"

"Apparently he's heard his estate manager there isn't keeping a close eye on things."

"A bit dodgy, this estate manager?"

"Perhaps. But you know how it is with rumors—it's probably nothing more than gossip."

Jasper frowned. "I don't like it."

Olive looked up from pulling on her gloves. "Don't like what?"

"You going up there alone. If this estate manager—who is it?"

"Frank Carter."

"If this Frank Carter is doing something shady, he'll resent your intrusion."

"That's the whole idea—to catch him unaware *if* he's up to something."

The frown deepened on Jasper's face. "Sebastian should go with you or do it himself."

"Sebastian? Inventory his own art?"

Jasper sighed. "You're right. Too menial a task for him, I'm sure."

Olive tapped her chest. "Thus, a job for me. If Sebastian announces his intention to travel there and anything untoward *is* going on, Mr. Carter would have time to cover his tracks. With me arriving unexpectedly, Mr. Carter won't have time to do anything like that. I'm sure he'll see me as nothing more than a glorified secretary, not a threat at all." Olive had performed another job, arriving at a country house in the role of editorial assistant and found that despite her job description, the lady of the manor considered Olive a stand-in for a personal secretary.

"That would be a grave mistake on his part," Jasper said.

"What do you mean?"

"If Mr. Carter thinks you're inconsequential, he's underestimating you."

"Why, thank you, Jasper."

"But I don't think it's a good idea for you to go up there alone."

"Oh, what could happen? I'm only going to look at some paintings."

Zoe

Present day

The rattle of the garage door pulled Zoe back to the present. Jack came into the kitchen, loosening his tie. "All packed?" he asked as he kissed her.

"Hardly." Unlike Jack, who'd had his suitcases ready for several days, Zoe's was empty, her clothes strewn across the bed.

He grinned. "I didn't think you would be. You like to leave it to the last minute."

"The last minute is when I do my best work." She tilted her head as she studied Jack's face. He looked worn out. "You okay?"

He rubbed his forehead. "Yeah. Just a long day. Lots of following up leads."

"And that's your least favorite thing to do."

"Got to be done, though. Have to keep the clients coming in the door." Jack glanced at the thick file folder. "What's this?"

"A new case." Zoe glanced at the clock and reluctantly put Olive Belgrave's report down. "Just provenance research for a painting. I'll make copies and bring those on the plane. Should make good reading for the flight. Right now, I've got to find my passport."

The next afternoon Zoe sat in one of the uncomfortable chairs in the gate area. Her passport was tucked into her messenger bag. It had taken all evening to find, but she'd finally discovered it at the bottom of her jewelry box.

Jack returned from his reconnaissance of the terminal and sat down beside her, cracking open the lid on a bottle of water. He offered it to her and took a second bottle out of the plastic bag. He gestured with his water to the stack of papers in her lap. "Anything useful?"

"Nothing about *Woman in a White Fur* so far, but it's fascinating reading. This report was written by a woman named Olive Belgrave. I looked her up this morning. There's a couple of articles about her online. She was known as the 'high society lady detective' and solved problems for the posh set in the nineteen twenties."

A chime from Jack's phone signaled an incoming email. "I need to set my Out of Office reply." He capped the water bottle and reached for his phone. Zoe went back to Olive's report.

5 November, 1923

Hawthorne House

I arrived at three in the afternoon and received a lukewarm welcome from Mr. Carter. No one seems very happy to see me, but it may simply be resentment for the extra work I'm creating. I've begun inventorying the art . . .

6

Olive
5 November, 1923
London

Olive looked down into the mass of metal that made up the engine of her Morris Cowley motorcar. Beside her, Tommy, the boy who retrieved keys and ran errands for the owner of the garage where Olive parked her motor, shoved his flat cap up and scratched his forehead. "I'm afraid there's nothing else I know to do, Miss Belgrave. Herbert might know how to fix it, but he's on holiday until the end of the week. Can you wait a few days?"

"No, I need to leave London today."

For the last quarter of an hour, Tommy had cranked the engine while Olive tried to coax the Morris to start. Then they'd changed places and Olive had turned the hand crank while

Tommy tried to rouse the engine. But they didn't get even a sputter. Despite the frigid air sweeping in through the wide doors of the garage, Olive was a little warm from her efforts and blotted her forehead with her handkerchief. Tommy closed the bonnet, pulled a rag from a pocket, and wiped away his fingerprints from the glossy blue finish. "I'm sorry I don't know more about how to fix motors. Herbert's a right wizard with the engines, even the finicky ones. All I do is fetch keys and hand Herbert the tool he asks for."

"There's no need to apologize, Tommy. It's not your fault my motor won't start. Thank you for giving it a try." Olive picked up her handbag and took her suitcase, which Tommy had retrieved from behind the driver's seat.

"I'll have Herbert look at it as soon as he gets back."

"Thank you, Tommy. I appreciate it." A gust of icy air swept over Olive as she emerged from the garage and retraced her steps along the pavement back to her boardinghouse. This evening the city would be bustling with Guy Fawkes celebrations, but the streets were fairly quiet now. She ran through alternative transportation possibilities as the wind buffeted her. The train was out of the question. Hawthorne House was a good distance from the railway line, and Sebastian had been quite clear he wanted her visit to be a complete surprise. Cabling that she was on her way and expected to be met at the station this afternoon would give the occupants of Hawthorne House several hours' notice of her arrival, and that just would not do. Not many of her friends had their own motors. Those who did have motorcars weren't exactly the reliable types one wanted to bring along when engaged in professional work. There was really only one option.

She let herself into the boardinghouse, plunked down her

load in the hall by the telephone table, and asked the operator to connect her to Jasper's lodging.

Jasper's man, Grigsby, grudgingly turned the phone over to Jasper, who said, "It's awfully early, old bean. Don't tell me you woke up with a hankering to see more avant-garde art?"

"No, I have a spot of bother. I hope you can help me out."

Olive explained the situation, and Jasper said, "I'll be around in an hour."

"An hour?"

"No matter how dire the situation, Grigsby won't allow me to leave the house without achieving a basic level of sartorial acceptability."

Jasper might blame his delay on his gentleman's gentleman, but Olive knew Jasper was more finicky about his appearance than she was about her own clothing. But she was in no position to argue. "Thank you, Jasper. I'll see you soon."

Despite their late start, they made good time once they were on the road. Jasper wasn't one to tool along admiring the view at a sedate pace. After they left London, they sped along the country lanes. The tall hedgerows dotted with autumn berries flashed by in a blur. While Jasper liked to be perfectly turned out in his clothing, his preference for luxury didn't extend to his motor. He drove an aged Austin 10-hp that rattled and creaked as they raced along. Wind whistled through gaps between the canvas top and the windows. Olive spent most of the drive with her hands shoved into the pockets of her coat, thinking it would have been wiser to have worn her thick tweed ensemble instead of her stylish knit sweater and skirt.

"I can see why Grigsby prefers the train," Olive said over the rumble of the engine.

"What?"

Olive repeated herself, and Jasper nodded and raised his voice to be heard over the noise of the motor and the wind. "Yes, I think Grigsby was right—it is going to rain."

Olive didn't attempt more conversation after that. The temperature dropped as they traveled north, and a bank of low charcoal clouds blotted out the sun. Except for a brief stop for a plowman's lunch at a pub, where Olive snagged a table beside the fire so they could warm up, they didn't stop. The rain held off until they left the main road at the signpost for *Hawthorne Village*, which pointed up a country lane. Fat raindrops splattered against the windshield for a moment, then a torrent of water pounded down. With the wipers swishing back and forth like mad, Jasper hunched forward, slowing the motor to a creep as they jounced along the rutted road, which quickly turned into a muddy mess.

They traveled through the village, which was a single High Street with a few shops, a post office, and a scattering of houses, some of which had front gardens with profusions of Michaelmas daisies and chrysanthemums. Dahlias surrounded one particularly pretty cottage, the heads of the flowers drooping under the onslaught of the rain. Once they left the village behind, Jasper took the second right, turning in at a wrought-iron gate set in a hawthorn hedge with bright crimson berries. A deep forest closed around the road, cutting off the incessant drum of the raindrops. Some of the trees were bare, but autumn leaves still clung to some of the branches of the oak trees, glowing gold and copper even on the rainy day. Under the thick screen of tree limbs, the underbrush was hard to make out, but Olive could see drifts of fallen leaves among the brambles.

The lane abruptly came out of the trees and into a gravel forecourt fronting a brick manor house in the Jacobean style, which was covered in scarlet Virginia creeper. Three-story bay windows on either side of the central entrance were topped with parapets and gave the impression of turrets flanking an entry.

As soon as they cleared the trees, the motor plunged into a curtain of rain. Jasper raised his voice over the clamor of the water lashing against the motor. "I'll stop right at the base of the staircase. You make a dash for it."

By the time Olive opened her umbrella and climbed the four shallow steps, she felt as if she'd walked through a monsoon. Hawthorne House's door was a thick wooden affair. Two narrow mullioned windows on either side of it were nearly covered over with vines. She freed the bell pull from the encroaching twist of the Virginia creeper's flaming tendrils and rang the bell, which set off a gong-like echo inside the house. The small overhang above the door didn't protect Olive from the slanting rain that drummed on her umbrella and gurgled through the down-spouts around the house.

Nervousness sparked through her. She couldn't imagine Mr. Carter would be pleased to have someone descend on him unannounced. Once he realized she was here to check up on him . . . well, he certainly wouldn't be pleased—with her or the situation. She pushed those thoughts away and told herself not to be a rabbit. Sebastian had offered her a job. She'd accepted it and would complete it. Mr. Carter's opinion of her didn't come into it.

Jasper splashed up the steps as Olive rang the bell again. She shifted the umbrella so that it partially covered both of them. Water drenched one of her sleeves and her stockings around her ankles. The last deep vibrations of the gong were fading away when the door was wrenched open.

A man in his early forties said, "Goodness. Have you had a

breakdown in this weather? Come in. Come in. Let's get you out of the rain. Nasty day."

He had a sweep of thick black hair that curved away from his forehead and heavy eyebrows over liquid dark eyes. He wore a cashmere sweater with a silk ascot at his throat and held a half-eaten biscuit. "I do apologize. You caught me during my afternoon tea. Your ringing was so insistent, I came along myself instead of waiting for Mrs. Lum." He popped the biscuit into his mouth and motioned for Olive and Jasper to come in as he dusted crumbs from his sweater.

They stepped inside, leaving copious puddles on the parquet floor. When the man closed the door, it cut off most of the light in the vast entry. Olive had a quick impression of ornately carved heavy wood, a monstrous staircase, and a fireplace on one side of the room that would have been large enough for both Olive and Jasper to walk into. Wan light coming from the narrow windows on either side of the door illuminated a small section of the room, and Olive was able to pick out two paintings, one with horses and hounds on a misty morning, and another of a landscape done in the picturesque style with a crumbling ruin.

Before Olive could tell the man who she was and about her assignment, he said, "Come along to the drawing room," and set off toward a thin string of yellow light that Olive hadn't noticed. It came from around a partially closed door at one side of the entry. Olive propped up the umbrella by the door and followed him. Moving through the gloomy room was a bit like walking about in the dark, and Olive put out a hand to make sure she didn't run into any furniture. As they crossed the old wooden floorboards, they set off a cacophony of creaks and squeaks.

The man threw open the door. "Come warm yourself by the fire. I'll ring for a fresh pot of tea."

Olive entered the room and sent up a silent prayer of thanks that she wasn't inventorying the décor. The spacious room was crammed with heavy Victorian pieces, and every surface was packed with porcelain figures, silver picture frames, fringed lamps, and all sorts of preserved specimens like flowers and butterflies under glass globes. A thick layer of dust covered all the bric-a-brac.

Once Olive looked past the décor, she saw the room itself had once been beautiful. Pilasters with classical capitals framed the fireplace. The walls and ceiling were covered with strapwork. Intricate plaster carvings of birds, flowers, and draped swags of fabric circled the top edge of the walls. The grooves in the carvings were layered with grime, and large chunks of plaster had crumbled, leaving gaps in the design. The ceiling strapwork with its less complex geometric design of ovals and squares had fared better than the walls and was mostly intact.

A blaze crackled in the fireplace, and they all gravitated to it. Olive sidestepped her way between a console table and an enormous world globe that came up to her waist. The furniture had been shoved back to create a little alcove of space in front of the fire, which must have been where the man was before they had disturbed him. A floor lamp curved over the back of an upholstered chair. The ottoman in front of it still showed the imprint of his heels. A crinkled newspaper lay on a nearby table beside a tea tray. A button-back Chesterfield sofa completed the little area of habitation.

When they'd entered the room, the man had yanked on a bell pull, and now an older statuesque woman entered the room. She wore a simple black dress, which was the same shade as her close-set eyes. Wiry gray hairs had escaped from her bun and frizzed out around her face. He murmured something to her, and the gaze she turned on Olive and Jasper before leaving the room was not friendly.

The man joined Olive and Jasper in front of the fire. "Mrs. Lum will return in a moment with tea." He jabbed at the logs with a poker, and sparks sprayed out from the wood. "We don't have many visitors, so you'll have to excuse us."

"It's we who should apologize for dropping in on you unexpectedly, Mr. Carter," Olive said. "You *are* Mr. Carter, aren't you?"

He looked sharply over his shoulder at the mention of his name, then he replaced the fireplace tool. "It appears you have the advantage of me."

Olive extended her hand. "I'm Olive Belgrave." Mr. Carter automatically reached out to shake her hand, but his expression had become guarded. "Sebastian has sent me to do an inventory of the paintings here. I'm sorry to arrive without warning, but Sebastian insisted I leave straightaway." Olive took Sebastian's letter from her handbag. "You'll find all the details in here."

Mr. Carter held the envelope between two fingers as he stared at Olive for a long moment, then he transferred his gaze to Jasper. "And who's this?" Olive opened her mouth to explain why Jasper had brought her, but then she realized if she told the truth, she'd immediately convey the urgency of her visit, and she couldn't do that. After a second, she said, "This is my assistant, Mr. Jasper Rimington."

Olive felt Jasper turn to look at her, but she kept her gaze on Mr. Carter.

"Indeed," Mr. Carter said. "He's your *assistant?*"

"Yes. Mr. Rimington is quite a valuable chap to have around."

Mr. Carter made a humming noise as his gaze darted back and forth between Olive and Jasper. Then he ripped open the envelope and skimmed the letter. "Well. This is a surprise."

Clearly, it was not a happy surprise for him.

He stuffed the letter back into the envelope. "Most irregular. We only have a skeleton staff here, and we do not have the ability to put up guests."

"We won't be any trouble at all. We'll discharge Sebastian's commission and be on our way. It probably won't take us more than a few days." As Mr. Carter's gaze continued to cool, Olive was glad the Morris hadn't started. It was much easier to stand up to Mr. Carter with Jasper at her side.

"I'm sorry, but your staying is out of the question." He smiled as he said the words, but there was no regret in his tone.

"Well, I have my instructions from Sebastian, and I intend to carry them out. If you have any concerns, I suggest you contact him and discuss your thoughts on altering his plan."

Mr. Carter seemed outwardly calm, but his breathing was a little heavy. Olive could see the rise and fall of his ascot. After a few seconds, he looked away from Olive's steady gaze and tapped the envelope. "I'll have to confirm this, you understand."

"Of course. We're sorry to turn up unexpectedly, but Sebastian was quite insistent that I begin at the first possible moment."

"That's not surprising. My dear cousin is not one for considering the impact of his actions on others."

"Oh, I didn't realize you were related."

He waved the envelope. "Distant cousin, several times removed."

Mrs. Lum entered with a rattle of crockery. Jasper moved to shift the tea tray to make room for the new tray she'd brought with fresh tea and more cups. After she'd set down the tray, Mr. Carter said to her, "It appears Miss Belgrave and—ah—Mr. Rimington, was it?—will be staying with us for a short time."

Mrs. Lum turned a sour expression on Olive and Jasper. "I'll prepare two guest rooms." Her tone indicated that she considered them as welcome as a trip to the dentist for a tooth extraction.

Her attitude was insolent, and if anyone had spoken in that manner at Parkview, the stately home owned by Olive's aunt and uncle, the servant would have been turned out immediately. But Mr. Carter only nodded and said to Olive and Jasper, "Please have a seat." Mrs. Lum left, closing the door with such force that the thud reverberated around the high-ceilinged room. Olive expected bits of plaster to rain down after the slam of the door, but only a little dust spiraled through the air. Olive and Jasper sat on the Chesterfield sofa opposite the fire, releasing a puff of dust from the cushions.

Mr. Carter seemed to have recovered a smidge of his bonhomie. "You'll have to excuse Mrs. Lum. Her feet pain her greatly. Corns. You know how difficult it is to keep anyone on, especially in such a remote location as this. Help yourself to tea. I've already had mine. If you'll excuse me for a moment, I'll ring Sebastian."

As soon as he left the room, Jasper turned to Olive. "Assistant?"

"We had to have some sort of explanation for you to stay here as well. I'm not about to send you out into the gale."

"And I'm not about to leave you in this mausoleum." He brushed a dusting of plaster from his shoulders before pouring a cup of tea and handing it to her. "You'd better drink up. It looks like you have your work cut out for you."

Olive hadn't really looked at the paintings yet. She'd been so overwhelmed with the number of furnishings in the room, then she'd been focused on the confrontation with Mr. Carter. She swiveled around, surveying the room. One wall was taken up with windows, which were covered with threadbare drapes that looked as if they'd disintegrate if they were touched. The fireplace dominated another wall. The remaining two walls were covered with art. Rows of oil paintings, one on top of another, rose from the wainscoting to the ceiling. "And this is only one room." Olive tilted her head back as she looked up to the ceiling. "How many rooms do you think a house like this has?"

"At least fifteen or twenty, I'd imagine."

"I think we're going to need more tea."

7

Zoe

Present Day

Zoe flipped to the next page, eager to see what Olive had found when they inventoried the artwork, but there were no more pages.

"Where's the rest of Olive's report?" Zoe muttered as she flicked back through the papers. She looked at each page, but she hadn't missed them. There was nothing else from Olive Belgrave.

Jack touched her arm. "Zoe, we're boarding."

"What?" She looked up. People were standing and shrugging into jackets or reaching for their suitcases. Zoe had been so wrapped up in Olive's report that she'd completely lost track of what was going on in the gate area.

Jack tilted his head toward the folder Zoe was cramming into her messenger bag. "Something wrong?"

"There are some pages missing. It's a report from the woman I was telling you about, the high society lady detective. She went to the country house in nineteen twenty-three to do an inventory of the paintings. I have the beginning of her report to the owner, but then it just cuts off. I'll need to get in touch with Ava and see if she has the rest of the pages and the inventory Olive did for Blakely." Zoe grabbed her rolling suitcase and joined the line. "Maybe she forgot to send them."

"That doesn't sound like Ava."

"I know. Maybe Harrington took them out to read them and they didn't get put back in the file."

Jack looked doubtful.

"It's a long shot, I know, but I need the rest of Olive's report. If the inventory from nineteen twenty-three lists *Woman in a White Fur*, that will go a long way to filling out the provenance."

By the time they'd inched their way down the crowded aisle of the plane and stowed their suitcases, Zoe was on the phone, poised to leave a message for Ava.

Zoe dropped into her seat and tucked the phone against her shoulder. She was surprised when Ava's smooth voice answered. "Hi, Ava. It's Zoe. You're working late." It was evening in London.

"I'm finishing up an assessment that has to go out tomorrow. How can I help you?"

Zoe described the missing pages, and Ava said, "I sent you copies of everything we have." Her tone was matter-of-fact and assured. "I checked with the archive at the Blakely estate, and they say there's nothing else."

"There *has* to be more. This Olive Belgrave went up to Hawthorne House to do an inventory of the paintings. Surely she completed it. And if she didn't, there should be a note or summary indicating she wasn't able to finish."

"I agree. I'm just passing on the information I've received." Ava's tone was calm. She was one of the most mellow people Zoe had ever dealt with. No matter what drama was going on around the office, she remained as cool and unmoved as an iceberg. Zoe had told Ava she should become a professional poker player. With her head for "maths," as Ava called them, and her unflappable personality, Zoe thought Ava would make a fortune. Besides her unflappable nature, Ava was organized and methodical. If she said she'd sent everything, the last pages of the report hadn't been misplaced somewhere around the office. Ava would have sent them if she had them.

"Well, I've got to find them," Zoe said. "I'll try the Blakely Archive again. Thanks, Ava."

Zoe reached for her messenger bag, which she'd tucked under the seat in front of her. The strap caught and wouldn't budge. Jack leaned forward to unwind it. "Ava doesn't have the missing pages?"

"No." Zoe took the messenger bag from him. "And if she doesn't know where they are, then you know they're not in that office." Zoe took out the folder and flipped back to her copies of the inventory and the typed report. The top corner of each piece of paper had been stamped with the words *Property of the Archive of Sebastian Blakely*. A string of numbers was printed under the text.

Zoe typed in a quick search on her phone for the Blakely Archive and dialed. Passengers were still shuffling down the aisle, but it wouldn't be long before she'd have to put away her phone for takeoff.

An automated voice announced, "You have reached the Archives of Sebastian Blakely. Our hours are . . ."

Zoe left her name and phone number along with the details of what she was looking for, reading off the inventory number printed on the top corner of the report. "I look forward to your call."

Zoe sat in the hotel breakfast area, trying to keep her eyelids open. They'd had several delays before their flight had taken off, which had pushed their arrival time in London to nearly noon. By the time they'd cleared customs and traveled to their Knightsbridge hotel, it was edging toward teatime. They'd eaten an early dinner at a nearby restaurant and called it a day, but even after hours of sleep, Zoe's internal clock was still messed up —and she wasn't exactly at her best in the morning to begin with.

With jet lag adding to her already sluggish morning disposition, she felt as if it was the middle of the night despite the sunshine glinting off the buffet's silver chafing dishes. She'd already downed one cup of coffee, which helped her move up the scale from sleepwalker to marginally human. Her fingers were curled around her coffee cup, which she held just below her chin.

A familiar noise permeated her semi-comatose state. Her phone. By the time she'd extracted it from her messenger bag, the call had already gone to voicemail. Harrington. She took another gulp of coffee and pressed the phone to her ear while watching Jack as he made his way across the room with two plates. In his blue dress shirt, tie, and dress pants, he stood out from the tourists in their windbreakers and jeans.

Harrington's recorded message came on the line. "Zoe, I had a call late last night in regard to a negotiation, and I must fly to Taipei this morning. I apologize, but I have to cancel our dinner. It looks as if I'll be returning immediately, but I believe you'll have already left by the time I get back. Again, sorry for dashing out of town at the last moment. If I don't see you before you leave London, have a lovely time."

Zoe put the phone down as Jack handed her a plate. "I brought you a chocolate croissant, and the waitress is on the way with more coffee."

"You do know how to treat a girl." A few delicate flakes of pastry sprinkled onto the plate as Zoe picked up the warm croissant.

Jack slid into the banquette seat beside her, and Zoe smiled.

Jack gave her a quizzical look. "What?"

Zoe gestured at the banquette with her coffee cup. "Old training dies hard. You still won't sit with your back to the room." Jack's spycraft training had never quite left him. There was still an element of caution in everything he did—even years on from that life, his habit of critically assessing their surroundings influenced his every action and thought.

He looked at her over the rim of his orange juice, a small smile on his face. "So the coffee *is* working its magic—you're teasing me." His gaze swept the room. "Besides the unobstructed view, I have a few other reasons for being on this side. First, sitting here prevents you from curling up on the bench and snoring."

"True. Falling back asleep is one of my faults, but I take issue with the snoring."

"Trust me, you snore. And"—he bumped his shoulder against hers—"I like sitting beside my wife."

She leaned into him for a moment. "I like you over here too. It's cozy."

Jack turned his attention to his plate, which was loaded with an English breakfast of eggs, bacon, sausages, beans, fried bread, and grilled tomatoes and mushrooms. He picked up his fork and knife. "Did you hear back from Ava? It seems early even for her."

"No. It was Harrington canceling our dinner. He had to leave for Asia this morning."

"What happened?"

"He didn't go into detail, but I know he's been working on a negotiation for weeks, trying to recover a painting that was stolen from a private home ten years ago."

"What do you plan to do while I have my appointments?"

Zoe popped the last bite of the croissant into her mouth. She felt as if her brain was finally beginning to function. "I'll follow up with the archive. That may take a while, but they don't open until noon. I'm sure I can find something to do until then. I might drop by the art gallery that has *Woman in a White Fur* on display—a place called the Janus Gallery. Then I'll wander around London."

8

————

Once breakfast was over, Jack slipped into his all-business mode and went silent, his thoughts on his upcoming meeting. A few years ago, Zoe would have been hurt or annoyed at the change in his manner, but now she knew he was mentally preparing himself, going over possible questions his clients would ask and how he'd answer. He buttoned his suit jacket, gave her a kiss, and was out the door in under two minutes.

Zoe had no need to rush. The gallery didn't open until ten. She was tempted to crawl back into bed but fought off the desire. She'd dragged herself into a mostly coherent state. If she went back to bed, she might not wake up until evening—and then she'd be even more messed up than she was now. She turned her back on the invitingly rumpled sheets and sat down with her laptop instead. She'd received an email from the estate of the artist with a copy of the bill of sale. Zoe clicked on the scanned document. The neat cursive handwriting certainly looked like something written decades ago. No one wrote that neatly now. The ink was faded to a sepia brown and enumerated the sale of two paintings to Sebastian Blakely, both original one-of-a-kind pieces. One was listed as *Woman in a White Fur*. The dimensions of the paintings were listed along with the note about packaging the canvases. The bill of sale certainly looked authentic, but they might need an expert to examine the original document. She made a note, then since she still had some time to burn, she did a couple of online searches, scanning the links about Sebastian Blakely and the painting.

Zoe found an article about the current owner of *Woman in a White Fur* in the online archives of a small regional newspaper. They'd run a profile on Rosalind Kingwood, interviewing her when the Sebastian Blakely Museum and Archive opened at Hawthorne House. It seemed Rosalind was the driving force behind gathering Blakely's photographs and papers into a central location. Zoe skimmed the text, pausing to read Rosalind's comments on opening day. "It's been a rather large project but incredibly satisfying. My great-granduncle's work was incredibly innovative. Having the majority of it here will let viewers experience the whole range of his career from the early nineteen twenties until his death in the seventies."

A few photographs accompanied the article. One was the black and white self-portrait of Blakely that had been attached to the file. The next image was one of Blakely's photographs of a Hollywood actress from the forties. She wore a sparkling evening dress. Her sweep of blonde hair covered one eye as she looked into a full-length mirror, which reflected her small smile that seemed to hint she had a secret and might share it with the viewer.

The article included a smaller color photograph of Rosalind. She sat at a desk, her gaze focused on her laptop as she typed. A pair of glasses pushed up on her head held back her pale brown hair, which fell straight to her shoulders. Rosalind projected an air of focus as if she really didn't have time to look up from the laptop and smile while her picture was taken. Zoe couldn't see any physical resemblance between Rosalind and Sebastian Blakely.

Zoe checked the address of the Janus Gallery and the hours of the Blakely Archive, then headed out. The gallery was located in a three-story white-painted brick building on a quiet Kensington street. It was too early for it to be open, and the glass-fronted ground floor was dark inside. Zoe peered through the large window, but *Woman in a White Fur* wasn't visible. She headed for Hyde Park and strolled among the business-suited men and women striding purposefully along while a smattering of early-bird tourists snapped selfies.

She found a little café and had another cup of coffee but avoided the chocolate croissant this time, then made her way back to the art gallery. By the time she returned, the lights were on and the door was unlocked. The soft notes of classical music floated through the gallery. It was a long, narrow space with a low ceiling and a staircase along one wall with waist-high glass sections serving as a banister. A mixture of Impressionist and Abstract paintings hung on the walls. A piece of art made of strips of metal suspended on wires hung from the ceiling at the center of the room. A scuffed ladder-back chair was positioned below the wires, and a chunk of concrete rested on the seat of the chair. The bits of metal spun on the wires in the air current Zoe created as she walked by. An arrangement of Dutch pottery was displayed on the small console table by the stairs.

A man who was probably in his early forties came out from behind the sleek marble-topped counter at the back of the room and greeted her. He wore a pale gray suit, and he had a deep tan and dark black hair.

"Hello. I'm Zoe Andrews." She shook his hand and gave him one of her cards. "I'm working with Throckmorton Enquiries on the provenance for *Woman in a White Fur*. I'd like to take a look at it in person."

"Of course. Of course. I'm Daniel Janus, owner of the gallery. I'll be happy to help you. Right this way." He led her up the stairs to the next floor, which was more open. "It's here in the alcove." He paced the length of the second floor, his hand extended to the back wall where the Tamara de Lempicka painting hung. It was the only artwork in that section of the gallery, but even among a crowded grouping of paintings, it would have stood out with its rich purple dress and arresting style.

Janus had stopped a few paces behind Zoe, giving her the ability to view the painting from any angle. Zoe looked at it for a moment from a distance, then she stepped forward and examined the layers of paint. Zoe expected him to leave her, but he waited at her side. He was silent, but a slight air of impatience radiated from him. He didn't do anything so gauche as tap his foot, but he did check his watch several times.

After a few moments Zoe turned to Janus. "It's stunning."

"Quite." He stood with one arm crossed over his waist and the other propped on his wrist, his fingers curled against his chin. "I agree." He pulled his fingers away from his face, gesturing to the canvas. "You realize we have no doubts as to its authenticity?"

"I'm glad to hear it. Might I see the back?"

A winkle appeared between his thick brows. "It could be arranged, but we'd need to deactivate the security plates and remove it from the brackets fastening it to the wall."

"So it's an involved process."

"Yes. Our insurance requires it—and we'd take the precautions regardless of their stipulations." He looked at his watch again. "The photographs we sent Mr. Throckmorton are an exact likeness of the back."

Jack would approve of the security arrangements. "Then I won't put you to the trouble right now." Zoe understood the headache it would be to remove the canvas from the wall, especially if it was wired with pressure-sensitive plates. It wasn't her job to examine the painting itself. Someone else would do that if the provenance checked out. "What are your thoughts on the painting?"

"We all agree it's marvelous. No tests of a scientific nature have been done, but you can see for yourself that it's a masterpiece."

"All you need is the paperwork to go with it."

"Correct," he said with a smile.

"Thank you for letting me see it. I won't take up any more of your time."

"Allow me to walk you out." He handed her his card, and Zoe noticed he had a better manicure than she did. Janus motioned for her to lead the way down the stairs. "Please let me know if you have any other questions or if you'd like to see the painting again."

"Thank you. I will."

As soon as they reached the bottom of the stairs, a woman rushed across the room to Janus, brushing by Zoe without looking at her. She was slender and wore black leggings, chunky ankle boots, and an oversized oatmeal-colored sweater with an asymmetrical hem that fluttered around her hips as she walked. "Oh, Danny. There you are. They look *spectacular*." She flung her hands up by her shoulders, emphasizing each syllable of the last word as she patted the air, her fingers spread wide. "I just had to see them."

Her white-blonde hair was cropped close around her neck in

the back, but her bangs fell in long strands over eyes that were as bright blue as the Dutch pottery on the console table. She twitched her long fringe aside and leaned in to kiss Janus on both cheeks in the continental manner.

"Hello, Farina," Janus said. "I didn't realize you were in London."

"Just a brief trip, then I'm headed back to Amsterdam tonight."

Janus pivoted to include Zoe. "Allow me to introduce Zoe Andrews. She's with Throckmorton Enquiries. Zoe, this is Farina, one of our up-and-coming artists. You might have noticed her work when you came in."

Zoe had only one painting on her mind when she'd entered—*Woman in a White Fur.* She'd barely glanced at anything else, but she kept that observation to herself.

Farina extended her hand. "That's Farina Vee." She spelled her last name for Zoe as if Zoe were a reporter taking notes for an article. Then she added, "But I sign all my canvases as Farina V—with the single initial." She circled a hand. "It is a gimmick, of course. We starving artists must do what we can to stand out. And I'm Dutch—my last name is actually Veenendaal, which is difficult for English speakers."

Zoe had noticed a slight accent in Farina's speech but hadn't been able to place where she might be from. Farina tilted her head, causing her thatch of white hair to fall farther away from her arched eyebrow. "Throckmorton . . . where have I heard that?"

"We handle all sorts of inquiries related to fine art and antiquities. Art recovery, provenance research, and the like."

"Oh—the Tamara de Lempicka. You're the one working on that."

"Yes." Zoe gave Janus a sideways glance.

Farina placed a hand on Janus' arm. "Oh, don't be upset. He's not giving away confidential information. *Woman in a White Fur* is the talk of the art world right now. Everyone knows it's here and wants a peek at it." She swiveled to face Janus, not so subtly excluding Zoe. "Are you sure I can't talk you into bringing it downstairs? Even just for a couple of hours? It would be so amazing to have my work displayed alongside hers."

Janus gave a perfunctory little smile. It was obviously not the first time he'd fielded that request. "No, that's not possible. Insurance reasons, as I've said."

"Oh well." Farina swiveled her gaze to Zoe and leaned forward in a confiding way. "I keep trying. Eventually I'll get him to give in." Zoe doubted that, but thankfully she didn't have to reply because Farina didn't wait for an answer. "Let me show you my work."

Farina was already moving away, and since the paintings were in the window by the door, Zoe followed her. Farina threw out an arm. "Those two. *Titled* and *Untitled*." Excitement suffused her voice.

Two medium-sized canvases hung side-by-side near the gallery's front window. They were mirror images of a sort. One was entirely covered in white paint and had a single black dot in the middle. The other was covered with black paint and had a single white dot in the middle.

"Interesting." It was the safest thing Zoe could say.

Janus said, "We've had quite a few inquiries about them."

"I imagine so," Zoe murmured.

"They're meant to be a pair," Farina said. "I do hope the same person buys both of them. Their statement about the void of the modern world and the contextual dichotomy of emptiness and fullness only works if they're side by side. You must sell them as a pair, Danny. I *insist*."

"I agree," he said, and Zoe wondered if it was more a financial motivation than an artistic one.

"I must be off," Zoe said, partly because she couldn't think of anything else to say about the paintings and partly because, while her mother had not been the best person to teach manners, Zoe had learned that if she didn't have something nice to say, it was best to not say anything at all.

As she walked away from the Janus Gallery, Zoe took out her phone to see if an industrious employee at the Blakely Archive had arrived early and returned her call. Nothing. No messages or missed calls. It was only ten thirty, and Jack wouldn't be done until late afternoon. Zoe did a quick search of the train schedules, then she set off at a brisk pace, sending Jack a text to update him on her plans. She could be in Warwickshire by the time the Blakely Archive opened at noon. She'd grab the photocopies she needed of Olive's report and inventory. She'd be back in London before dinner.

9

Zoe gripped the armrest and cringed as the car drifted toward the tall green hedgerow. A car was approaching from the opposite direction. Zoe waited for the scrape of metal on metal, but her driver maintained her loose one-handed hold on the steering wheel, and the two cars slid by each other without incident.

Getting to Hawthorne House had proved to be harder than Zoe expected. The Sebastian Blakely Museum and Archive was off the beaten path. It was too far to walk from the train station, and Zoe had no desire to drive on what she considered the wrong side of the road, so she'd opted for a rideshare. Her driver, a chatty young woman, shouted over the pop tunes blaring from her radio as they whipped along the narrow lanes.

Zoe caught a glimpse of a signpost that read *Hawthorne* before they raced through a picturesque village of stone and brick cottages with beautiful gardens. A few miles later, the driver turned at an iron gate set into a hawthorn hedge, and they plunged into a thick forest. The short lane curved through the trees for a few seconds, then they came out of the belt of foliage.

The driver wheeled the car onto the gravel forecourt in front of Hawthorne House. "Quiet today, isn't it? No kiddies or mums." Seeing Zoe's puzzled expression, the driver added, "The park area around the house is open for picnicking, and people come here quite a bit during the summer for the gardens and the hiking trails in the wood."

"I see."

"But it's a little too cold for that now. You'll probably have the place to yourself. Tours run from now until October, then they shut everything down."

"Does the family live here?"

"No, it's just a museum now. At least people get to enjoy the park."

Zoe thanked the driver and climbed out. The car pulled away, and she paused for a moment, taking in the castle-like appearance of the red brick manor. Vibrantly green Virginia creeper softened the edges of the building and gave it a fairytale aura that reminded Zoe of illustrations in storybooks, except that it was a smaller version of those rambling and multi-turreted affairs. The house was larger than many of the mansions in the more exclusive neighborhoods in Dallas, but she supposed it was only modest in size compared to some of the castles and grand stately homes in England.

She climbed the shallow steps, but before she reached the hefty wooden door, it opened. A plump lady with curly dish-water blonde hair said, "Oh, hello. You're right on time for the tour."

"Actually, I'm here to visit the archive."

The woman looked a little disappointed. "I'll call Mona for you as soon as I get this set up." She wrestled a sandwich board out of the door.

"Here, let me help you. Over there?" Zoe unfolded the board with bold letters. *Tours start here.*

"Yes, there by the edge of the steps. Thank you. Come in."

A huge chandelier lit the vast hall of rich dark wood. A massive hearth filled one wall, and a grand staircase marched up another.

"Mona came down a moment ago. She should be back—yes, here she is."

A young woman entered the hall from a side door, holding a mug. She had a peacock-blue bob, and her brightly colored head was tilted down as she studied a notepad as she walked.

"Mona," the older lady called out. "You have a visitor for the archive."

Zoe crossed the room to her. Mona's hair and makeup were perfectly and elaborately done. Her lash extensions and bright red lipstick contrasted with her casual jeans, scuffed boots, and a poncho-like sweater that was trailing threads from the hem. Zoe extended her hand. "Hello. I'm Zoe Andrews."

Mona tucked the notepad under her arm and switched her mug to her left hand. "Mona Lake." Her eyebrows, one of which had a piercing in it, flared. "You're with Throckmorton Enquires. I just listened to your message. I thought you were in America."

"I usually am, but I'm visiting London and had a free afternoon. I decided to run up here and save you some time. I'm happy to photocopy the rest of Olive Belgrave's report and the inventory she completed." An expression that Zoe couldn't identify chased across Mona's face, and Zoe quickly added, "Olive Belgrave, the woman who did the inventory here at Hawthorne House in nineteen twenty-three."

"Oh yes. I know exactly who Olive is. Can I see some ID?"

"Um, sure." Zoe took out her Texas driver's license, which

Mona scrutinized for longer than Zoe would have thought necessary.

Mona handed it back. "Thank you." She let out a small sigh, then gestured with her mug to the grand staircase. "You better come up."

The paper square on the string attached to a teabag fluttered around Mona's mug as they climbed the steps. "Care for a cuppa?" Mona asked.

"Thank you, but no. I had lunch on the train." Zoe wanted to get her copies and get back to London.

Enlargements of Sebastian Blakely's color photographs lined the stairs, and Zoe slowed her steps to give each a quick look.

Mona, who'd been trotting up the steps at a rapid pace, slowed down. "Sorry. I see them every day and forget how eye-catching they are."

"He did photograph some famous people, didn't he?" They'd already passed photos of a First Lady, two princesses, and several actresses from Hollywood's Golden Age.

"Blakely was the go-to photographer. He could make anyone look amazing." They reached the top of the staircase, and Mona led the way down a corridor with a creaky parquet floor. A series of small chandeliers hung from the lofty ceiling, and a few flower arrangements perched on side tables, but the main focus of the décor was again Blakely's photographs. These portraits were all black and white and looked from the clothes as if they'd been taken in the twenties, but Zoe didn't recognize the people in these images. While they might not have been famous, they were glamorous. In one, a beautiful woman with blonde hair posed with her folded hands on a mirrored surface, her cheek resting on the back of her top hand. The mirror reflected her face and hands as well as the multi-strand pearl bracelet she wore. In another, a man in a tux—probably one of the Bright

Young People—stood in a formal garden gazing at a classical statue.

Through the open doors along the corridor, Zoe could see the rooms upstairs had been turned into galleries. Photographs lined the walls, and the only furnishings were couches at the center of the rooms. They reached the end of the hallway, and Mona stopped in front of a panel door that was nearly twice her height. A gold plate beside the door had the word *Archive* on it. Mona blocked Zoe's view, punched in a code on a lock, waited for a beep, then flicked back the deadbolt.

She held the door so Zoe could follow her in. Rows of metal shelves filled the room, leaving tiny, narrow aisles. Archival boxes of all sizes were stacked to the ceiling. An antique desk with a rope-edge carving stood in one corner. Mona moved behind the desk and gestured to a single straight-backed chair in front of it.

Zoe sat down and wondered if Mona ever felt claustrophobic with the rows of shelves towering over her.

"I'd offer to take your coat, but it doesn't get warm in here until the sun hits the back of the house in the afternoon. It's actually a good thing for the documents." Mona dropped the notepad on the desk beside her computer and set down her mug. "I'll find the box you're interested in."

Mona disappeared down one of the aisles. The shelves were so close together that the hem of her long sweater brushed against the boxes as she walked. She returned and put an archival box on the desk in front of Zoe. "You're free to have a look, but I have to warn you, you're going to be disappointed. I sent everything we had to Throckmorton Enquiries. The reports and inventory you're looking for aren't in there."

"Reports? There's more than one?"

"There were. Olive Belgrave sent several reports to Blakely, but they're gone."

Zoe took off the lid. "They're lost?"

"Missing." Something in Mona's tone made Zoe frown. A trace of anger? Mona motioned to the box, and her tone returned to normal. "But feel free to double-check." Her vivid lips broke into a smile. "I can see you're the sort who likes to chase down every angle, and since you came all the way from London, I thought you'd like to see for yourself."

Mona sat down and gave her full attention to her computer, her fingers tapping away on the keyboard.

Zoe pulled the box closer. It contained the originals of Olive's letter to Sebastian and the few pages of the report Zoe had read along with the family tree, legal documents, and the photographs of the painting. When she'd finished looking through the box, she returned everything and fastened the lid into place. "Could the rest of Olive Belgrave's reports have been misfiled?" Zoe asked with a glance at the box-filled shelves looming behind Mona.

The clacks from the keyboard cut off, and Mona spun her chair toward Zoe. "No. I'm sure Mallory has them." The shift in tone was back, and it was definitely anger. "I can't prove it—or do anything about it."

"Mallory?"

"Mallory Tredmont."

Speaking the name aloud obviously annoyed Mona. Her bright lips flattened as she pressed them together.

"Well, if this Mallory Tredmont has them, I'll have to find her and convince her to let me see them."

"Good luck with that. She's very . . . possessive of them. Even though they're not hers."

"Why is that?"

"You've looked over the genealogy chart?" At Zoe's nod, Mona sat back in her chair and picked up a paperclip, turning it over in her hands. "Then you know Rosalind Kingwood is a direct descendant of Sebastian Blakely. Mallory Tredmont is on the chart, but she's such a distant relation she's barely on the paper—a *very* distant cousin. But from the way she carries on, you'd think she was Blakely's daughter! She's writing a book about Blakely—or that's what she *says*, although I have yet to see evidence of an actual manuscript. Mallory wants access to the archive to 'double-check some facts.' I told her she had to show me the manuscript before I'd give her access. She's banned after what happened."

"Banned?"

"There was something about her visits to the archive that made me uneasy. I couldn't put my finger on it, but I always made sure to stay in here with her when she came to do research. But then one day she convinced one of the museum docents to let her in here while I was at lunch. When I returned, I found Mallory scattering papers across the floor as she bulldozed through the boxes—including that one you've been looking through." Mona had twisted the paperclip, folding it over on itself. "I kicked her out, of course, but I didn't think to check her bag." Mona threw the paperclip onto her desk. "I was so angry about the mess, it never crossed my mind that she'd actually steal documents. But once I'd cleaned up her chaos, I discovered several items were missing." Mona dragged the mangled paperclip across the desk and tossed it in the trash. "At least she didn't take any of the original photos or negatives. That would have been a disaster." Mona flicked her hand to the door. "Mallory is the reason we had to have a deadbolt lock installed."

"Well, if she has the reports, that's what I need. I will just have to convince her to let me see them."

Mona gave Zoe a long look, then said, "Perhaps you can. Don't tell her I set you on her trail. She hates me. I'm the reason she can't finish her book. It has nothing to do with writer's block —or laziness."

"I read one of her blog articles that mentioned her book about Blakely."

Mona snorted. "I doubt she's got more than a couple of chapters finished, if that. She's one of those people with grand plans but no follow through."

"She has some sort of secret about Blakely . . .?"

Mona rolled her eyes. "Mallory has no new information. She's quite good about creating fiction—her own truth. There's nothing new out there about Blakely. She thinks the hint of a juicy bit of gossip will draw in a publisher or an agent."

Zoe stood up and handed Mona her card. "Thank you for seeing me and letting me look through the materials myself. You're right, I had to check them."

"I understand."

Zoe put her messenger bag on her shoulder, letting it drape across her chest. "Can you give me any information about where I can find Mallory Tredmont?"

"I'm afraid it will be a bit of a journey."

"Is she in some remote village in South America or something?"

"Not quite that far. She's in Amsterdam."

"Actually, that works out perfectly."

10

"That's who we're meeting?" From his seat beside her in the airplane, Jack studied the photo of a young woman that Zoe had brought up on her phone.

"Attempting to meet. Yes, Mallory Tredmont. I wasn't able to track down a good phone number for her. The number Ava found was disconnected, but I do have directions to the houseboat she's sharing with a boyfriend."

Zoe zoomed in on the image of Mallory to make it larger. Zoe had found many photos of Mallory Tredmont online—she had a big social media presence with thousands of followers—but in most of her selfies, she wore a hat, either a wide-brimmed fedora or a floppy sun hat, and it was hard to see her face. Zoe had only found one clear photo of Mallory. She sat at a desk with a fountain pen poised over a stack of paper as she held a thick book open. Behind tortoiseshell glasses, her eyes were deep set. Dark brown shoulder-length hair fell in fashionable loose waves around her face. She looked like a college student who'd been interrupted in the library cramming for final exams.

Zoe had spent their short flight from London to Amsterdam

skimming Mallory's blog posts while Jack slept. He'd seem preoccupied and tired after his meetings, and Zoe had learned to give him some space when he was in that state. He'd bring up whatever was bothering him soon enough. "There's very little information about her and only a smattering of posts about her book, which are vague and brief. Tons of posts about living in Amsterdam—lots on cycling as well as the best museums and restaurants, how to get to Keukenhof Gardens to see the tulips— I bookmarked that one. I think there's a bus service, but it's been a while since I proofread the Amsterdam *Smart Travel* guidebook."

"There's a bus. All-day departures from the airport as well as several locations around Amsterdam." Jack's preoccupation slipped away as he talked about the tourist sites. He pulled out a printed list that had been tucked between the pages of the guidebook.

"You *did* make an itinerary for us."

"Don't worry. It's not written in stone."

"Really?"

"Yes, really." He grinned. "Although I will admit I created a color-coded highlighting system to help me find everything in the travel guides."

"Ugh. You can color-code all you want, just don't expect *me* to use it. You know systems and plans make me twitchy."

"Oh, I'd never do that."

The flight attendant announced they were preparing to land. Jack moved his seat forward one inch, out of the so-called reclining position. "Do you want to see if we can find this Mallory person before we go to the gardens or a museum?"

"If you don't mind."

"No. I did a little work on this trip. Now it's your turn."

Zoe wrinkled her nose. "We're both sort of workaholics, you know."

"Perhaps just a touch. But this stuff you're working on *is* interesting. It's not like you're shut away in a conference room pitching potential clients or inputting data in spreadsheets."

"I draw the line at spreadsheets on vacation. I do have some boundaries."

"And I promise no more client meetings, not even video calls."

"Okay," Zoe said. "It's a pact. I'll get the report and inventory from Mallory, then it's all vacation, all the time."

Jack nodded. "Deal."

Zoe considered the photo of Mallory one more time before switching off her phone. Jack said, "That's a serious look on your face."

"Just trying to figure out the best way to approach Mallory. I'd like to get her to tell me firsthand about her dramatic scoop on the painting."

"You think she'll talk to you about it?"

"You're thinking like a spy." Zoe tightened her seatbelt. "*You* wouldn't tell some new acquaintance the tiniest bit of info about yourself, but most people aren't so guarded. They like to talk—especially about themselves. If I can get her talking, she might just tell us the big secret. Big secrets are hard to keep. People are usually bursting to tell someone."

"So we treat her like a source. Gain her trust and use her knowledge to our benefit."

Zoe wrinkled her nose. "That sounds so callous. I prefer to think of it as getting at the truth. If there's an issue with the painting, the buyer needs to know. If not, we need to convince Mallory she's not doing any good spreading rumors to the contrary."

"Do you want to go by yourself? She might be more willing to talk if you're alone."

"Maybe. Let's play it by ear. If it seems like she wants to talk to me alone, you're good at fading out. But—well, let's just say having you along might be an advantage."

Jack frowned. "You think we need to tail her?"

Zoe laughed. "No, you're good-looking. You might be able to break the ice, strike up a conversation with her."

"Oh, so I'm eye candy now?"

Zoe kept a straight face and lifted a shoulder. "Don't you like the idea of being eye candy?"

"I think I'd rather fade out."

"Yes, that does sound more like you. Okay, I'll do the talking and only call on you if eye candy is absolutely necessary."

A few hours later, after they'd dropped their bags in their room and had taken a few pictures of themselves beside a planter bursting with red tulips outside their hotel, they set off to amble around Amsterdam. They were walking along a suburban street with a mix of modern and more aged apartment buildings and shops. Small cars were parallel parked bumper-to-bumper on each side of the road, and trees with tender pale green leaves lined the wide sidewalk. They could have been in any European city, but then a blast of the sweet yet pungent smell of marijuana engulfed them as they passed an open doorway.

"No doubt about what they serve in that coffee shop, is there?" Jack said.

"We're definitely in Amsterdam."

They came to a cross street, busy with small cars jouncing along the bricked roads. The light changed, and Zoe was about to step off the curb, but the tinny sound of a bell rang out, and she jumped back as a cluster of bicycle riders swept by. Most of them were adults dressed for work in business casual clothes, with their purses or messenger bags worn across their chests. They rode sturdy bikes, sitting with perfect posture as they zipped by, the wind ruffling their hair and clothes. Zoe turned to Jack. "I forgot, bikes have the right-of-way here. Can you imagine how healthy we'd be if we rode bikes everywhere?"

"We wouldn't have to go to the gym as much, but it's not practical when your work is twenty or thirty miles away."

"Yes, but I'd love it."

Jack grinned. "Says the woman who works from home."

"True, but I could ride down to get my morning coffee."

"That could be extremely dangerous unless you'd already had at least one cup of coffee—"

Jack broke off as they turned a corner and came to a canal. Zoe checked for swift-moving bike riders, then crossed to the edge of the canal. "Now, this is iconic Amsterdam."

It was a beautiful day, bright and cloudless. The still waters of the canal reflected the lacy pattern of the elms and the buildings that towered over the trees. The flat-fronted brick buildings rose on either side of the canal to steep-pitched roofs with false fronts in a multitude of shapes—some curved like a bell, others rose in straight lines to a triangular point, while still others sported a stepped outline. A glass-enclosed tourist barge putted along through the serene water, sending out ripples behind it.

Zoe and Jack leaned on the metal railing that edged the canal. Zoe pointed above the trees. "Check out the hooks at the top of the buildings." They were mounted on sturdy pieces of wood protruding from the peak of the gables. "They attach pulleys to them, then hoist furniture up to the windows. They've used them for centuries."

"That's my travel-lover. I knew you hadn't forgotten all those details from your guidebook-proofing days." Jack tilted his head back, his chin rising as he took in the building directly behind them. "Using a pulley would be much better than taking the stairs, especially when you've got five or six flights."

They strolled along the canal, stopping to photograph an incredibly narrow house that was only a few feet wide, then they dropped into a shop to order Vlaamse Frites—not French fries —at a stand-up counter. The chef dipped the thick-cut strips of potatoes into sizzling oil, tossed them with salt, then served them in a paper cone. The variety of sauces to choose from was extensive, but they went with a heavy dollop of ketchup. Jack motioned to a couple of bar stools that lined the shop's window. "Want to sit?"

"No, let's keep walking. There's so much to see." They nibbled fries as they wandered along the canals and over bridges, making their way to the Prinsengracht Canal, where Mallory's houseboat was located.

The canals of Amsterdam ran in concentric half circles. The central train station was at the center of the half circle, perched between the Old Town and a channel that ships had used to reach Amsterdam for centuries. The canals moved out from the central point in ever-larger arcing half circles. Roads and bridges bisected the canals, creating a fan-like pattern. If they took the correct canal and cut through on certain bridges, they could save themselves quite a few steps and a lot of time—not that Zoe wanted to cut their rambling short. She was soaking up the atmosphere and enjoying every step of their walk, but the sooner they found Mallory and tracked down Olive's reports, the sooner they could focus solely on their vacation.

Zoe ate her last fry and tossed the empty paper cone in a trash bin. "I think we're almost there." They crossed over an arched bridge, then went along a short street with clothing shops and cafés, weaving in and out of tourists loaded down with backpacks and shopping bags, catching snatches of English, German, and what sounded like Russian or an Eastern European language. Tulips were everywhere, their bright colors and straight stems bursting out of round stone planters spaced along the streets as well as in pots and buckets on the steps leading into the shops.

Rows of houseboats lined each side of the next canal. "Looks like the right place," Jack said.

"So interesting how they're all so different." Some were squat houses on floating platforms, but others were actual boats that had been converted to homes. One was painted bright orange and had a colorful contrasting blue trim, while the next houseboat had a sleek gray exterior and a modern style. Farther down the canal, another one looked to be made of slats of teakwood. Another was covered with a mass of low-growing plants, like a rooftop garden. Flowers in pots with trailing ivy decorated the decks of some of the houseboats, while other owners had created container gardens along the edge of the canal.

Zoe consulted the map and the note from Ava. "Mallory's is the third one from this bridge on the east side of the canal, by the bistro with green awnings. There, I see it."

Zoe navigated around a tangle of bikes propped against a row of metal racks. Only a couple of the bikes were locked with chains.

"Trusting lot around here," Jack said, noticing Zoe's gaze.

"Yes. I've heard the way to keep your bike from being stolen is to ride one so old that no one would want to steal it."

Mallory's houseboat was low and barge-like, painted a dull brown with small portholes lining the cabin. "It looks closed up," Jack said as they approached.

Zoe wasn't sure what the protocol was when visiting a house-boat, but since there was no one around to ask if she could come aboard, she crossed the wooden gangplank with Jack following her. They walked along the narrow passage at the side of the low cabin to reach the front—the bow, she supposed—gliding her hand along a waist-high rope that was obviously meant to prevent someone from falling off. The boat had barely shifted under their weight when they crossed the gangplank. If Mallory was onboard, could she tell someone had stepped onto the boat?

The narrow passage opened to a deck at the front of the boat with a pair of plastic chairs and a low table. A pot of drooping pink tulips with frilly-edged petals sat on the water-spotted table. The entrance to the boat had to be a metal hatch on the cabin's roof. Zoe knocked on it.

Silence. The boat didn't rock with movement from inside the cabin. Zoe knocked again, pounding harder. After a moment, she stepped back.

Jack angled to the side and peered through one of the port-holes. "No light on inside. She's probably at work." They made their way back to the gangplank. "We can come back this evening. We'll have a better chance of finding her home then."

"Yes, you're right. We can come back to this part of Amsterdam for dinner."

"Sounds good." Once they'd crossed the gangplank to the road that edged the canal, Jack paused to allow a woman with a wooden box the size of a wheelbarrow mounted on the front of her bike to trundle by. As she passed, a toddler with curly hair peered at them from inside the cart. A small dog and a string bag of groceries were nestled beside the little kid.

"Wow." Zoe's gaze followed the mom. "I think that was the Amsterdam version of an SUV."

"Impressive."

"I bet she never has to go to the gym." Zoe realized they were blocking the view of a man with gray hair pulled back into a thin ponytail who was taking a photo of the canal from his café table at the bistro. They moved out of his way, and Jack took out the map that came with the guidebook. "So . . . where to now? Art, tulips, or more wandering the canals? I'm good with anything."

Zoe settled her sunglasses on her face. "It's such a gorgeous day. Let's look at flowers."

11

The bus was covered with images of tulips. "Well, that makes it easy to find the right one to take us to the flowers," Zoe said before she and Jack climbed aboard, squeezing into the last pair of open seats. "Popular destination today," Zoe murmured.

"Keukenhof Gardens are only open for about six weeks each year, so I imagine it's busy all the time."

"I love it when you speak guidebook."

Jack flared an eyebrow. "I'll have to remember that."

They left the city center behind and skimmed along the highway to the outskirts of Amsterdam, where modern buildings lined the freeway. The sun streamed through the window, and the steady hum of the wheels created a soothing white noise. Zoe's eyelids felt heavy, and she put her head on Jack's shoulder.

A soft voice sounded in her ear. "Zoe, take a look." She sat up straight, rotating her shoulders to work out a kink in her neck as she followed the direction of Jack's gaze out the window. Strips of brightly colored lines marched away from the bus across the flat land toward the horizon, each one a vibrant color—startling yellow, crimson, lush purple, shocking pink. Zoe reached for her phone to take a picture. "Are those tulips? We're going by so quickly I can't tell."

A woman in the seat in front of them twisted around. "They're hyacinths. Aren't they gorgeous?" She had a British accent, and she was clearly prepared to spend hours looking at flowers. A canvas hat dangled between her shoulder blades, sunglasses were perched on her head amid her white curls, and a bulging fanny pack encircled her waist. "You'll see lots of those today too, not just tulips."

"You've been here before?" Jack asked her.

"My third visit. It's a gardener's heaven."

The bus maneuvered around a massive parking lot where the sun glinted off thousands of cars, then stopped near the entrance to the gardens.

They made their way through the gates and into a forecourt area where people were milling about, heads bent over maps. Jack surveyed the multiple paths that branched off from the entrance area. "I had no idea this place was so large."

Zoe skimmed the map she'd picked up as they walked in. "It's like Disneyland for flowers."

They set off down a random path and worked their way through the open-air displays. The tulips were planted in a mixture of patterns, some of them masses of straight lines of a single variety of tulip. Other flowerbeds contained many varieties of flowers and mixed shades and tones of the same color or contrasting colors, like one that contained pink and white hyacinths along with tulips so dark purple that they almost looked black.

Some of the flower beds were arranged in geometric shapes, while others undulated through the landscape, a meandering blaze of scarlet or brilliant white. And there were indeed plenty of hyacinths and crocuses along with the tulips. The hyacinths in particular had a strong aroma, and when they rounded a corner and came to a sweep of hyacinths under a stand of tall pines, the scent was so intense that it seemed as if they'd walked into a cloud of perfume.

They wandered in and out of several of the display halls with rows of unusual tulips. The variations of the tulips were endless, ranging from color to petal shape to height. Zoe scanned the seemingly endless diversity. "These are amazing but a little over-whelming. I think I like the outdoor gardens the best."

"Then let's go back outside." Jack pushed open a glass door, and the scent of hyacinths engulfed them again. They strolled along the path and came to a long bed of sunny yellow tulips that contrasted with the dark green lawn. "This demands a picture with us in it." Zoe looked around to ask someone to take their picture and caught sight of a familiar figure. "Look, it's that man from the café—the one who was trying to take a picture and we blocked his shot. The guy with the gray ponytail."

Jack moved his gaze over the crowd in an unhurried fashion. "I see him."

"It's kind of weird to see him again." It was his position that caught Zoe's eye, with his arm extended for a photo.

"Probably just a coincidence. The canal with the houseboats is a tourist attraction, and this is another major one." Jack glanced around. "We'll probably go to dinner at the same restaurant as some of these people later tonight."

"I suppose you're right." They moved on, but Zoe noticed Jack glanced back and gave the man a long look.

They were strolling around the delicate white blossoms on some massive cherry trees a little later when Zoe's phone dinged with a text. "It's from Ava." Sheltering the screen from the sun with her hand, Zoe read, "*Woman in a White Fur* stolen during the night!"

"What?" Jack pushed his sunglasses up on his head and leaned in to look over her shoulder.

"Ava sent a link to a news video."

An image of the Janus Gallery filled the screen as a voice-over announced, "A London art gallery was the target of thieves last night. Entering through a back window, they made off with a Tamara de Lempicka painting, *Woman in a White Fur*, along with two paintings from an up-and-coming artist. The Tamara de Lempicka paintings are popular with collectors and have appeared in music videos. We caught up with the other artist whose work was taken, Farina Vee, this morning."

The video cut to a close-up of Farina. She brushed her white-blonde bangs out of her eyes. "I'm shocked. I don't know what to think. It's stunning—that someone would take a Tamara de Lempicka painting along with mine." Her lips, shiny with lip gloss, parted in a small smile. "It's flattering—horrible, but flattering at the same time, if you know what I mean."

The shot shifted to include both the reporter and Farina. The reporter's red windbreaker seemed garish next to the subdued tones of Farina's taupe cashmere scarf and flowing cream-colored dress. The reporter asked, "Tell me about the paintings of yours that were stolen."

"They were two of the ones most special to me—*Titled* and *Untitled*—they speak to the void and blankness of modern life—"

"Wait," the reporter said, "one of your paintings is called *Titled*? Do I have that right?"

"Yes. And *Untitled*. Only by examining the ambiguous can we bring the perceptible into focus. It's all about egocentrism . . ."

She drew a breath, but the reporter cut in again. "Have you had any ransom demands?"

Farina blinked. "No, nothing like that."

"Would you pay a ransom demand?"

Her glossy lips widened into a full smile. "I'd have to receive one first before I made that decision."

"Thank you for speaking with us. And best of luck. We hope your artwork is returned unharmed."

"Thank you." Farina looked directly into the camera. "So do I."

Zoe closed the video. "Well, Farina didn't look *that* upset."

"You know what they say—there's no such thing as bad publicity."

"That should be helpful if she ever gets them back. I'd better call Ava. The news clip barely mentioned *Woman in a White Fur*. I guess that means the provenance research is on hold."

A few moments later Zoe put her phone away. "Ava wasn't in. I left her a message. She's probably at lunch right now."

"Lunch is an excellent idea. Here or back to Amsterdam?"

"Honestly, I think I'm all tulip-ed out. I'm ready to head back to Amsterdam."

"I'm okay with that."

Once they were on the bus, Zoe twisted around and looked up and down the rows, but she didn't see a man with a gray ponytail. As she settled back into her seat, Jack said, "I didn't see him either."

Once they were back in Amsterdam, they strolled along the canals until Zoe saw a sign for an Italian restaurant. "This sounds good. We need the carbs after walking all those acres." They shared a pizza and a bowl of pasta, then headed back to the hotel.

The streets were busier than they had been earlier in the

day. Zoe and Jack threaded between pedestrians, bicycles, and trams, then halted at a corner to wait for the light to change. Jack turned around.

"The hotel is just a couple of blocks ahead," Zoe said, thinking he was checking the street signs for their location.

"I know." The light changed, but instead of moving with the foot traffic across the street, Jack tugged on Zoe's hand. "This way." She followed his lead as they turned left and walked down a side street at a quick clip.

Zoe was itching to glance behind them, but she made herself look straight ahead. "What's going on?"

"Mr. Gray Ponytail is behind us."

Zoe wanted to turn around even more and get a look for herself, but she focused on the street in front of them. If Jack said the guy was behind them, he was. "So you agree that the third time we see someone it's not a coincidence."

"Could be, but it's doubtful. How about a little test?" The skin around his eyes crinkled as he smiled.

"I'm not going to put the brakes on your fun." Jack so rarely got to exercise some of his best skills. She waved a hand. "Have at it."

"Excellent." He slowed his pace and nodded to a shop window.

They stopped in front of the large plate-glass window, seemingly to check out the rather unusual displays. Zoe said, "I don't need to look at the map to know we're on the edge of the red-light district."

"Appears so." Jack's gaze was on the window's reflection, not the merchandise inside.

Zoe shifted her focus to the hazy image of the street behind them. "Is he still there?"

"Yes. He's stopped to look in a window as well."

Zoe and Jack resumed walking, dodging through pedestrians and bikes. "Why is he following us? Who is he?"

"No idea."

They worked their way back to the main street, which was packed. Bicyclists threaded their way through the throngs of tourists posing for selfies as the trams slid silently by. After a while their hotel came into sight, and they made directly for the maroon awning over the sidewalk. The hotel lobby was a hodge-podge of nooks and crannies with the reception desk and elevators tucked into the building at odd angles.

They paused at a grouping of couches and chairs in the only open area of the lobby where they could see out the double glass doors. Jack took out the map and pretended to study it. "Is he still there?"

"He's on the corner across the street . . . he's turning . . . looks like he's headed away." Zoe took in the intent look on Jack's face. "And you're going to follow him."

"You can come too."

They'd played this game before, and Jack was a better choice to tail someone. For one thing, her bright red hair tended to stand out, and she didn't have a hat or scarf to cover it up. She gave him a quick kiss. "You go ahead. I need to try Ava again."

"Okay. Back soon."

Upstairs in their room, Zoe went to the window. She spotted Jack's lean dark-haired figure moving away from the hotel as he stayed several yards behind Mr. Gray Ponytail, who was striding quickly up the street without glancing to the side or behind him.

Zoe turned away from the window and dialed Ava. She picked up after the first ring. "Hello, Zoe. Perfect timing. I was about to ring you."

"I can't believe *Woman in a White Fur* has been stolen."

"Awful, isn't it? I have Harrington on the line. Let me merge the calls."

A few clicks later, Harrington said, "Zoe, how is Amsterdam?"

Zoe glanced out the window, but Jack was too far away to see now. "It's turning into an interesting stay. How's it going where you are?"

"Slowly. Criminals are rather lax about keeping to a schedule. No developments here, unlike in London."

"Yes, Ava sent me the details. Do you have any news on the theft?" Zoe asked.

"Nothing official. I have spoken with the buyer."

"And everything is on hold now, isn't it?"

"On the contrary. He has complete confidence that the authorities will recover the painting shortly. He wants us to continue to pursue the provenance research. Perhaps the investigators have shared some information with him that makes him very certain the art will be recovered, but . . ." A breathy sigh came down the line. "I'm afraid I'm not so confident."

"Who's the buyer? Can you say?"

"Yes, of course. I just prefer not to put it in documentation that will be sent through the mail. It's Mr. Best."

"Hmm . . . I'm not familiar with the name."

"Hedge fund manager. He keeps a low profile," Harrington said. "Are you interested in continuing to pursue this for Mr. Best? After all, you are on holiday. It would be perfectly acceptable to put everything on hold until the painting is found."

"No, I don't want to do that. I'm so close to locating the reports, and I want to complete the job. I'm in the same city. I might as well try to close that loop." Zoe had emailed an update to Harrington with her plans for tracking down the missing documentation in Amsterdam. "I think I'm on the right track to find them. Mallory wasn't in earlier today, but I plan to go by again later tonight. Besides squaring away the provenance, I'm curious on a personal level. I want to read the rest of Olive Belgrave's reports. Since I'm here, it would be silly not to spend a few moments trying to get in touch with Mallory Tredmont."

"As long as it's not interfering too much."

"No, not at all. If I can meet with the woman tonight, I may be able to wrap everything up in a few hours. Then if Mr. Best is right and the painting is found, the other testing can be done right away."

12

Later that evening, Jack groaned and rubbed his hand across his stomach. "That was a dinner of a thousand plates."

Zoe tucked her arm around his elbow as they emerged from the restaurant. "Not quite, but close. The flavors were amazing. I've never had a meal quite like that. And your stomach looks exactly the same as it always does. How is that possible?"

Jack had returned from following Mr. Gray Ponytail, who had gone to a hotel near the train station. Although Jack had hung around for a while, the man hadn't emerged from the hotel, and they hadn't seen him since then. Jack had seemed preoccupied during dinner, and Zoe had to repeat a question that he'd missed. He'd seemed to give himself a mental shake, and for the rest of the meal, he'd been his usual charming self. But something was on his mind, pulling his attention away from their conversation. Zoe wasn't sure if it was the fact that a guy was trailing them around Amsterdam or something else, but before she could broach the topic, their food had arrived and the moment passed.

They'd dined at a restaurant that served rijsttafel, a style of dining that the Dutch had adapted from Indonesia. The only thing Zoe could compare it to was tapas, but instead of ordering a small selection of a few different plates, the rijsttafel meal was a seemingly endless array of dishes of various textures and spiciness.

Jack sidestepped around a group taking a selfie. "My favorite was the chicken coconut curry."

"How can you pick just one? The spicy beef was incredible, and the spring rolls and the fried rice—oh, and the banana fritters—they were all so good. I'll have to go for a run in the morning, but I regret nothing. Good thing we're walking back to the hotel. We can work off some of our dinner."

"Do you still want to stop by Mallory's houseboat?"

Zoe checked the bank of clouds that was drifting over the city. "Yes, I think we can make it before it rains." The weather, which had been clear all day, was changing. When they went into the restaurant, a gossamer layer of clouds had covered the sky. Now a breeze with the scent of rain buffeted the pale green leaves of the trees, and a denser layer of clouds, thick and dark gray, was edging across the evening sky.

They left the main road and crossed a few bridges, finally arriving at the Prinsengracht Canal, which was more crowded than it had been during the day. They slowed at the curb before crossing to the side of the street next to the canal, and Jack glanced behind them.

Zoe watched the phalanx of bicycle riders glide by. "Is our favorite gray-haired man behind us?"

"Nope. Still nothing."

Despite his relaxed appearance, Zoe had noticed the alert way Jack had scanned the street when they left the hotel for dinner. No one else would pick up on his heightened awareness, but Zoe knew he was being extra watchful. A cold gust of wind whipped her hair across her face. "I may have been wrong about the rain." She tucked her hair behind her ear.

"Well, now that we're on this canal, we'll walk right by the houseboat. Might as well check."

Restaurants were pulling café tables under awnings as they paced along the street. The clouds hadn't covered the sinking sun yet, but it was low in the sky. One side of the canal was already in shadow, but there was enough light for Zoe to make out the figure of a woman walking across the gangplank of the brown and white houseboat.

"Oh, I think that might be her." Zoe hurried ahead and called out, "Mallory!"

The woman turned, removing a backpack as she dug into her pants pocket.

She was at least a decade older than Zoe had expected, but the deep-set eyes were the same as the photo Zoe had found online, even if there were dark circles under them.

Zoe moved up the gangplank, her hand extended. "Hi, I'm Zoe Andrews. You're Mallory, right?" The photograph Zoe had seen online must have been airbrushed and touched up, smoothing the blotchiness of her skin and removing the dark circles under her eyes. And instead of the shiny chestnut waves, a lopsided clip held back her stiff, crinkly hair.

Mallory fumbled with the keys, dropping them, and muttered a curse as they hit the boat's low railing with a jangle.

Zoe lunged forward and caught them before they disappeared down the gap between the boat and the edge of the canal. "I'm sorry. I didn't mean to startle you." Zoe held out the keys. "I've been reading your blog and wanted to catch you before you went inside."

Mallory took the keys and relaxed her arms, letting the backpack sag toward the deck. "You've read my blog?" Her accent was British. "How? The site is, like, down."

Small drops of rain began to patter around them, spotting their shoulders and beading on the boat deck. "I found the archives online. You can find everything online now."

"Oh. Well, that's good—I guess. The site should be back up soon. There was, like, a little hiccup with the hosting site, but that should be taken care of any day now." Mallory's gaze shifted to Jack as he joined Zoe on the gangplank.

"This is my husband, Jack. We're vacationing here in Amsterdam, and I wanted to look you up."

"Because of my blog?" Her accented tones took on an incredulous note.

"Well, partly because of your blog, and partly because I'm interested in Sebastian Blakely. I gather you're something of an expert on him."

"That's true."

"I'm doing some research on Blakely." Mallory's expression closed down, and Zoe hurried on, "I think you might be exactly the right person to answer my questions."

"I might."

The raindrops were falling faster, needling into the canal and Zoe's scalp. Mallory glanced up at the sky. "You'd better come in. We'll, like, get drenched if we stay out here."

She led the way to the deck at the front of the boat, unlocked the hatch on the cabin, and pushed it back, revealing a ladder, which she clambered down quickly, the rain creating a leopard-spotted pattern on the back of her dark T-shirt.

Zoe followed her down, and Jack came after her as Mallory switched on lights, illuminating a single open room with white walls and pale wood flooring. Mallory pointed to a handle on the underside of the hatch. "Just pull there," she instructed

Jack. "It, like, sticks sometimes. Give it a good shove if you need to."

A futon and small television filled one side of the room. The other end of the space had a minuscule kitchen with a two-burner gas stove, mini-refrigerator, and tiny sink heaped with crusty dishes. A wooden table that looked as if it had been made from an old door was positioned near the kitchen. There was an open laptop on the desk, its cord snaking over piles of papers, boxes, books, and a tangle of clothing. A scaled-down version of a pot-bellied stove sat at the midpoint of the room. A closed door beyond the kitchen was probably the bathroom.

In a recessed area behind the ladder, Zoe could see the corner of a bed. The comforter had been flung back, revealing rumpled sheets. The windows on the other side of the bed looked out of the front of the boat and gave a view of the canal. Raindrops pockmarked the glittering reflections of lights from the buildings and other boats.

Jack joined Zoe at the base of the ladder, tucking his hands into his pockets, probably so he wouldn't be tempted to start cleaning up. The golden hardwood floors and clean white walls would have made the small area feel spacious, but discarded clothes, stacks of books, wrinkled magazines, and used plates and mugs filled every flat surface.

Mallory cleared a pile of laundry from a futon. "Let me just move this. There you go. Have a seat." She carried the pile of clothes around the ladder and dumped it on the bed. "Sorry about the mess. I've been working double shifts at the restaurant, so there isn't much time to tidy up."

Zoe settled onto the futon but shifted as something poked into her hip. "This is so cozy. It must be quite a unique experience living in a houseboat."

"It's all right. It belongs to my boyfriend's father, so at least the rent is good, you know." She smiled briefly as she pulled a chair over from the table. "The crowds can be, like, a little over-whelming, especially on weekends. So what do you want to know about Blakely?"

Zoe shifted around and pulled a remote control from between the cushions of the futon. "You're working on a book about him, right?"

Mallory tossed the remote on a small table on top of a tilting pile of magazines on the floor. "I was, but I had to take a break." Her face seemed to take on an extra glow, making her look more like the younger version of her image online. "Since I got a book contract, that has to be my focus now."

"Oh, that's exciting. Is it for a different book about Blakely?"

"No, it's about sorting out your life, finding your stride, you know. Living your best life."

"Sounds interesting."

"Yes. It's all about, like—you know—getting organized, making good choices, and—um—changing from the inside out, all that—"

Zoe was sure Mallory had been about to say "all that crap" or something along those lines but stopped herself.

"It could be a whole series," Mallory continued. "Mind-body harmony and finding balance and—um—other things."

"How exciting."

"It is. It's, like, such a big step for my personal brand. Moving into self-improvement is the perfect opportunity. I want to help people live, like, their best life, you know?"

Zoe didn't have to turn her head to know Jack's gaze was skipping around the mess that coated the cabin of the house-boat, and he was biting back a comment about a self-help guru who couldn't find time to fold laundry or do the dishes. But Jack had excellent self-control. He'd never say anything to derail the conversation between her and Mallory, so she willed herself to ignore the vibes of disbelief coming off Jack. She focused on Mallory. "Will you go back to the book about Blakely?"

"I doubt it, especially since the publisher is talking about more self-improvement books. Blakely's great and all, but kind of dated. Who's interested in a dead photographer, you know? Self-help is a much bigger market. It's the way to go. So much more earning potential." She glanced around the tight quarters. "Then Rolf and I can get a bigger place."

A scraping sound came from overhead, and the metal hatch slid back. A pair of scuffed men's shoes appeared, then long legs encased in jeans.

Mallory said, "Oh, this is Rolf," as a lanky man descended the ladder, shifting it closed in a practiced motion. His light brown hair was tousled, and he had a few days' worth of stubble. "Rolf, this is—um—"

"I'm Zoe, and this is Jack."

Jack was in the process of rising from the futon, but the guy barely paused. He greeted Mallory, lifted his chin toward Jack, then said, "Hey." He continued on to the bedroom behind the ladder. He shut the door, leaving behind a whiff of marijuana.

Mallory didn't seem to find anything rude about his behavior. She turned to Zoe. "So what did you want to know again? Something about Blakely?"

"I'm doing research, trying to fill a gap in a painting's history. It's for *Woman in a White Fur*. Do you know it?"

"Know it? I've seen it many, many times. Did you hear about it being stolen?"

"Yes, but that's not why we're here. I'm strictly interested in the history of the painting."

Mallory's brow wrinkled. "Okay. That's kind of weird, but whatever. What do you want to know?"

"I'm looking for a set of reports and an inventory of paintings that were done by a woman named Olive Belgrave."

Mallory squinted at one of the portholes that lined the cabin. "Belgrave . . . sounds familiar."

"It was in nineteen twenty-three."

Her face cleared. "Oh. Right. I remember now." She glanced out of the corner of her eye at the stacks of papers and books tilting at precarious angles on the table. "She went down to Hawthorne House. Why do you want it, again?" Mallory's gaze focused on Zoe, really concentrating on her for the first time during the conversation.

"It's provenance research for the painting."

"But the painting is, like, missing."

"I know. I'm only tying up a loose end regarding the provenance. Since I'm here and you live here, I thought you might be able to help me out since you've done some research on it."

"Well, I do know a bit about Olive Belgrave."

"Have you read her reports?"

"Yes." She tilted her head, and her face took on a coy expression. "In fact, I have them."

"Wonderful," Zoe said. "If you'd let me have a look, that would be terrific—"

"You can see them—for a fee."

Zoe lowered her chin. So it was going to be like that, was it? Okay, she could play the game. "How much?"

Mallory's eyes narrowed as she studied Zoe for a moment. "I'll let you see them for five thousand."

Zoe blinked, but before she could form a complete sentence, Mallory added, "Just see them—no photos or anything. And that's euros, by the way."

Zoe stood up. "No. That's not going to happen."

Mallory rocked back in her chair. "But they're an important

piece of the history related to a painting that's worth millions. I saw the news reports, so don't try to con me and say they're not worth that much. Five thousand euros is cheap compared to the price of the painting."

"But the painting is missing, as you pointed out. The buyer doesn't want to spend thousands of euros researching a painting that might never be recovered." Zoe handed her card to Mallory. "I'm at the Premier Hotel for a few more days. Call me if you change your mind." Jack had stood when Zoe did. He'd already climbed the ladder and opened the hatch.

"Wait." Mallory hopped up. "I suppose I could go down to three thousand."

Zoe, her foot on the first rung of the ladder, shook her head. "I can't do that."

Jack slid the hatch open, and rain sprinkled down on Zoe's head.

Mallory came over and gripped the edge of the ladder. "Okay, a thousand."

"Where are they?" Zoe asked, her gaze skimming over the cabin. A thousand dollars to Mr. Best was probably equivalent to the change Zoe tossed in her car's cup holder after a run through a drive-through.

Mallory casually flicked her hand toward the desk. "Around here." A trace of disbelief must have crossed Zoe's face because Mallory added, "It may look a tad disorganized, but I know exactly where they are."

Zoe looked up at Jack, sighed, and infused as much reluctance in her tone as possible. "I don't want to do this, but . . ." She sighed. "Okay. Two thousand."

Mallory's eyebrows shot up. "Gre—"

"But for that price, I'm *buying* them, not just looking at them."

Zoe held her gaze, and Mallory lifted a shoulder after a second. "Okay. Like, fine. I don't want them anyway."

A pulse of satisfaction beat in the center of Zoe's chest, warming her despite the cold breeze sweeping over her and the rain pelting her head. She kept her tone neutral. "I don't have that kind of money on me, of course."

"Can you get it by tomorrow?"

"Yes." *I hope so.*

"Good. Right. Okay, then. Come back tomorrow afternoon. That'll give me time to, like, get everything ready for you."

"Three o'clock?" Zoe asked.

"Sure."

"See you then." Zoe began to climb.

"Oh." Mallory bounced up on her toes. "Cash. It's got to be in bank notes. No wire transfers or anything."

"Of course."

O nce they were clear of the houseboat, Jack said, "You negotiated like a pro back there."

Rain streamed down, soaking into Zoe's shoulders as they splashed along the street. "I just hope my expense account can handle it—and that Mr. Best actually does want the provenance wrapped up—*and* that the painting is recovered. That's a lot of variables."

Zoe halted and gripped Jack's upper arm. "What day is today? Tomorrow isn't the weekend, is it?"

Jack checked his watch. "It's Wednesday."

Zoe sagged with relief. "Thank goodness. The banks will be open tomorrow. With all our travel, I'd forgotten what day of the week it was. Of course, I'll have to figure out how to get that much cash. I can't withdraw such a big amount from a business account at an ATM."

"I'm sure Ava will be able to help you out."

"You're right." A trickle of water ran down Zoe's collar. "Let's go over there." Their hotel was several blocks away. They'd be soaked through by the time they got there. She darted under an awning of a clothing store and opened her messenger bag. "I have an umbrella."

Jack stood outside the shelter of the awning and turned up the collar of his jacket. She shifted over a step. "There's room." He joined her, water dripping from his hair onto his forehead as she shifted the contents of her bag. "Of course it's under everything else—oh, here we go."

The area was nearly deserted—only a few pedestrians were out, and they looked like locals. An older man walked by with a Jack Russell terrier on a leash, then a woman carrying an armful of flowers and a string bag strode by. Jack watched both people as they passed, then swept his gaze around the street and the canal.

Zoe unfastened the umbrella strap. "Still looking for Mr. Gray Ponytail?"

"I'm not looking anymore." Jack turned toward her, his back to the street. "Found him. Over my left shoulder, inside the bistro on the other side of the canal, at the table by the window."

"That's just odd how he keeps showing up." Zoe popped the umbrella open. "Let's see if he's up for a walk in the rain."

They set off for their hotel at a brisk pace, but the man didn't follow them.

Back at their hotel, Zoe came out of the bath, towel-drying her hair to find Jack standing out of sight beside the window, studying the street. "No sign of him."

"Why didn't he follow us tonight?"

"No need. He knows where we're staying."

"I find that slightly disturbing. Do you think we should change hotels?"

Jack let the edge of the curtain fall into place. "No. If we already had the couple of thousand euros you're planning to get, we might consider it, but I think we're fine where we are now."

"You think so?"

"Yes."

"Okay." The thought of a man dogging their steps around a foreign city was disturbing, but if Jack said they were fine, then they were.

Jack checked the display on his phone, then set it on the desk. "Did you get the money sorted out?"

"Ava's on it." Zoe had contacted Ava as soon as they got to the room. "She said it shouldn't be a problem; we'll be able to pick it up by noon tomorrow. She sounded as if I'd asked her to order up a curry for us instead of a bundle of bank notes. So that's fixed up. We'll get the money, pick up Olive's reports from Mallory, and then it'll be full-on vacation mode. Oh wait, we're not meeting Mallory until three tomorrow. We can do some sightseeing in the morning." Zoe picked up the guidebook. "Where should we go tomorrow? The Rijksmuseum? We don't need advance tickets like the Van Gogh Museum."

"Let's figure it out tomorrow." Jack came across the room to her. "You're overdressed."

"I'm wrapped in a towel."

"I know."

"But what about the plan—the itinerary?" Zoe took the paper out of the guidebook and unfurled it. "We might miss something."

Jack plucked the paper from her hand and tossed it aside. "The beauty of a good plan is that it can be modified"—he brushed her hair aside and kissed her neck—"as needed."

"Mmm . . . true. So you're okay if we don't see everything on your list? You have so many must-see places."

He raised his head. He'd been working his way across her collarbones, dropping kisses as he went. "You're the only *must* on my list."

"Excellent. You know how I love flexible schedules."

The next morning, after a lazy breakfast in bed provided by room service, they decided the Rijksmuseum would be a good place to avoid the rain, which was still coming down, but in intermittent bursts rather than a steady downpour. Zoe enjoyed the contrast between the small, quiet Vermeer paintings that were flooded with clear light and the massive canvas of Rembrandt's painting of the civil guard with its deep shadows. However, she wasn't completely in tourist mode. Part of her thoughts were tied up with *Woman in a White Fur*. There was nothing new in the news on the missing painting, and she was concerned about the two thousand euros. It wasn't every day that she waltzed into a foreign bank and picked up that much cash.

After ambling through the cathedral-like atmosphere of the museum with its vaulted arches and stained-glass windows, they agreed they'd seen everything they wanted to and headed for the exit. They were crossing the modern and airy atrium when Zoe's phone rang with a call from Ava. She snatched it up. "Is there a problem?"

"Problem?"

"With the funds?"

"Oh no, that's not why I was calling. Everything's arranged." Ava gave Zoe the name of the bank and address. "You can pick it up there within an hour. I'll text you the information."

"Perfect. Thank you."

"All in a day's work." Ava's tone was matter-of-fact. "The reason I called is that I want to check with you about a potential client, a woman who will only speak to you. Of course, I told her you're on holiday, but she was quite insistent. Farina Vee."

"Oh yes. I met her at the Janus Gallery. It was her artwork that was stolen along with *Woman in a White Fur.*"

"Right. I hadn't put that together. I knew I'd heard her name recently."

"I'll call her."

"She refused to leave a number. In fact, she was quite huffy about it when I wouldn't give your number to her. Her number was blocked, so I don't know where she called from. I suspect she wants you to look for her paintings, but don't worry. I'm not going to add anything else to your to-do list. I just wanted to check with you and see if you truly did know her. I'll handle it if she calls back."

"I don't mind speaking to her if she does call again."

"But you're on holiday. Well, you're *supposed* to be on holiday. Not making a good job of that, are you?"

"We've seen the tulips, a museum, and toured a houseboat."

"Hmm . . . that does sound quite touristy, yet you need thousands of euros to complete a transaction for work. I think the lady doth protest too much."

"Unfortunately, thieves don't take holidays." Even small-time document thieves like Mallory.

"So true. In fact, they do their best work when people go on holiday."

"It's our bread-and-butter, so I won't complain."

They emerged from the museum into the tunnel and road that ran through the center of the museum. With cyclists whipping through the tunnel beside them, they headed in the direction of the bank, which took them across the Museumplein, a spacious park ringed with museums. They took one of the paths in the direction of the Van Gogh Museum. With its exterior of smooth glass and curved walls, it was quite a contrast to the elaborate architecture of the Rijksmuseum, which was a mixture of Renaissance and Gothic with a roof line that made Zoe think of a French chateau.

The Van Gogh Museum was on the far end of the space beyond a shallow reflecting pool that was dotted with circular planters filled with tulips. A line snaked out from the Van Gogh Museum shop and stretched beyond the shallow pool. "I'm glad we bought our tickets online." Jack's detailed plan for sightseeing meant he'd purchased the tickets weeks ago.

They stopped for a quick lunch at the food stalls near the museum, then headed for the bank, which was a few blocks off the Museumplein. Everything went smoothly. Zoe shoved the bank notes deep into her messenger bag, wondering what strings Ava—or Harrington—had pulled to have that amount of cash available on short notice. They had just enough time to hop on a tram that took them across the city to the stop near the canal where Mallory's houseboat was anchored.

As the tram glided away, Zoe put on her sunglasses. The clouds had completely dispersed. "Our gray-headed friend isn't with us today. I haven't seen him all morning."

"Neither have I," Jack said as they walked along the canal. "He must have lost interest in us."

"Odd that he'd disappear, though," Zoe said as they arrived at the houseboat. The hatch was open, and Zoe crossed the gangplank. She was walking along the narrow passageway to the deck at the front of the houseboat when Mallory's head popped up through the opening, her jaw clenched. "Came back to gloat, did you?"

Zoe halted as Mallory stormed toward her.

"Well, that was foolish. You should have left when you had the chance." She came at Zoe and hit both her shoulders, shoving Zoe backward into Jack. "Give them back."

14

Zoe fell back against Jack's chest. She wasn't in danger of falling, especially as Jack's arm encircled her waist and braced her, but she still grabbed the waist-high rope that lined the passageway and steadied herself. "What are you talking about?"

Jack eased around Zoe. Mallory faded back a step, but the cold fury on her face didn't change. "Some nerve you have. Coming back here after what you did."

Zoe moved forward, wedging her body beside Jack on the narrow space of the boat's passageway. "What are you talking about?"

"The papers." Mallory surged forward, her fists clenched. "You stole them."

"What?" Zoe said. "We did no such thing!"

"Of course you'd deny it."

"We came here to pay you for them." Zoe tossed back the flap of the messenger bag. Jack reached out to stop her, but Zoe was quicker and angled the bag so Mallory could see the wad of bank notes bulging out of an envelope at the bottom.

The sight seemed to penetrate the haze of anger that surrounded Mallory. Zoe snapped the bag closed and shifted it so that it hung over her hip on the side where Jack was pressed against her.

Mallory's state of paralysis lasted only a few seconds. She surged into Zoe's face. "I don't believe you. You're the only one who's interested in them. The day after you ask about them, someone breaks in and steals them."

Jack stepped forward. "We didn't take them. Would we be here, cash in hand, ready to pay for them if we did?" A sulky look crossed her face as Jack continued. "Why would we come back if we had what we wanted?"

Zoe said, "I understand you're upset, but we didn't take them. Could they have been misplaced?" It wouldn't be hard for a couple of papers to disappear into the mess of the cabin and not be found for ages.

"No. I know exactly where they were. I had them all ready to go. I left them on the desk chair this morning before I left for work. Rolf wouldn't move them. He never uses the desk."

Jack said, "Are you sure they were taken this morning?"

"Of course I'm sure."

Rolf emerged from the hatch, his hair even more disheveled than it had been yesterday. His stubble was thicker, edging toward a full-on beard. He wore a black T-shirt and jeans and held a half-eaten sandwich. The aroma of marijuana reached them at the same time he did.

"Tell them, Rolf."

"What?"

"About the papers."

"You're still going on about that?"

Zoe hadn't been able to distinguish from his muttered single-word greeting yesterday if he was British like Mallory, but now she could hear his faint Dutch accent. He spoke excellent English—as did most of the Dutch she'd met—but his words contained the same lilt and cadence she'd heard from the hotel clerk and their waitresses.

"Yes, I'm going on about that." Mallory jerked her head toward Zoe and Jack. "They were going to pay for them—two thousand euros, remember?"

He'd lifted the sandwich to take a bite but paused with it inches from his mouth. "Two thous—you never said that."

"Yes, I did. I told you last night. You weren't, like, paying attention, as usual."

Rolf turned to Zoe and Jack. "Two thousand?"

Jack nodded.

Rolf said, "Oh, man. I never would have gone out if I'd known that." He cut his gaze to Mallory.

She glared back. "I *did* tell you. I put them on the desk chair and told you not to move them."

Jack's deep tones cut into their argument as he addressed Rolf. "Did you notice the papers this morning?"

"No. All I know is that after Mallory left for work, I went out for a proper coffee. When I came back, the hatch was open. I just thought I'd forgotten to close it."

"Was anything else missing or disturbed?" Considering the messy state of the houseboat's living quarters, it was a long shot, but Zoe had to ask.

"No. Everything looked just as it always does." Rolf sent a dark look at Mallory. "I didn't notice a couple of pieces of paper were gone."

Mallory drew a breath to respond, but Jack cut in. "Have you had any unexpected visitors lately? People you don't know?"

"You." Mallory shot back.

"Besides us," Zoe said. "Maybe a repairman or a delivery

person, or even a city employee checking a meter? Something like that?" Did they have utility meters on houseboats? Zoe had no idea, but the question sparked something for Rolf.

"There was that tourist earlier today. He asked if he could tour the houseboat."

"We get that sometimes," Mallory said. "So rude, you know?"

"What did he look like?" Zoe asked.

Rolf waved the sandwich. "Just a guy—older."

Zoe leaned forward. "Hair color?"

"Um, gray, I think. It was hard to see it. It was pulled back in a ponytail." Rolf pointed his sandwich at them. "And he was American."

Jack said, "And this was earlier today, you said?"

"Yes. Right before I left to get coffee."

Zoe exchanged a look with Jack, then reached for another one of her cards. "If the guy—or the papers—turn up, give me a call, please."

As Zoe and Jack walked away from the houseboat, Zoe said, "Let's cross over to the other side."

"And check the café where we saw Mr. Gray Ponytail last night?" At Zoe's nod, Jack said, "My thoughts exactly."

The café was quiet. Only a few customers were scattered around the tables, and none of them were sporting ponytails of any shade. Zoe turned to Jack. "So this hotel where Mr. Gray Ponytail was staying . . . you said it was near the train station?"

When the multistory parking area for bikes came into view near the train station, Jack said, "Almost there. What did you think of Mallory and Rolf's story?"

"About the papers being stolen? I think they're telling the

truth. Her anger seemed genuine. She really did want the money."

"I agree. And Rolf didn't seem to know or care about them."

"But apparently he would have, if he'd understood their potential value."

A few more turns brought them into a narrow street with tall houses, some of them leaning slightly off-center. "This one." Jack led the way to a building with a plaque that read *Amsterdam Plaza North Hotel*. Without pausing in the lobby, he went directly to the elevator and punched in the button for the fourth floor.

Zoe raised an eyebrow. "You know which floor Mr. Gray Ponytail is on?"

"I know more than the floor. I know his room number."

"Impressive."

"If I'm going to do something, I'm going to do it thoroughly."

He grinned at her, and she knew he was thinking of other things. "Thoroughness is an excellent quality to have."

The elevator dinged. The doors opened, Jack gave a cautious look up and down the corridor, then they stepped out. "He's in room 410."

The housekeeping cart was parked outside of room 408, and the maid was working in the room with the door propped open. They eased around the cart, slowing as they came even with the next doorway. Someone inside was talking, but it was impossible to distinguish the words.

"Sounds like a guy," Zoe said in a low voice.

Jack nodded and tilted his head toward the elevator. "We shouldn't hang out here too long."

"Right." She followed him for a few steps as they turned back the way they'd come, then Zoe halted.

"Zoe?"

"Sorry." She drew her gaze away from the room where the maid was working and caught up with him. "I have an idea."

Downstairs in the lobby, Zoe went to the front desk and asked for a room. Jack joined her as Zoe leaned over the tall counter. "But not just any room. We want room 408."

"You want to stay in a specific room?"

"Yes. 408."

"We have quite a few rooms that are better situated."

She sent Jack her most blinding smile. "But room 408 has special memories for us."

Jack picked up on her cue and wrapped his arm around her waist.

The clerk consulted the monitor. "In that case . . . that particular room is being cleaned right now, but if you're willing to wait . . ."

"That's fine. We'll be in those chairs over there in the corner."

The clerk glanced at the bellboy stationed at the door. "And your luggage?"

"Delayed," Jack said. "It will be along soon."

As they moved to the chairs, Jack whispered. "Your glibness is rather frightening." He reached for her hand as they sat down. "We'd better at least hold hands—to keep up our cover."

She squeezed his hand. "Of course."

"Did you put this room on our credit card, or will your expense account cover a second hotel room?"

"Oh, I think Harrington will see the benefit of it. If Mallory's telling the truth—and I think she is—then she did have Olive's reports and someone stole them from her. The only person who's been interested in us and has been hanging around Mallory's houseboat is Mr. Gray Ponytail."

"Very clever to get the room next door."

"I could see an adjoining door between room 408 and 410."

A quarter of an hour later, they had the key cards to room 408 and entered as noiselessly as possible. The maid had finished with the room, and the housekeeping cart was parked farther down the hall.

As their door to the hallway swung closed, Zoe pointed to the door to the adjoining room, which had a gap of about an inch between the bottom of the door and the hardwood floor. She whispered, "Look at that. We should be able to hear absolutely everything."

Unfortunately, there was hardly anything to hear. Zoe and Jack settled down to listen, keeping quiet so their voices didn't carry. Except for a few words spoken in a deep voice a few moments after they entered their room, they'd heard no other sounds from room 410. After about an hour, Zoe stood up and paced back and forth across the room, alternating between checking the window and the peephole. She'd taken off her shoes so she wouldn't make any noise as she padded back and forth. Patience wasn't her strong suit, and she found waiting as irritating as a rash that she couldn't scratch. Jack had settled on the bed with his long legs stretched out and his ankles crossed. He'd turned on the television but muted the sound. He found a soccer game, and the figures of the men racing back and forth across the green field irritated Zoe, seeming to emphasize her confinement in the small hotel room.

Zoe plopped down on the bed beside him and whispered,

"We know there's a guy next door because of the voice we heard when we came in here, but we don't know if he's the right guy. Is he Mr. Gray Ponytail? We haven't seen him since last night. What if our guy checked out last night or this morning and it's a new person next door?"

Jack replied in equally subdued tones, "There's no way to know. We just have to wait until he makes a move."

"Couldn't we draw him out somehow?" Zoe reached for the booklet of hotel information and flipped to the menu page. "Let's order room service and tell them to deliver it to room 410. He'll at least have to open the door and speak to someone. We might be able to catch a glimpse of him then."

"Too risky. If there's a 'mix-up' in a room service order we called in from our room, the waiter would immediately bring it over here, and that would draw attention to us."

Zoe closed the booklet. "You're right. I'm sorry we're stuck in here waiting. We should be out sightseeing."

"Not a big deal. I'm as curious about what's going on with the papers as you are. We did a lot of walking this morning, and we didn't have anything specific planned for this afternoon. I figured you'd be reading Olive's reports and we'd hang out in our hotel room this afternoon for a couple of hours. There's not much difference between one hotel room and another. We can take a break here just as easily as we could in our original hotel."

"Well, I don't want to sit here all afternoon."

"Let's give it another half hour."

Zoe agreed, then hopped up to pace around the room, her arms crossed. The minutes ticked by with agonizing slowness. Zoe paced faster, while Jack's eyes seemed to get heavier and heavier. She expected to hear him snore at any moment.

"It's a good thing you look so handsome when you sleep," she muttered. There were times when Jack's ability to compartmentalize was absolutely the most annoying thing in the world. How could he relax at a moment like this?

The rumble of a masculine voice sounded from next door. She tiptoed across the room to shake Jack's shoulder, but he'd already sat up and swung his legs off the side of the bed. They crept to the adjoining door.

15

Zoe crouched down so that her ear was near the gap between the base of the door and the floor.

A deep voice said, "Hey." Zoe flinched. The man's words were so loud, it seemed he was only inches away.

The voice faded a bit, and a shadow traced along the gap. He laughed. "No, I'm not sitting in a coffee shop."

Zoe mouthed the word, *he sounds American.* Jack nodded his agreement.

The shadow along the gap at the base of the door faded. He was pacing around the room, just as Zoe had. The man's voice came through clearly after a pause. "I'm in my hotel room, packing up."

Zoe widened her eyes and shifted to stand, but Jack grabbed her arm and tilted his head to the door, indicating that they didn't want to miss anything.

He was right. Zoe stilled herself and concentrated on listening to the man's words. "Did you get the flight information I sent?" he continued. "Right. The first flight tomorrow . . . yeah.

It's not my fault all the flights were booked today. I'll be in New York by two . . . of course I'll come straight to the office. Okay, good. See you tomorrow."

Zoe sat back on her heels and murmured, "He's leaving tomorrow."

Jack's voice was barely above a whisper. "Don't worry, he'll have to go out to dinner. We can catch a glimpse of him then and make sure he's our guy."

"What if he orders room service?"

"Then we'll figure it out—"

The metallic snick of a latch disengaging sounded. They both froze. A few seconds later, the door in the next room thudded closed.

Jack was around Zoe and at their door to the corridor before Zoe got to her feet. Jack unlatched their door, easing the deadbolt back so that it didn't make a sound, then cracked the door and put his eye to the opening. After a second, he eased the door closed and smiled at Zoe. "It's him—Mr. Gray Ponytail. He's waiting for the elevator at the end of the hall now."

"Thank goodness. I'm glad we didn't waste hours and hours sitting around a hotel room doing nothing only to find out it was the wrong guy."

Jack glanced at the clock on the nightstand. "We've only been here for about two hours."

"Is that all?" Zoe pulled on her shoes. "Well, it felt like an eternity. Let's see where he goes."

Jack opened the door a smidge, then gave a nod. Zoe snatched up her messenger bag, and they headed down the empty hall. When the elevator doors slid open in the lobby, the man with the gray ponytail was trotting down the short flight of steps outside the hotel to the street. They followed, staying back.

It wasn't hard to stay out of sight once they reached Damrak, a major street where the crowds of tourists were thick. A few blocks later, he turned off into a coffee shop with the image of a marijuana leaf on the window.

Jack pointed to the other side of the street. "We can wait in that bistro over there and keep an eye on him."

"No, let's go back to the hotel and take a little peek in his room. He probably left Olive's reports there."

"And how will we get in?"

"We have a connecting door. Perhaps . . . the lock didn't completely fasten."

"Zoe, I'm shocked that you'd suggest something like that," Jack said, his voice taking on a prim tone. "Breaking and entering is illegal."

"All's fair in love and war and . . ."

"Document theft?"

"I'm only looking for Olive's reports so I can return them to the original owner—the Blakely Archive."

Jack raised an eyebrow.

"Okay, after having them authenticated and making copies, of course."

"Of course."

"This might be our only chance to get a look at them. I have to at least try. You stay here and keep an eye on him if you want. Call me if it looks like he's coming back."

Before she'd covered a yard, Jack fell into step with her. "I thought you didn't want to be involved."

"I'm better at lock-picking than you are," Jack said. "It'll be faster if I do it."

"True." She threaded her arm through his elbow. "Thank you, Jack. It's the little things like this that I appreciate so much."

"Little things, she says," Jack said, but Zoe could hear the smile in his voice.

The adjoining door between rooms 408 and 410 was actually two doors set into the wall. Each swung open in the opposite direction, so even if one door was open, the other door could remain closed and locked. It was easy to flip the deadbolt and open the door in their room, but then they were faced with the locked deadbolt on the other door. Jack set to work. He improvised, using a screwdriver-like tool from Zoe's keychain that she kept in her messenger bag and a bent paperclip he'd snagged from the business center.

Figuring that breathing down Jack's neck would only slow the process down, Zoe went to the window that looked out over the hotel entrance to keep watch. She didn't see any sign of Mr. Gray Ponytail returning, and after a few minutes, Jack said, "I think that should do it." He twisted the implements in the lock, and the door swung open.

"You are the best husband ever." Zoe gave him a kiss as she hurried by him into the adjoining room.

"I'm sure you could have finagled a key card from the maid if I hadn't come back with you, but this way keeps anyone else from knowing we're interested in room 410. I wouldn't touch anything."

"Do you really think we need to worry about that?"

"Like you said, old habits die hard."

"I suppose it's better to be cautious." Zoe dashed back into their room and grabbed a couple of washcloths from the bathroom.

Room 410 looked as if housekeeping had just finished. The

bed was perfectly made, and the only evidence of an occupant was the suitcase on the luggage rack. The lid was propped open, showing neat stacks of folded clothes. "Well, this shouldn't take long," Zoe said.

"No, not much to see." Using the washcloth, Jack slid the closet door back. One suit jacket, a shirt, and a single pair of slacks hung inside. Jack gestured to the wall safe, which was set into the wall inside the closet. "If he was smart, he'd have left Olive's reports in there or taken them with him."

"I hope not. Surely he doesn't want to walk around with them in his pocket. We're talking about the original reports and inventory. The paper is several decades old and would be fragile."

Zoe checked the interior pockets of the suitcase. It was difficult to do with the washcloth covering her fingers, but she managed to draw out a wad of bright white pages. "Lots of papers, but these are all receipts for hotel stays. Looks like his name is Ferris Thompson. He lists a post office box in Newark as his address." She put the papers aside. "Who is Ferris Thompson and why is he interested in Olive's reports?"

Jack had been checking the pockets of the jacket. "This answers one of those questions." He'd used the washcloth to cover his hand as he flicked open a business card holder. "Ferris Thompson, private investigator." Jack eased one of the cards out and handed it to her. "I doubt he'll miss one card."

"Maybe another buyer for *Woman in a White Fur* hired him, someone who wants an edge in the bidding." Zoe studied the card, then tapped it against her chin. "If the papers can't be located, the value of the painting could drop."

Jack returned the card holder to the suit pocket, and Zoe went back to the suitcase and replaced the hotel receipts.

A man's voice rumbled in the hall. Zoe froze with the papers half in the suitcase pocket, her gaze flying to Jack, who was poised over a bureau drawer he'd opened. They both waited, motionless, as they listened. The voice sounded again, closer, then faded out as the person passed the door.

Jack slid the drawer closed. "Let's finish up. No need to linger here. Looks like all these drawers are empty anyway."

"Right." She shoved the papers back into the suitcase and fumbled with the zipper because her fingers were trembling. She blew out a calming breath.

Jack closed the drawers of the nightstand. "Nothing here." The room phone's red light was blinking, indicating there was a message. Using the washcloth, he picked up the handset and followed the instructions on the phone, punching in the code to retrieve the message while Zoe unzipped the outer pocket of the suitcase.

"Found them!" She drew out the delicate pages, her heart fluttering with excitement. She was careful to not catch the fragile paper on the teeth of the zipper. Zoe laid them on the bureau and quickly flipped through the stack. "The dates are right. These are Olive's last reports . . . and yes, here's the inventory at the end."

"Zoe."

She spun around at Jack's serious tone. "What's wrong?"

He held out the handset that was still wrapped in the washcloth. "You need to hear this." Zoe left the papers spread on the bureau and took the handset as Jack used the keys from his pocket to punch in the code to repeat the message.

A female voice announced, "Hello, Mr. Thompson. This is Nina in guest services at the Amsterdam Plaza North Hotel. We're always delighted to have the employees and associates of the Best Corporation stay on our properties. We want to make sure you're enjoying your stay. If you have any problems or concerns, don't hesitate to give me a call. Thank you again for choosing the Amsterdam Plaza North Hotel."

"Best Corporation!" Zoe banged the handset down into the cradle. "Ferris Thompson isn't working for a competing buyer. He's working for Mr. Best."

"You look annoyed."

"I'm insulted. Mr. Best thought I wouldn't be able to complete the provenance research and hired someone else."

"Perhaps he was covering all the bases."

"Well, he shouldn't have done that. I didn't know it was a race. I'd have pressed Mallory harder yesterday if I'd realized."

"Feeling a tad competitive, are you? You're going to tear the washcloth if you keep wringing it like that."

Zoe loosened her grip on the fabric. "If I take a job, I want to *do* the job without people sneaking around, trying to cut me off at the pass." Zoe marched back to the suitcase and closed the zipper on the outer pocket with a jerk. She ran the washcloth around the zipper and its metal tongue, then wiped down the edges of the luggage rack.

"I think you might be losing sight of the big picture—the reports have been found."

"Yes. By us!" Zoe swept up Olive's reports. "These are coming with me." She rattled the paper. "I'll admit you do have a point about taking them. I suppose it *is* stealing, technically speaking—"

"Yes, taking something that doesn't belong to you is the accepted definition."

"Says the former spy."

Jack looked up from wiping down the phone and nightstand. "Details, details," he said, his tone light.

"As I was saying, we're taking them to *return* them."

"I don't think Ferris Thompson would agree with your

assessment, but if he has a problem with it, we'll just tell him our motives are pure."

"No, a better plan is to not have to deal with him at all. Let's get out of here. Are you with me?"

"You have to ask? Didn't I just pick a lock for you?" The skin around his eyes had crinkled into a smile. "Of course I'm with you—no matter what crazy plan you have, I'm with you. And I think getting out of this room and this hotel is a great plan." Jack motioned for Zoe to lead the way back through the open doorway to their hotel room. "I'll make sure the deadbolt is back in place on Mr. Thompson's side, then we can go."

"Why take the time to do that? When he realizes the papers are missing, he can't call the police and report the theft of stolen property. In fact, he might not notice the papers are missing until later—maybe not even until he gets back to New York."

"I doubt that. I'd check."

"You would have locked them in the safe. He's not as smart as you. He didn't even put these delicate papers in something to protect them, like a folder or binder."

"Thank you for the compliment, but I'll make sure his side of the door is locked. It's better this way."

"You can take the man out of the spy game, but you can't take the spy out of the man," Zoe said, reconciling herself to wait while Jack worked the deadbolt. "While you do that, I'll put the papers away." Zoe picked up a magazine from the table positioned between the room's single armchair and the window. She tucked the aged reports between the shiny pages, then put the magazine in her messenger bag. By the time she'd settled the strap of her bag across her chest, Jack had the deadbolt back in place. He closed the door on their side and snapped the deadbolt home. Then he took the washcloth out of his pocket and wiped down the lock and handle. "Okay, let's go check out. The desk clerk will have a story to tell. I bet they don't get many afternoon room rentals here, unlike some hotels in Amsterdam."

"I got the automatic checkout. We just leave the keys in the room, and they email the bill." She motioned to the key cards on the desk. "All done."

"Excellent. Let's go."

16

They hopped on a tram to make their way back to their hotel. Zoe kept a tight grip on the strap of the messenger bag. She'd once had a thief attempt to snatch her messenger bag by cutting the strap, and she wasn't taking any chances with Olive's reports. Jack was ever-vigilant, always surveying their surroundings, looking for anomalies that might turn into a threat, but the ride back to the hotel was uneventful.

But the whole time, Zoe felt as if her fingertips were tingling as she pressed the soft leather of her bag. She wanted to take out the reports and read them as she swayed with the gentle motion of the tram. But the pages were too delicate, and she knew it was better to leave them out of sight until they were back in their hotel room.

They left the tram at the stop near their hotel, waited for the bicycles to whizz by, then crossed the street to the awning over the hotel's entrance. The doorman in his gold-buttoned coat held the door, and Zoe's shoulders relaxed as she headed for the elevator.

Jack murmured, "There's a woman approaching us. Your two o'clock."

Zoe tucked the messenger bag into her side. Jack had already moved around so that he was between her and the woman, but Zoe put a hand on his arm. She recognized the fair-haired woman with the asymmetrical haircut striding toward them. "It's okay. I know her. It's Farina."

"The artist?"

Zoe only had time to nod before Farina joined them. "Thank goodness you're back," she said. "I've been waiting for hours. I was afraid you'd checked out."

"No, we're still here enjoying Amsterdam. Farina, this is my husband, Jack."

"Pleased to meet you," Jack said.

Farina shook his hand, then scrubbed her palm over an eyebrow and up into her rumpled hair. She didn't look nearly as carefully groomed as she had during the television interview. She hadn't bothered with more than a swipe of lip gloss. Instead of her hair falling smoothly to frame her face, it poked out at odd angles. "I'm sorry to, well—ambush you like this, but I must talk to you. It's urgent. It's about the paintings. I don't know who else to talk to."

"The police would be the obvious starting point, I think," Jack said.

"It's not that simple."

"Why?" Zoe asked. The elevator dinged. The doors swished open, and a group of people emerged. Zoe really wanted to put off Farina and escape upstairs so that she could read Olive's reports.

Farina put her hand on Zoe's arm. "Please, will you give me a few moments of your time so I can explain? I know you're on holiday, but you're here in Amsterdam, and art recovery is your specialty. I read the articles online. You found a Picasso! Yes, I did research you. Please, will you give me just a few moments?"

Zoe had told Ava she'd speak to Farina if she got in touch again. Well, she'd certainly done that. Zoe turned to Jack. "Okay with you if I take a few moments to listen to her?"

He said, "It's up to you."

"Okay, then. We can spare a few minutes." Zoe turned away from the elevator doors. She could take a few minutes to listen to Farina and pass the information on to Ava. Zoe glanced around the small lobby, which was crowded with a tour group waiting for room keys. "Perhaps we can find a café nearby."

"Oh, no. I don't want to take up any more of your time. What about Vondelpark? It's only a couple of blocks away. We could talk there and not be disturbed."

"Sounds fine," Zoe said, and they followed Farina out of the hotel as the doorman swept open the glass doors. They turned through the gates of the enormous park and strolled three abreast down the wide asphalt path. Puddles from the recent rain dotted the walk and the grass. A circle of bright purple tulips surrounded a statue, but instead of heading for the flowers, Farina indicated another path. "There's some benches along here." Zoe was about to broach the subject of the stolen paintings, but a flash of bright green darting through the trees caught her eye. "What kind of bird is that?"

The tension that lined her face eased as Farina smiled. "Those are . . . what is the English word?" She snapped her fingers. "Parakeets. Yes, that's right." She moved her arm in a wide arc, indicating the spacious grounds of the park, which were dotted with old-growth trees. "They're all over."

Now that Zoe had spotted one, she picked out the bright feathers of the birds in many of the trees. "Parakeets in Amsterdam. That seems unusual."

Farina shrugged. "It is. No one knows where they came from. There are all sorts of stories about how they came to be here, but no one really knows. However it happened, they're thriving." She paused at a bench which fronted the path. "Shall we stop here?"

"Yes, this is fine. Now tell us about the paintings." Zoe sat down beside Farina on the bench, but Jack remained standing.

Farina lifted her chin and fixed her gaze on the sky as she gathered her thoughts. "It's a long and complicated story. I do realize the police would seem to be the obvious place to go, but I can't go to them." She gave a quick shake of her head, which caused the long side of her hair to fall over her eyes. She tucked it behind her ear and swiveled toward Zoe. "I think I know who has the paintings. I'm almost positive it's Pieter, the younger brother of my friend Margot."

Jack said, "Then you really should go to the police."

Farina jerked her head toward him. "He does go on about the police."

"And he's not usually their biggest fan." Zoe sent him a look, and Jack stepped back and put his hands in his pockets. Zoe turned back to Farina. "Tell us why you won't go to the police."

"I told you—I can't. Margot and I have been best friends since we were seven. I cannot go to the police about her brother. I can't."

Zoe asked, "Why do you think this man is involved? What was his name?"

"Pieter. Pieter Ecker." Farina pressed her hands together palm to palm and put them between her knees. "It's partly my fault. Margot and I had dinner recently. Pieter came along too. I'd just found out that the Janus Gallery would be displaying my artwork while one of Tamara de Lempicka's paintings would also be on display. Pieter hadn't heard of Tamara de Lempicka."

Farina blew out a sigh. "I explained—at great length—about what a famous artist she was and how valuable her paintings were. I was trying to convince him that it was a very prestigious thing to have my paintings displayed in the same gallery as hers." She rubbed her palm across her forehead again. "At the time I didn't think anything about it. It's only now, looking back, that it seems odd."

Jack had been surveying the empty park, but now he asked, "What sort of questions did he have?"

"How many floors did the gallery have. How many people worked there. Was it busy with people coming and going all the time." She shook her head and looked at the puddles on the road. "It's only now that I realize how suspicious it sounds."

"Jack is right. You really should—"

"No." She gave a sharp shake of her head, and a long strand of hair caught in her fair lashes. She brushed it away. "I've told you. I can't do that. Pieter has been in enough trouble in the past. If I contact the police, it won't be good for him. I can't do that to Margot or to Pieter." She shifted, straightening her posture. "I think Pieter can be convinced to give up the artwork. That's where you come in." Her gaze traveled between Zoe and Jack. "He doesn't know either of you. You can approach him and convince him to return the paintings."

Jack leaned forward. "So you think he has your paintings as well as the Tamara de Lempicka?"

A frightened look chased across Farina's face. She transferred her gaze to a group of bicyclists flying down the path. By the time they'd swooped by, she looked more composed. "I think he does. I'm not one-hundred percent sure."

"Why are you so convinced?" Zoe asked. "Sure, he asked some specific questions, but that doesn't mean that he took them."

"He was in London when they were taken."

"But that doesn't necessarily mean it was him," Jack said.

Farina's shoulders slumped, and she squinted as she watched the birds flitting through the trees. "I didn't want to have to tell you. I was afraid it would color your perception of him, but . . . he's been involved in a burglary before."

Zoe tilted her head so she could see more of Farina's face. "Just one?" Farina stilled. "Or was it more?"

"Okay, yes," Farina said. "It was more than one. A few. He was involved in a few. But he doesn't break into houses anymore."

"Only art galleries," Jack said, sotto voce.

Farina either didn't hear Jack or ignored him as she continued. "I can't go to the police. But I can't sit around and do nothing. I know he's—what's the phrase? In over his head. A painting is different from a few bits of silver or jewelry. No, he needs a way out. And you can give him that." She pressed a slip of paper into Zoe's hand. "This is where he works. You can approach him and arrange for him to turn the paintings over to you. You deal in finding lost artwork. It won't raise any eyebrows if you recover the paintings. He's got red hair and a fair complexion. You'll recognize him the moment you see him."

"And what should Zoe tell the police when they ask her how the paintings came into her possession?"

Farina smiled, the first real smile since she'd told them about the parakeets. "That's the beauty of this situation. You don't have to say a word. You're here. You've been posting on social media. Pieter searched and found you after he decided he had to get rid of the paintings—they were too much trouble—and he dropped them off with you . . . or left them for you. He could even leave them at your hotel. It couldn't be simpler."

"I doubt that," Zoe said. "Say Pieter does have the paintings and does decide to give them up. You think the police will believe Pieter found me through social media?"

She blinked, her expression puzzled at Zoe's question. "Yes, of course. It's how I found you. I recognized your hotel in the picture you posted a couple days ago. The photo of you beside the big tub of red tulips made it easy to find you. The awning with the hotel's name on it was right there in the background." Farina put her hand on Zoe's arm. "Please. Will you try? I'm not worried about my paintings, but the Tamara de Lempicka . . . well, it deserves to be found."

Zoe put the piece of paper in her pocket. "I can't make any promises. But I'll see what I can do."

17

Z oe fingered the piece of paper Farina had handed her with Pieter's work address as she and Jack walked back to the hotel from the park. "Well, Farina certainly isn't giddy now."

"Yes, it was quite a change from the news interview. She's worried, but I think there was something else going on too."

Zoe stopped walking and turned to Jack. "That's what I thought. Do you think she *knows* Pieter actually stole the paintings but didn't want to admit it?"

"Could be. Or it might be something else. Only one way to find out." He dipped his head toward the slip of paper.

"But we're on vacation."

Jack laughed. "I don't know if we're ever really on vacation. With our jobs, we're on call all the time."

"True. Neither of us has work that runs on a normal schedule."

"And we both want to know if Pieter has the paintings." Jack reached for the paper. "Where does he work? I wonder if it's nearby."

"Good question." Zoe tapped the address into her phone. "It's a shop called Lux in the Nine Little Streets area."

Jack looked over her shoulder at the screen. "It's open until six. Let's take a stroll up there and have a look around. We can have dinner there."

Zoe put her arm through his as they began walking. "Sounds good. First, though, I want to stop at the hotel and put Olive's reports and the cash in the safe in our room. I don't want to carry them around Amsterdam any longer."

"I haven't seen any sign of Ferris Thompson."

"Good." If Jack said he wasn't around, then Zoe was sure he was right. "I'll feel better if I don't have them in my messenger bag, though."

"Okay." Jack checked his watch. "You can read them before we put them in the safe."

Zoe squashed her sense of disappointment and shook her head. Finding a stolen painting worth millions took priority over documents. If they had a chance to find *Woman in a White Fur*, that had to come first. "I'd only have time to skim the reports anyway. We'll be cutting it close on time as it is. I want to give Olive's reports my full attention. I'll read them after we go to Lux."

Jack looked from the street sign to the map. "Left here, then another two blocks, and we'll be at Lux." He put the map away. "How do you want to handle this?"

"I don't think the direct approach is the way to go. If Pieter has the artwork, he could have it hidden away anywhere. In fact, he could've left it in London."

"That wouldn't be the smartest move."

"No." Thieves usually tried to move artwork across a border as soon as possible to make it more difficult to track down. "Leaving it in London would be a long shot. But there's plenty of places Pieter could have stashed it here in Amsterdam—the shop where he works, his house, or even a friend's home. And we don't know him at all. If he's already hidden it away somewhere, we could trail him for days and never come close to figuring out where he has it."

"Unless we broke into his house, and I know you wouldn't want to do that." A grin teased at the corners of Jack's mouth.

She gave his arm a gentle punch. "You know that was a one-time thing, a special circumstance."

Jack tilted his head from side to side. "I don't know . . . I think this might fit the same pattern. Stealing something that was stolen."

"Okay. You have a point. But we could waste hours—or days —tagging along after Pieter, hoping he'd give us a hint about where the paintings are. No, I think the direct approach is best," Zoe said. "Let's go in separately, though."

"Good idea," Jack said. "I'll give you a couple minutes' lead, then come in and browse. We'll act as if we don't know each other."

They arrived at Lux fifteen minutes before closing time. Tucked away on one of the cross streets between the canals, the narrow shop was wedged between a clothing boutique and a restaurant that sold stroopwafel, the thin waffles with caramel in the middle. The line from the restaurant curved out the door and in front of Lux, partially blocking the store's front window. Zoe and Jack paused a couple of yards away from the shop.

"Looks like high-end merchandise," Jack commented, his gaze roving over the display of vintage Louis Vuitton handbags.

A short stocky man with red hair and a fair complexion

came outside and picked up a folding A-frame sidewalk sign with a chalk drawing on it. Jack said, "Looks like that's our man."

Zoe started walking. "And it looks like he's closing up. Pity I won't have time to browse for real. Some of those bags are gorgeous."

"I didn't know you liked any designer bags."

"Not normally, but these are vintage. Vintage stuff is always interesting."

"Try not to get too distracted by the merchandise," Jack said as he stopped and pretended to examine his phone so Zoe could enter the shop first.

Zoe said over her shoulder, "A girl can browse."

18

An electronic chime sounded when Zoe entered the shop. A single thin aisle ran from the front window to a counter at the back. It was so narrow that if Zoe extended both arms, her fingertips would brush the walls on either side. Vintage leather bags filled the shelves and glass display cabinet, mostly Louis Vuitton handbags, luggage, and even a few steamer trunks, but there was a smattering of Chanel purses as well.

Zoe would have liked to have lingered over the vintage trunks, but she went to the back, where the man with the ginger hair was stacking receipts into a pile. He'd already turned off the lights in several of the glass display cases.

"Hello," he said in English with a barely perceptible Dutch accent. "Looking for anything in particular?"

"I'm looking for Pieter."

He glanced up and smiled quickly, an automatic customer-service smile, and went back to squaring the edges of the receipts. "I'm Pieter. How can I help you?"

Zoe put her business card on the counter. "I'm Zoe Andrews.

I'm a recovery specialist. I was told that you might be able to help me locate certain pieces of art that have gone missing."

His only reaction was a small hitch in the movement of his hand as he slid the receipts into a drawer. He closed the drawer with a thud. His voice was pleasant as he said, "Well, there's no artwork here. Handbags, purses, change purses, even a couple scarves and an occasional piece of jewelry. Everything Louis Vuitton, that's what we do."

Freckles were scattered across his nose and upper cheeks, reminding Zoe of a Norman Rockwell painting. He practically radiated innocence. Zoe plowed on despite his wholesome appearance. "My . . . source tells me that this has nothing to do with this shop. That it's sort of an extracurricular activity."

The electronic chime rang, and the mirror on the wall behind Pieter showed Jack's silhouette as he came through the door. Jack stayed at the front of the shop, his head bent over one of the glass cases. Pieter glanced over Zoe's shoulder, and he must have been satisfied that Jack didn't need further assistance, because he transferred his gaze back to her. "I can't control what you've heard. I can only tell you what I know. And I don't know what you're talking about."

He was shorter than Zoe and had a small stature, but he obviously spent a lot of time at the gym. His bulging biceps and chest muscles strained against the fabric of the button-down shirt he wore, giving him the appearance of a balloon that had been blown up just a tad too much and might burst at any moment. His muscled body was at odds with his guileless face, giving him a disproportionate bobble-head-like figure.

"Those art pieces are difficult. Sometimes people—um— acquire them, then realize they're a millstone, not a windfall. You might want to get rid of them. I can help you with that," Zoe said, thinking all the while that Farina was wrong—Pieter didn't have a care in the world, and the only thing he was interested in was locking up the shop.

He crossed his arms, tucking a hand under each armpit, which made his biceps expand even more. He took up a stance with his feet spread wide apart. "You have a terrible source. They're telling you nonsense. Now, if you'd like a bag or purse or trunk, I'd be happy to help you. Otherwise, I need to close up."

Zoe pushed the card across the counter to him. "I'll leave this in case you need to get in touch. I'll be in Amsterdam a little longer."

Zoe walked around Jack as she left, never making eye contact with him. She ambled slowly down the street and took a twisty path through the canals, confident Jack would trail along and catch up with her when he was sure they weren't being followed. She'd stopped to read a restaurant menu when Jack materialized at her shoulder and said, "Pieter sounded pretty adamant."

"Either Farina is completely wrong or Pieter's lying. I'm leaning toward the first option. I think she's got the jitters about her paintings and she's grasping at straws."

"Could be." Jack looked over the menu. "Or he could call you."

"I think that's unlikely. He probably tossed my card into the trash the moment I left."

"No, he didn't. He put it in his pocket."

Zoe popped the last bite of the stroopwafel into her mouth and savored the mixture of the crunchy waffle exterior and the sweet layer of caramel. She crumpled the paper wrapper and stuffed it into her pocket. "Well, that was worth the wait in line."

"Yep, I agree. A quintessentially Amsterdam kind of dessert."

They'd stopped at a street stall to pick up a stroopwafel as they made their way back to the hotel. They paused at the gentle peak of one of the arched bridges and watched as a tour boat putted away from them. The lights of the tall buildings on either side of the canal glittered in the wake of the boat. A few moments later, Zoe pushed away from the railing with a sigh.

"That was quite a sigh."

"I'm debating. Should we contact the police with the information Farina gave us about Pieter?"

"We don't have any proof, just hearsay."

Zoe looked up at Jack out of the corner of her eye. "You were all for going to the police earlier."

"I was all for *Farina* going to the police. There's obviously something going on there, and she's not telling us the full story. If we go to the police with that information . . ." He shrugged. "I don't think they'll take it too seriously. It's secondhand."

"It might give them a lead."

"Now you're the one sounding like you want to go to the police."

"I just want to do the right thing. But you're right. It's not much for them to go on." They walked a few more yards, passing by shops that had closed for the night. The rows of brightly packaged tulip bulbs and wooden shoes stood out even inside the dimly lit stores. "I'll give the information to Harrington," Zoe said. "I'm sure he knows someone in the police force here in Amsterdam. He can pass it along to his contacts."

"That's a much more effective way to convey it than you and I going to the local police station. That could take up most of our day tomorrow."

"Okay, then. I'll contact Harrington." With that decision made, Zoe felt a little lighter as they walked along. "Speaking of tomorrow, what's on our agenda?"

"The Van Gogh Museum in the morning, then the afternoon's open."

Zoe twisted toward him. "You've actually blocked in free time?"

"All the best tours have one free afternoon," he said with a laugh. "And then we switch to your schedule. What's our next destination?"

"Well ..."

"You haven't given it a thought, have you?" There wasn't a trace of accusation in his tone.

"Honestly, no. I'm sorry. I've been a little preoccupied."

He wrapped his arm around her shoulders and squeezed. "There is no rush—especially since we're just taking the train. We'll get our tickets tomorrow morning. You have Olive's reports, and you've been waiting days to read them. You should do that first."

Zoe snuggled into his shoulder. "Thanks for being so understanding."

"I've had my city tour. Now we can do things your way and ramble around, looking at whatever takes our fancy."

The doorman wished them a good evening as they went inside the hotel. Upstairs in the room, Zoe changed into a pair of yoga pants and a T-shirt, left a message for Harrington about Pieter, then opened the safe.

Earlier that evening, they'd used the hotel's business center to make two copies of the reports. She'd put the first copy in an envelope and addressed it to Ava at the London office, then dropped it off at the front desk to be sent overnight. She'd put the originals of the reports along with the second copy in the safe in their room.

She punched in the code, and even though she expected the papers to be there, she still breathed a tiny sigh of relief when she saw the crisp copies on top of the faded originals. She left Olive's original reports and removed the copies. The pages were sturdy, and she didn't have to be careful handling them. She curled up on the bed. "Do you want me to pass the pages to you as I finish them?"

Jack sat at the desk, the faint blue light of his laptop reflecting on his face. "No, you go ahead. I'll read them later. I have to answer these emails."

Zoe adjusted the lamp and settled in to read.

Olive
5 November, 1923
Hawthorne House

"There you are, old bean." Jasper handed Olive a sheet of paper filled with his neat handwriting. "Those two walls, all done."

"Thank you, Jasper. You are a dear—not only to drive me up here, but also to help me inventory the paintings." Olive rubbed her neck, which had a crick in it from tilting her head back to see the paintings at the very top of the wall. "It would take me weeks, not days, if I had to do it myself."

Once they'd finished their tea, Olive had decided to get right to work. It would be much harder for Mr. Carter to force her out if she were already industriously working away, but he hadn't returned since he'd announced he was going to contact Sebastian.

Olive had come to Hawthorne House armed with a tape measure, paper, and pens. She was working from the inventory done before the war that Sebastian had given her before she departed London. She checked off the paintings on the original inventory as she found them, then transferred the details to her new list. She put down a brief description of what the painting depicted, the type of frame, and noted any signature along with the size of the painting. For the larger paintings that were high on the wall, she'd transferred the dimensions from the original inventory list with the notation that she wasn't able to measure them at that time. For the smaller canvases that were within her reach, she used her tape measure and double-checked the dimensions.

"At least we've finished in here. I hope the other rooms aren't brimming with paintings like this one." Olive looked at her wristwatch. "Since it seems Mr. Carter isn't going to return, let's take a little tour of the house. I think we have time before dinner."

Jasper waited for Olive to precede him through the maze of tightly packed furniture to the door. "If we're so fortunate as to be served dinner."

"The welcome has been decidedly chilly."

They left the drawing room and paused in the gloomy entry to get their bearings, then explored the rooms on the ground floor, which were the library, the dining room, a small sitting room, and a morning room. The rooms were much smaller than the drawing room and contained less artwork, with only a few paintings decorating each wall.

After their quick survey, Olive suggested they go to the morning room and work there. "I think we'll be able to list all the paintings in that room before it's time to change for dinner."

Jasper held the door. "After you, old bean." The morning room was papered in a busy pattern of vines intertwined with yellow roses. Heavy velvet drapes in what might have once been deep green had faded to a sage color. Their frayed hems spread across the floor, and Olive had to wipe her fingers on her handkerchief after switching on several dusty lamps.

Olive shuffled her papers and pulled out a fresh sheet, tucking her handwritten pages to the back of the stack. "I'll copy these out in a fresh list to send to Sebastian when we finish."

"Or you could type them up." Jasper nodded to a desk in the corner of the room. A typewriter sat on it behind a stack of books. "If you're in luck, there'll be carbon paper in the desk. You could type up your list and make a copy at the same time."

"I wish I could type, but my education focused on the classics, not practicalities. It's something I should look into, I know."

"Well, you're fortunate you brought me along." Jasper tugged the handwritten pages out of her stack and went to the desk. "Allow me."

"You know how to type?"

He began opening and closing the drawers. "Ah, there we are —carbon paper, quite a healthy stash of it, along with plenty of paper too. I'm sure Sebastian won't mind if we help ourselves." He settled into the chair, dusted off the typewriter with his handkerchief, and settled a pair of spectacles on his nose. "It's a skill I picked up during the War. Had to make myself useful, you know. The old peepers were too weak for the battlefield, but not the War Office." He took two sheets of paper, slipped a carbon between them, and rolled them into the typewriter with a practiced motion.

He poised his fingers on the typewriter keys, fixed his gaze on the list beside on the desktop, and began clacking away at a rapid rate.

Olive said, "Very impressive."

Jasper didn't look up from the paper and didn't slow his typing. "I have to fulfill my designation as *a handy chap* to have around." The typewriter bell dinged, and he threw the carriage back with barely a pause.

"You are full of surprises."

Jasper's finger stilled, and he looked at her for a moment over the rim of his glasses. "Hidden depths, my dear. Hidden depths."

With a smile, Olive took up a new blank sheet of paper and a pen.

They worked away, Olive's pen scratching across the paper while Jasper clattered away at a truly impressive rate on the typewriter, the counterpoint of the bell ringing out at steady intervals. It took Olive about half an hour to list the paintings in the room, and Jasper had just typed up the last line of her notes when a man with a slight build opened the door and froze when he saw them.

19

The man hesitating on the threshold of the morning room wore rough work clothes and a heavy cardigan. He held a lamp with a fringed shade in one hand. "Beg your pardon, miss, sir." He ducked his head and reached to close the door.

Olive said, "No, it's fine. Please come in. We don't want to keep you from your work."

The man didn't move.

Olive stepped forward. "I'm Olive Belgrave, and this is Mr. Rimington." She motioned to Jasper, who'd replaced the chair under the desk and was moving across the room, the typed pages in his hand. "We're staying at Hawthorne House for a few days."

The man wiped his hand over his forehead, pressing down his thinning pale brown hair as he stepped into the room. "Pleased to meet you. I'm Hendricks."

Carter appeared in the doorway behind the man and said, "Hendricks sees to the gardens as well as repairs around the house."

Hendricks started at Carter's voice, and his free hand shot

out to hover over one of the pockets of his cardigan. A square-shaped bulge made the fabric sag on that side.

Carter surveyed the stack of typed pages Jasper was handing to Olive, but he spoke to Hendricks. "Were you able to fix the lamp?"

"Yes. It was a fault in the flex. Works fine now. I'll set it up quickly and be out of your way."

"Good." Carter waved his hand, indicating that Hendricks should go ahead with his work, then he turned to Olive and Jasper. "As I said earlier, we don't stand on ceremony here. No need to change for dinner. Mrs. Lum has laid out cold sand-wiches in the dining room, if you'd like to join me."

"Sounds lovely." Olive and Jasper followed Carter into the dim entry hall. "We were able to get a good start on the inven-tory. I'll just put the papers in my room, then I'll join you."

"Suit yourself," Mr. Carter said. "I believe Mrs. Lum intends to put you in the chintz guest room. Turn right at the top of the staircase, then it's the third door on your left."

Hendricks, who'd come out of the morning room without the lamp, said, "I'll bring up your luggage and show you the way, Miss Belgrave."

"Thank you," Olive said. "That's most kind of you." And the least someone could do for a guest. Was Carter doing as little as possible for them to make a point, or was he simply a poor host? Olive suspected it was the former.

Carter said, "Take the gentleman's bags to the north guest room, Hendricks."

Hendricks bobbed his head and went to the shadowy corner of the hall where Jasper had left their luggage. He'd retrieved it during a break in the rain while they were cataloging the paint-ings in the drawing room.

Olive followed Hendricks to her room, which was a small,

musty space with a plain white counterpane, one chair covered in chintz, and a bureau. Hendricks put down her bags and left.

The room was surprisingly warm, and Olive was happy to see a modern radiator. She wouldn't shiver all night. The walls were a faded blue above scratched wainscoting. Cobwebs festooned the corners of the ceiling, and a layer of dust covered the bureau. Olive pulled the thin drapes closed, blocking out the grimy windows. The intermittent tap of rain spattering against the window indicated the storm had abated. Had it passed over, or was it only a respite? Depsite the lack of welcome and the sad state of housekeeping, Olive was glad to be warm and dry. Even if they'd wanted to leave now, she was sure the road to the village was a muddy, impassible mess.

A quick inspection of the bed showed fresh sheets—another thing to be thankful for. Olive put the papers away in her luggage and freshened up in the bathroom down the hallway from her room. The basin had a copper-colored streak running from the faucet to the drain, but the tub looked clean, and fresh towels were stacked on a stool.

Olive went downstairs and followed the low rumble of the men's voices to the dining room, which was a long room with gray walls and gilded trim. The mahogany table must have been the only thing in Hawthorne House that wasn't coated in dust. Its polished surface reflected the light from the massive chandelier above, which looked as if it were pulling the ceiling downward. Olive decided it must be the shadows from the chandelier and her rather overactive imagination. Surely the beams of the ceiling wouldn't actually bow in that alarming manner.

The edges of the room were in darkness, and Olive crossed from the shadows into the light under the chandelier and joined the men at the table. The room had the same tinge of musty aroma as the chintz guest room. Mr. Carter probably had his meals in the chair in front of the fire, not in the dining room.

Dinner that evening was a platter of roast beef sandwiches and a cheese plate. While the meal was not elaborate, the bread was soft with a hint of warmth from the oven, and the roast beef was well-seasoned.

Conversation was strained until Jasper mentioned an acquaintance that both she and Carter knew. The discussion moved from their mutual friend to clubs to a recent gallery opening in London.

"I myself can't do more than admire the art," Carter said as Mrs. Lum removed their empty plates. "I must leave the art collecting to Sebastian. Fortunately, he has a rather good eye—most of the time."

"He certainly has quite an extensive collection here," Jasper said. "I didn't realize he was such an avid admirer of art."

Carter waved a hand at a painting of a man in a doublet and thick lace ruff. "He inherited most of these paintings. They've been in the family for generations. Much of the furnishings and artwork were sent here from the town house in London to keep it safe during the War. Because of the Zeppelin air raids, you know."

So that explained the warehouse-like situation in the drawing room, Olive thought as she sipped the last of her wine.

"Not many of the things here are from Sebastian's collection," Carter said. "He keeps most of the paintings he's purchased himself in London."

Jasper offered the cheese plate to Olive. "Very sensible. It would be awful to lose some of these works of art."

"Terrible," Carter agreed as he settled back in his chair. "We had even more artwork here during the War, you know. The house was bursting at the seams for several years. The National

Gallery crated up some of their art and sent it here during the War. Too risky to leave it in London."

"Goodness, where did you put it all?" Olive asked.

He motioned around the dining room. "We had heaps of it in here. Had to use the morning room for all our meals. Of course, we only had a small portion of the art from the National Gallery. They divvied it up. Some of it went into unused tube tunnels in London, while some were sent to various homes in the countryside."

"Spreading out the risk of loss." Jasper's tone was approving. "Did you receive any of the more well-known pieces?"

"A da Vinci or a Rembrandt?" Carter smiled and shook his head. "No, nothing like that. And everything was so cramped, we couldn't admire the artwork anyway."

Jasper said, "I noticed a painting in the small sitting room, a woman in a white fur stole. It's quite arresting."

"Now that painting *is* actually one of Sebastian's acquisitions, one of the few of his we have here."

Olive had noticed the painting as well on their speedy tour of the ground floor. It was striking—dramatic and modern—but art appreciation wasn't her main concern at the moment. She was interested in whether Carter would try to shove them out the door in the morning. "Speaking of Sebastian, were you able to get in touch with him?"

Carter's mellow mood seeped away. "Yes. He confirmed that you are his ambassador." Carter tossed his napkin on the table. "I'm to welcome you with open arms." He gave her a brief smile that only involved moving the muscles around his mouth. There was no warmth in his eyes. He was following orders, but only because he absolutely had to.

"Wonderful." Olive infused her tone with sincerity despite Carter's cold eyes. "I promise I'll complete the task here as quickly as possible." Olive pushed back her chair. "I'll leave you gentlemen alone to enjoy your port."

Carter and Jasper stood when Olive did, but Carter said, "There's no need for you to depart. As I said, we're very informal here. Afraid I can't linger. I have paperwork to attend to. It must be sent off in tomorrow morning's post." He turned to Jasper. "You're welcome to stay on and sample the port. It's excellent." He bid them good night and left the room.

Olive waited until the echo of his footfalls in the corridor faded. "The effusive hospitality continues."

Jasper put his napkin down beside his plate. "Let's be glad we're not out in the storm, searching for an inn or a pub with rooms to let."

"Or stuck in the mud. I'll leave you to your port."

"I'll skip this evening." Jasper crossed the room and held the door for her. "I'm going to toddle along and have another look at the modern painting in the small sitting room."

The sun had set, and the entry was pitch black. "I'll come with you. I'd rather not bump around in the dark on my own." Olive extended her hand in front of her as she inched along. "Feels rather like walking through a cave. How do the servants find their way through here?" Her hand brushed against the fabric of Jasper's coat.

He shifted his arm and took hold of her hand. "I doubt the servants do much walking back and forth between their quarters and the rooms upstairs."

She hadn't changed for dinner and wasn't wearing her gloves. The connection between their hands sent little pulses of warmth up her arm, and she realized how few times she'd actually touched a man's hand skin to skin. "I suppose you're right. It looks as if there's only Mrs. Lum and Mr. Hendricks." Her voice sounded a bit breathless, and she cleared her throat.

They rounded the stairs and came to a hallway where a few wall sconces had been switched on. The sconces threw out weak circles of light, spotlighting sections of the passage, which was lined with closed doors that reached to the lofty ceiling. "I think this is the small sitting room, isn't it?" Olive headed for a door midway down the hall. She was very aware that her hand was still linked with Jasper's, even though there was no need to hold onto each other to navigate now that they were in the light.

"I believe you're right. Although it is hard to tell with it so dim."

"Oh, this *is* it." Olive reached for the handle. "I remember this painting of a naval battle beside the door."

Olive opened the door. The fresh scent of rain permeated the air, which was so different from the usual dusty, musty smells of Hawthorne House. She felt along the wall for a switch, but before she found one, a light cut across the room, blinding her. A shuffle of movement sounded, then a crash, and darkness descended again.

Olive's fingers connected with the light switch, and the small chandelier overhead came on, illuminating the small room. "Goodness, what was that?"

Jasper crossed the room to the French doors that overlooked the back of the house. One door stood open. Cool rain-scented air gusted in, ruffling the fringe on the drapes. "An intruder, I believe."

Olive scanned the room. "Everything seems to be in place, though."

When they'd peeked in the room during their quick tour of the house earlier that evening, Olive had thought it the most cheerful and inviting of the rooms. The walls were paneled in a dark wood, but a mixture of chairs in faded chintz and sofas upholstered in pale colors gave the room a cozy, relaxed feel. Tall bookcases brimming with gold-tooled leather spines had filled Olive with a longing to explore the shelves, but she'd restrained herself. The French doors were set in the middle of a wall of windows. The drapes hadn't been drawn, and now the windows were rectangles of blackness, reflecting the glare of the chandelier.

Jasper studied the door handle. "We must have surprised him—or her. I suppose I should add that caveat since I didn't get a look at the person. Did you?"

"No, the beam of light—it must have been a torch—hit me right in the eyes. I only saw a white glare."

"I'm sure the chap is long gone, but I'll just take a quick look outside." Jasper disappeared out the door. Olive was about to follow him when she noticed a muddy footprint on the parquet floor a little beyond the open French door. The footprint was the first of several. The muddy prints ranged across the hardwood to the faded rug that covered the center of the room. They stopped near one of the bookcases that flanked the modern painting of a woman in a white fur stole.

Jasper returned and stamped his feet before stepping into the room. "They scampered. No one's around now." Droplets of water clung to his wavy hair and dotted his shoulders. He elbowed the door closed but didn't touch the handle.

"It seems they were interested in something on this side of the room." Olive pointed. "You can see the footsteps there."

"Perhaps the intruder was admiring the painting."

Olive tilted her head and studied the canvas. "I noticed this earlier today too. There's something about this painting that's . . ."

"Impressive?"

"Oh, yes."

Jasper stood beside her and stared at the painting for a few moments. "What do you think of the modern aesthetic?"

"I quite like it." Olive turned away from the painting. "I suppose we'd better find Mr. Carter and inform him he's had another uninvited guest this evening."

20

Zoe
Present Day

An intermittent ringing penetrated Zoe's thoughts, pulling her out of nineteen twenty-three and back to the hotel room. The muffled ringing was coming from her phone, which was in her messenger bag. Snuggled up among the stacks of pillows on the bed, she'd been reading Olive's report. She swung her legs over the side of the bed, but Jack picked up her bag from the floor beside the desk and tossed it to her. "Here you go."

Zoe threw back the flap. Of course her phone was at the bottom of the bag. She dug it out. "It's Harrington."

"Probably calling about the message you left for him," Jack said as he turned his attention back to his laptop.

Harrington's clear enunciation came through the line. "Good evening, Zoe. I hope I haven't caught you at a bad time."

"Not at all. I finally located Olive's report. We're having a quiet night in so I can read it. I'll send you the details once I finish it."

"Excellent."

"You got my message?"

"About the possible lead on the Tamara de Lempicka theft? Yes, I did. I had a chat with Superintendent Sven Visser and passed on the information."

"What was his reaction?"

"Tepid interest. Not really his department, if you know what I mean, but he'll send it on to the relevant team. I'll forward you his contact information in case you need to speak to him again and I'm out of pocket. I told him you're handling this for Throckmorton Enquires."

"How are things going for you? Still waiting?"

"No, things are starting to move, which is one reason I decided to contact you. I'm sorry to disturb you again during your holiday—that's getting to be quite a habit, I'm afraid—but I felt that you should be informed of a development related to the de Lempicka painting. Quite a lot of activity around it today."

Zoe pushed the messenger bag out of the way so she could sit cross-legged, her back straight. "What's happened?"

"Something that may explain why your lead there in Amsterdam seems doubtful. A collector has contacted me about *Woman in a White Fur*. He's been out of touch for several days and has just heard the news about the theft. He says he has the painting—"

Zoe sucked in a breath. "He has it?"

"So he says, but there's more. He says it's been in his collection for years, that he inherited it from a relative."

"Well, if he's had it for years, it can't be the de Lempicka painting. It must be a copy."

"Normally that would be the assumption, but he's . . . a rather slippery character."

"Oh." Zoe realized what Harrington *wasn't* saying. "You think he wants to use Throckmorton Enquiries as a way to get a hot painting off his hands. The story about his family owning it for years is a lie."

"Possibly. Highly probable, in fact. He's arranged for an authenticator to look at the painting. He'd like a representative from Throckmorton Enquiries to be on hand when the authentication is carried out."

"So he can hand it off to us and we can return it to the officials."

"All handled with discretion, of course." A gusty sigh came down the line from Harrington. "Recovering the art is always my top priority, but it does rankle to be used as a sort of return service."

"I agree, but if we can recover the painting . . ."

"Yes. It's definitely something we should do. And I'm sure that Darias Vokos has a cordial relationship with the authorities. Any charges against him would never have a chance of materializing. We're just another layer of protection for him."

"Darias Vokos? I haven't heard of him."

"Because he's very good at keeping a low profile. Although nothing was ever proven, it's well-known that he was active in organized crime. His organization controlled quite a bit of trade in the Mediterranean region for years. I've never met him, but I know colleagues have a nickname for him, *The Jester*. He's always smiling."

"Like a clown with a painted-on smile?"

"Exactly."

"I've never been fond of clowns."

"Me neither. He's retired now—supposedly. So, to return to

the authentication of the painting in his possession . . . because you're working on the provenance, I wanted to check with you and give you the first right of refusal, so to speak. Would you like to represent Throckmorton Enquiries? Vokos likes to move quickly, so you'd have to take a break from your holiday. I'd reimburse you for any changes you have to make to your itinerary. And since I'm suggesting an interruption to your holiday, Jack is welcome to accompany you." Before she could answer, Harrington hurried on, "If you're not interested, I understand completely. I can handle it. I'll just have to delay Vokos until I finish up here."

Zoe strained to reach for a pen and notepad on the nightstand. "Let me have the details of the meeting. I'll discuss it with Jack." As Zoe jotted notes, a smile crossed her face, then she said, "I'll call you back in a few moments."

She punched the End button on her phone. Jack lifted his fingers from his laptop keyboard and tilted his head. "Do we have our next destination?"

"Possibly. But you heard me, I didn't make any promises."

"So where are we off to?"

"Athens . . . if we'd like." She explained about Harrington's offer.

Jack said, "Sounds good to me. This is your leg of the trip." He smiled. "And I'm sure we can squeeze in a visit to the Acropolis while we're there."

"All right. I'll call Harrington back and tell him we're in."

When she told Harrington they were willing to travel to Athens, he said, "Brilliant. I'll have Ava arrange your flights and hotel. She'll send your airline tickets along with the details about the meeting."

Zoe hung up. "If the painting in Athens is *Woman in a White Fur* and we can get it back, that would be perfect." She picked up the pages she'd been reading. "With Olive's report and the painting recovered, it would close both open loops."

She settled against the headboard with Olive's report. She'd barely found the page where she'd left off when her phone pinged with an email. "It's from Ava. As usual, she's super-efficient. Our airline tickets are attached."

Zoe tapped out a reply to Ava. *That was quick.*

Ava's response appeared in Zoe's inbox almost immediately. *Harrington and I were pretty sure what your answer would be. Hotel reservations to follow shortly.*

Zoe typed out a note of thanks, then opened the attachment with the airline tickets and surged upright.

Jack looked up. "What is it?"

"We're booked on the 6:00 a.m. flight tomorrow."

Jack closed his laptop. "Then we'd better pack and get ready because that means we'll only get about four hours of sleep."

Zoe was already scrambling off the bed. "You can pack up in about three minutes. I'll need a little bit longer than that." She put away Olive's report, pushing down the wave of reluctance that bloomed in her. She really wanted to continue reading, but she had a painting to study. So far, she'd focused mostly on the documentation related to *Woman in a White Fur*, but since she was going to see the painting itself, she needed to know every detail about it by heart before the meeting with the authenticator.

Ava's next email came in with the hotel reservation and the details of the meeting. *The meeting with the authenticator is tomorrow afternoon at four.*

Zoe rubbed her forehead. "That doesn't give me much time to prepare."

"You can do it. You have tonight, and the time in the airport and during the flight."

"That's true. All the same, I'd better get moving."

———

Late the next morning, Zoe followed the bellman into their hotel room in Athens. As he opened separate closets and positioned their suitcases on luggage racks, Zoe turned so her back was to the man and mouthed the word *wow* in Jack's direction. Plaster ornamentation, some of it picked out in gold, decorated the high ceiling and wainscoting. A king-size bed layered with white linen filled one side of the room while a couch with delicate curved legs sat at the opposite end beside a table with a wood inlay. Two pairs of glass doors stretched to the high ceiling. One of the doors was open, and a warm breeze caused the sheer drapes to puff out. Jack tipped the bellman, and once the door closed after him, he flipped on the light in the marble-tiled bathroom, which was nearly as spacious as their room, and gave a low whistle. "We should always have Harrington make our hotel reservations."

"Ava said this was all that was available on short notice."

"Lucky us."

Zoe drew back the sheer curtain and stepped out onto the balcony. Their hotel overlooked Syntagma Square, a mix of cypress and plane trees along with paved walkways filled with people either lounging in the sun or striding quickly by, briefcases and purses bumping against their bodies. The pulse of car horns, the buzz of mopeds, and the rumble of motorcycles floated up from the busy streets that ringed the green space. The square was directly opposite Parliament. Zoe stepped to the railing to get a better view of the throng of people gathering in front of the building. "Look, it's the changing of the guard," Zoe said, and Jack came out onto the balcony with her.

"With the elite unit assigned to the Tomb of the Unknown Soldier, the evzones," Jack said, after pulling out the small guidebook from his back pocket. He'd picked it up at the airport that morning. They watched in silence as the men moved into position, the pleats in their kilt uniforms flaring out with each stiff-legged step. Jack tucked the guidebook under his arm. "If you squint, you can see the red pompoms on their shoes. Quite an outfit, but it's what the mountain guerrilla fighters wore when they rebelled against the Ottoman Empire."

They watched the ceremony from their high point several floors above street level, then they slipped back into the room. Zoe reached for the well-thumbed file on *Woman in a White Fur*. "Back to work for me. Let me just look over this one more time and then"—she glanced at her watch—"we can go out for a look around."

"Good plan." Jack settled on the other end of the couch, guidebook in hand.

After about an hour, Zoe rubbed her eyes. "Okay, I've read over this so many times that I'm starting to see double." She had spent half of the previous night and all that morning memorizing the file, first in the gate area at the airport, then during the flight. After she had the specifications down by heart, she'd pored over the images of the painting. She'd used her phone to zoom in and study the painting in detail. She'd memorized the pattern of brushstrokes in one area of the painting, the small section where the white fur brushed against the woman's ear. In that area, they crossed each other, creating a distinctive X pattern in the paint. Zoe snapped the file closed and slipped it into her messenger bag. "Time for some fresh air."

21

Zoe paused, her hands braced to push herself up from the couch, taking in the fact that Jack had a map spread out on the cushion between them. "You have a map now too?"

"Came with the guidebook. A good tourist is always prepared in case of a spotty cell phone connection." He reached for her hand and pulled her up.

As they rode downstairs in the small elevator, Jack leaned against the wall, his gaze on Zoe's face. "How are you feeling about the meeting?"

"Nervous."

"Probably a good thing. I'm always nervous before a big meeting."

"Yes, but you're very good at hiding your nerves." Zoe wiped her palms on her hips. The elevator doors opened, and Zoe reached for Jack's hand. "Let's enjoy Athens for a little while. A break will be good for me. I can come back and go over everything one last time before the meeting." They paused on the hotel steps. "What do you recommend we see?"

"Well, I think our driver was right. The Acropolis will be

wall-to-wall—or column-to-column—tourists at this time of day. Let's start with Ermou Street."

"That's the pedestrian shopping street, right?"

"Good memory. I thought the details from your guidebook copyediting days would start coming back once we were here. I had to buy a guidebook of my own to keep up with you." After a glance at the map, Jack slipped it into his pocket. "This way." They left Syntagma Square and strolled along the gently sloping street. It was dense with stores and boutiques, mostly modern, high-end chain stores. They came to a Byzantine church with arched windows and a cupola topped with a cross. Set in the middle of the road, it was apparent the church had been there much longer than the shops around it. Its mellow brown stones and faded red tile roof contrasted with the stores' plate-glass windows and mannequins wearing the latest fashions.

Jack consulted the guidebook. "Eleventh century, the Church of Kapnikarea."

The church was closed, but they admired the mosaic over the door that glowed with gold leaf. After Zoe snapped some pictures, they went on, rambling down a street that branched off the pedestrian mall. The tension that knotted Zoe's shoulders gradually relaxed as they admired more churches, studied a statue of Constantine, then found the Plaka neighborhood, where the streets became narrower and were lined with small shops selling clothing and all sorts of souvenirs from the two-toned blue evil-eye amulets to olive oil and T-shirts. Another street was lined with umbrella-covered tables outside tavernas.

"Lunch?" Zoe asked.

"Let's take a little detour first," Jack said. "I think you'll like this."

She followed him through the twisty streets, which were lined with cars parked bumper to bumper. Finally, Jack said, "I think it's around this corner . . . yes, here we are." He waved his arm at a gate-like structure with an arch that was topped with four Corinthian columns and glanced at the guidebook. "The Arch of Hadrian, built in 131 A.D. to mark where the old town of Athens ended and the new city of Hadrian began."

"Very impressive. And if I remember, that means we're close to the Temple of Olympian Zeus," Zoe said as they moved toward the arch.

"We are."

Once they neared the arch, the massive Corinthian columns were easy to spot, even from blocks away. They stopped by the arch for more pictures, then Jack motioned across the street. "Want to go across to the temple?"

"Of course."

He didn't have to check the map. They went around the arch and up another street to the entrance to the temple, where they bought a ticket. The temple was set on a flat plain, and they crossed the stubby grass to the columns that towered over them. "How high are they?" Zoe asked, just to see if Jack knew the number off the top of his head.

He checked the guidebook. "Fifty-six feet high. Fifteen are still standing. Originally there were one hundred and four—" He was rattling off the specifications when he glanced up and caught Zoe's eye, then stopped speaking mid-sentence. "I suspect you're humoring me, letting me go on about the details."

"The details are fascinating." Zoe waved her hand at the gargantuan columns. "I want to know more about what was here originally. Read on," she said in a mock-commanding voice. "Tell me how it looked originally."

Jack read off the description of the original layout, which included statues of both Zeus and Hadrian, then he tucked the guidebook into his pocket and they just stood and took in the immense scale. The Acropolis was visible in the distance, and Zoe had to take a picture of it framed with the columns of the temple in the foreground. They asked another tourist to take their photo, and when Zoe studied the result, she said, "We look like ants."

"That's about the scale of it."

Zoe said, "Let's go look at the fallen column."

They had to troop around to the far side of the temple to see the toppled column, which showed how they had been constructed with giant stone sections stacked one upon another. Grass was growing between the fallen stones. "Reminds me of a stack of Ritz crackers when you empty the whole sleeve at once," Zoe said.

"I was going to say a fallen stack of pennies," Jack replied. "But it must be lunchtime if you're thinking of food comparisons."

"Yes, I'm starving. Let's find a gyro."

"Sounds terrific." They found a restaurant that had formal seating inside, but also had a walk-up window on the sidewalk. They chose the fast method, and once their gyros were ready, they took a seat at a high table on the sidewalk in front of the restaurant. Zoe was glad for the umbrellas that shaded them. The afternoon was heating up. It was much warmer than Amsterdam. The gyros were a mix of rotisserie lamb, tomato, onion, and French fries, topped with dollops of tzatziki and ketchup, all wrapped in soft pita bread and served in paper wrapped into cone shapes.

It was delicious. Zoe was so involved in watching the foot traffic and enjoying her gyro that she didn't notice a buzzing sound.

Jack glanced at her messenger bag. "Is that your phone?" He reached out a hand. "Here, let me hold your gyro."

"Thanks, but no sneaking my fries."

"Wouldn't dream of it."

Zoe found her phone. "It's Ava."

"I have an update on the schedule," Ava said after they'd exchanged greetings. "Mr. Vokos' assistant called. The meeting's been moved to two o'clock."

Zoe checked her watch. "But that's in thirty minutes."

"I know. I'm sorry, but Mr. Vokos isn't one to consider others when he makes his plans. Where are you?"

"We're having a gyro . . . somewhere in Athens."

"Can you make it to the meeting?"

"We'll have to."

22

The address where Zoe was to meet Mr. Vokos was a neoclassical building not far from their hotel. Zoe would have liked to have changed out of her khaki pants and black cap-sleeved shirt, but her outfit would have to do.

As they approached the building, Jack's phone rang. He checked the screen, and an expression Zoe couldn't identify chased across his face.

"What is it? Is something wrong?"

"What? No. It's one of the businesses I had a meeting with in London."

Zoe gave him a long look.

He glanced up and caught her watching him. "It's nothing. Just something I've been working on. I have to take this."

"Okay." Zoe gestured to a café across the street. "I'll meet you there when I'm done."

Jack wished her good luck before answering his call.

"Thanks." Zoe blew out a breath as she climbed the flight of stone steps, telling herself that just because she was meeting someone who was suspected of being a player in organized crime, there was no need to be nervous—he was retired, after all.

She climbed the flight of stone steps and entered the hushed atmosphere of the lobby. The opulent building had probably once been a mansion owned by a single wealthy Greek family, but it had been converted into luxury apartments. Mr. Vokos lived on the top floor.

Zoe found the elevator on the other side of a large modern sculpture of fused cubes and triangles. She punched in the code that Ava had given her and found a hair clip in her messenger bag. She was sure she looked windblown from the quick jog she and Jack had taken across Athens. She pulled her hair into a ponytail as the elevator zoomed up. She fingered the file with the information about the painting, but she didn't have time to even take it out of her bag before the elevator glided to a stop.

A gorgeous woman met Zoe as soon as the elevator doors opened. With glossy black hair and high cheekbones, she looked like she'd stepped off a Milan runway. She also had the sulky look that most supermodels displayed on the catwalk. "Mrs. Andrews?"

"Yes. I'm here for a meeting with Mr. Vokos."

"This way."

The elevator opened directly into Mr. Vokos' apartment. Zoe followed the sharp clack of the woman's stiletto heels as she crossed the marble entry, which was lined on each side with a row of Corinthian columns that looked like miniature versions of the ones they'd just admired at the Temple of Olympian Zeus. The woman strode quickly through a large open room furnished in heavy wood-frame pieces upholstered with various animal prints. Onyx statues of sea creatures were spaced around the room. Mr. Vokos—or his decorator—seemed especially partial to dolphins. The woman paused beside a red-figure amphora with a row of athletes depicted on it. "Mr. Vokos, Mrs. Andrews is here."

One side of the room was a glassed-in balcony with a view of the Acropolis. A table had been set up there, and a man in a checkered shirt and baggy pants was bent over the painting. Zoe could see the vibrant purple and sharp white from several feet away.

Zoe gave the amphora a wide berth because it looked as if it belonged in a museum. She wished she had time to look at it closely, but she had to focus her attention on the man who was crossing the balcony to her, his hand extended. The light streaming through the glass panels behind him threw his face into shadow except for his white teeth, which stood out as he smiled. "Mrs. Andrews. I've never had the pleasure of meeting Harrington Throckmorton, but I'm delighted to have one of his associates here today."

He had a slight Greek accent, but his English was very good. "Please call me Zoe." They shook hands, and he pivoted slightly, which allowed Zoe to see him better. Vokos had jet black hair with gray at his temples, and now that he wasn't in the shadows, Zoe could see the smile only occupied the lower half of his face. His pale blue eyes were icy and assessing.

A slight movement in Zoe's peripheral vision drew her attention to a man who stood completely still at the far end of the room. He was much younger, probably in his twenties, and had a solid muscular build. His elegantly tailored suit didn't hide the bulge under the man's shoulder. Was he carrying a gun to protect Mr. Vokos or the painting?

Vokos noticed Zoe's glance and waved a dismissive hand at the young man. "My associate." Unlike the young man, Mr. Vokos wore a cream-colored shirt and a pair of designer plaid shorts along with cork-soled sandals.

"Come see my wonderful painting." He moved to the plastic-topped trestle table, which was set up so that it caught the natural light but wasn't directly in the sun. A pair of bright lights were aimed at the painting, and a magnifying glass on an arm was clamped to the edge of the table.

Vokos' figure threw a faint shadow over the painting. The man who was bent over the painting, his face inches from the canvas, said, "Please step out of the light."

Vokos didn't move.

The man, who was wearing magnifying glasses attached to a headband, straightened with a barely suppressed huff of irritation, then saw it was Vokos directly in front of him. He flipped the magnifying glasses up and swallowed. "Sorry, sir." He spoke with an American accent.

"Mr. Ewing, allow me to introduce Zoe Andrews, a representative from Throckmorton Enquiries."

"Right." He was a short man on the heavy side with a grizzled mustache and goatee. "I'd shake hands but . . ." He waggled chubby fingers, which were encased in gloves. "I'm in the middle of something rather delicate." He added, "Pleasure to meet you," as he snapped the magnifying lenses down over his eyes and returned his attention to the painting.

"Likewise." Zoe moved around the table so that she was on the same side as Ewing. At first glance, the painting looked very similar to the painting she'd seen in the gallery.

Mr. Ewing shuffled back and forth from the painting to the laptop, typing in notes as he muttered under his breath, lost in his own world.

Vokos put both of his hands in his pockets and tilted his head down as he examined the painting upside down. "It's always been a family favorite. I was quite shocked when I heard the news."

"About the painting being stolen?"

"Yes. I've been on my yacht for a week with my family. I have a strict policy. Everyone must disconnect. No mobiles, no computers, no television. No exceptions. They grumble—you'd think I'd banned them from eating—but in the end, everyone enjoys it."

He gave a shake of his head as he continued to look at the painting. "I couldn't quite believe the news when we docked, that the painting had been stolen." He patted his chest. "My painting. I knew it couldn't be true. I had the painting." He gestured to the wall in the room that Zoe had walked through. "It's hung there since I was a child."

He certainly sounded convincing, but his insincere smile, which hadn't slipped for a second, decreased Zoe's faith in his words. "How did your family acquire it?"

"My grandmother bought it. And"—he pointed a finger at her—"I have the paperwork to prove it."

"So you're saying the painting that was in the gallery in London was a copy?"

His shoulders went up. "I do not know about that painting. All I know is *this* painting." He knocked his knuckles against the frame.

Mr. Ewing whirled around from where he had been typing. "Please, do not interfere."

Vokos didn't say anything, but his smile vanished. He stared at Ewing for a few seconds. Ewing glanced at the man in the suit, who'd taken a step forward.

Ewing cleared his throat. "Sorry. Of course, it's your painting. I'm just trying to be—careful."

Vokos waited a moment, then his fixed smile returned. "Carry on."

The sulky woman entered with a cell phone. She and Vokos

spoke in low tones, then he said, "Excuse me. I must take this call." He moved away, and Zoe inched closer to the painting. Ewing glared at her. "There's no need for you to be here. I'm happy to send you a copy of my report."

"I'm here at Mr. Vokos' request."

Ewing blew out a breath through his nose and turned away. Zoe watched Ewing work for a moment, his movements delicate and gentle despite his gruff manner. She had been around other authenticators who shared their thoughts as they worked, but clearly that wouldn't be the case with Ewing.

Ewing picked up a metal box from under the table and unsnapped the latches. He opened the lid, exposing a machine packed in black foam padding. While he worked on removing the piece of equipment, Zoe stepped forward and peered at the painting through the magnifying glass that was attached to the arm. She shifted a little so that her line of vision was perfectly positioned to magnify the section of the painting she had memorized. Zoe was so absorbed in what she was looking at that she didn't realize Vokos had returned until the light changed and his shadow fell over the painting again.

"Beautiful, isn't she? It's one of my fav—" He broke off as Zoe looked up and he caught her expression. "What is it?"

"It's not what I expected." Zoe shifted the magnifying glass and gave the area of the painting another look. No, she was right; the brushstrokes on this painting hadn't been applied in a crosshatch pattern. These were straight up and down with no angle to them. "This painting is different from the one that was stolen from the Janus Gallery."

"Of course it's different. That one was obviously a fake." His smile was in place, but his gaze bored into Zoe.

Her heartbeat kicked. She'd just insinuated that she'd expected to find Vokos owned a copy of a very famous painting, not an original—and Zoe didn't want to be on Darias Vokos' black list.

His smile went down a few degrees. "This is the true Tamara de Lempicka painting of *Woman in a White Fur*. It's been in my family for decades."

"The Blakely family says the same thing, that the painting from their collection of *Woman in a White Fur* has been in their family for decades."

"They are wrong."

Ewing slammed the lid down on the now-empty box. "*This* is why I don't like amateurs hanging around. All my tests so far indicate that the materials are consistent with the early twentieth century, but it's too early to make a definitive statement. Now, if you'll let me get on with my work . . ."

Zoe stepped back, her thoughts churning. Vokos' eyes narrowed as he watched her for a moment. His gaze paired with his constant smile gave her the creeps. She sent him a fixed smile of her own. "Of course, I'm sure Mr. Ewing's report will help us sort it all out," she said, thinking, *I've got to read the rest of Olive's report and find out exactly what happened at Hawthorne House in nineteen twenty-three.*

23

It was late afternoon by the time Zoe rode the elevator down from Mr. Vokos' apartment. She dashed around the modern sculpture, her footfalls echoing through the quiet of the lobby. She sprinted down the hotel steps and rushed across the street to the café. Jack was at one of the outdoor tables under a red umbrella. An empty coffee cup sat at his elbow, and he was scrolling on his phone.

He pulled out a chair for her. "How did it go?"

Zoe dropped into the seat and threw back the flap of her messenger bag. "The bottom line is that there are two nearly identical paintings of *Woman in a White Fur*. I've got to finish reading Olive's report." She pulled out her copy of it. As she flipped through the pages, she told Jack about the meeting with Mr. Vokos. "So the question is, which painting is the original and which is the copy?"

"Wouldn't the original be the one from the Blakely collection?"

"Maybe. Remember Blakely sent Olive to Hawthorne House because there were rumors circulating about dodgy things going on? When Harrington called, I'd just read a section of Olive's report where she reports a break-in and an intruder. What if someone stole the painting at Hawthorne House and replaced it with a copy?"

"Did they?"

"I don't know. Olive says the painting was still there in the small sitting room after the break-in. But Carter, the estate manager, wasn't pleased that Olive showed up unannounced, so that makes me wonder if Carter was up to something. Mr. Vokos swears the painting he owns has been in his family for years—since nineteen twenty-three, to be exact."

"Popular year, that one." Jack studied the underside of the umbrella, his brow wrinkled. "Perhaps the artist painted two versions—same model, same pose. Van Gogh did that with his paintings of sunflowers. I read about it in the guidebook before we went to the Van Gogh museum. There are five versions of the painting."

"Yes, that's true. And Edvard Munch painted several versions of *The Scream*, but with *The Scream* and *Sunflowers*, the versions have easily discernible differences, either with composition—the number and positioning of the flowers—or with the materials used to create the art." Zoe glanced up at the top floor of Vokos' apartment building. The glass panels reflected the sun. "The painting I saw today looked *exactly* like the one at the Janus Gallery in London. The colors and composition and materials were the same—only the brushstrokes were different. Vokos showed me the documentation for his painting. It states the painting is an original one-of-a-kind piece, and it's similar to the provenance paperwork that the de Lempicka estate sent me for the painting in the Blakely collection. I didn't get a close look at it, though, only a glance. Ewing packed it up to take back to his lab for analysis."

Jack pushed his coffee cup away and leaned his arms on the table. "So what was the authenticator's assessment of the painting?"

"Ewing was cagey. He had equipment trouble. His portable x-ray machine wasn't working, so everything is on hold. Mr. Vokos refused to let Ewing take the painting. In fact, Vokos said the painting hasn't left the apartment in nearly a hundred years. Ewing said he'll return as soon as he has the equipment repaired, or he'll get another X-ray machine. But either way, it will take several days. Without the X-rays and full lab analysis of the pigments, Ewing refused to say anything definite today. He did allow that the materials, the paint and the canvas, appeared to be consistent with a painting produced in the early twentieth century, but that's as far as he'd go. It didn't go over well with Mr. Vokos. He wanted a definite declaration from Ewing. I think the best bet is to finish reading Olive's report." Zoe tapped the stack of papers.

Jack signaled for the waiter. "Coffee?"

"Sure. Want to read along?" Zoe offered him the pages she'd already read.

"It sounds more interesting than the thriller I picked up for the trip."

Zoe scooted her chair closer to the table and found the place in Olive's report where she'd left off.

Olive
5 November, 1923
Hawthorne House

Olive and Jasper found Carter in the drawing room. He was settled in his chair by the fire and hidden behind a raised newspaper. When they related what had happened, Carter reluctantly folded his paper. "Well, I suppose I'd better come along and check."

It seemed to be the least he could do. He was the estate manager, after all. Of course, Olive didn't voice her opinion aloud. Guests—even uninvited ones—didn't comment when their host's behavior was lacking.

As they made their way through the maze of furniture to the door, Carter asked, "Where did you say this happened?"

"In the small sitting room."

Carter paused at the door, his alert gaze fastened on Olive. "The small sitting room? Are you sure?"

"Yes, the cheerful room with French doors and paneling."

"Right." Carter let Olive go out the door ahead of him and lead the way, but he nearly trod on her heels as they walked to the small sitting room. He threw open the door and went directly to the painting of the modern woman with the white fur stole, his gaze scanning the canvas.

"The lock wasn't forced." Jasper had crossed to the French door and was pointing at the handle.

"What?" Carter turned a distracted look on Jasper.

"It appears the door was either unlocked or the intruder had a key."

"Hmm." Carter examined the door and the muddy footprints. "Someone probably forgot to lock the door. An oversight, you know. Must have been a tramp looking for warmth on a cold night."

"Perhaps you should—" Olive broke off. It was too late to mention fingerprints now. Carter had opened the door. The roar of the downpour suddenly filled the room. The patter of rain

Olive had heard earlier in the evening must have just been a brief break in the storm. Carter glanced outside, then closed the door, shutting out the pounding rain. He rattled the handle to make sure it was locked.

Carter turned to Olive and Jasper. "Thank you for alerting me, but nothing seems to have been disturbed. Don't let me keep you from retiring for the evening."

"You don't think a call to the constabulary is in order?" Olive asked.

"At this time of night and in this weather? No. There's no need to make a fuss. And you don't know our local chaps. You might ring up the police in London, but out here they're only interested in stolen farm animals and keeping the speed of motors down in the village."

Carter opened the door to the hallway for Olive to precede him out of the room, but she hesitated. Surely a break-in—even if someone had just entered the house to get out of the cold—should be reported, no matter how lackadaisical the police were in the area? "I do think Sebastian would like to know—"

"Of course I'll inform Sebastian next time I speak with him. I assure you, there's no need for you to worry. We're quite a back-water here." He dipped his head. "I'll bid you good evening. I'm sure you want to get your rest. So many pictures to inventory, you know."

24

Olive
6 November, 1923
Hawthorne House

When Olive awoke the next morning, daylight was seeping through the Virginia creeper, which almost completely covered the windows. As the wind ruffled the vines, filtered sun and shadow shifted across the walls and floor, giving her room an underwater ambiance. It reminded her of the summertime swims she and her cousin Gwen had taken in the river that twisted through the grounds of Parkview Hall.

She pulled on her dressing gown and went to the window. If she stood on her tiptoes, she could see out of a section of glass that wasn't covered with vines. Her room overlooked the lawn at the back of the house. Olive was sure that in the summer the view would be a verdant green, but autumn had leached away any emerald color. The view was a sepia-toned landscape in shades of beige, brown, and muted green. The lawn stretched out in a series of gentle slopes to a belt of trees. Unlike the subdued colors of the land, the sky was bright blue.

A figure emerged from the thicket of trees at the far edge of the lawn. The person was too slender to be Carter, whose middle was quite thick. It was difficult to tell because of the distance, but it seemed to be Hendricks moving across the lawn, carrying a rake propped on his shoulder. He disappeared behind a tall hedge that concealed a small outbuilding or shed. The shingles of the building were just visible from Olive's high vantage point.

A few seconds later the man reemerged pushing a wheelbarrow. He trundled it across the grass and out of Olive's line of vision. Despite the clear, cloudless day, the unencumbered view unnerved her for some reason. She hadn't realized the grounds around Hawthorne House were so deserted. Beyond the swath of lawn, the trees extended out as far as Olive could see without another rooftop or chimney in sight.

She shook her head at herself as she lowered her heels to the floor. Surely her short time in London hadn't given her a city-dweller's aversion to the empty countryside? She picked up her sponge bag and told herself not to be a silly rabbit. She was a countrywoman, born-and-bred walking the hills and fields of Derbyshire, not some cosseted city girl who exclaimed about her nerves when she experienced the silence of the country.

She went along to the bath to prepare for the day. She was glad to have this assignment from Sebastian, but she would complete the task as expeditiously as possible. She didn't want to linger any longer than she had to in Hawthorne House. It was simply because of the limpid welcome and had nothing to do with the sudden feeling of discomfort that had just come over her. Of course that was it.

Jasper was not the sort to jump out of bed at first light, so she was quite surprised when she found him in the dining room. "Jasper, what are you doing up so early?"

"Paintings to inventory, old bean. I know you can't get on without your trusty assistant."

"It will go much faster with you. I'm certainly glad to see you. How is the breakfast?"

"You arrived at just the right moment. Mrs. Lum brought fresh toast and coffee moments ago."

"Excellent news." Olive help herself to eggs, toast, and bacon, then poured herself a cup of coffee and sat down at the table across from Jasper. "Any sign of Mr. Carter?"

"No. Mrs. Lum hinted he won't be down for several hours."

"Then we should be able to get quite a bit done." As they ate, they planned a strategy, deciding that they would aim to finish cataloging all the rooms on the ground floor before moving upstairs.

Olive put down her flatware and picked up her coffee cup. "Did you happen to see which direction the intruder ran off last night?"

"No. But using keen observation, I can conclude he—or she—must have gone toward the back of the house."

"Really? Why do you think that?"

"There's a tall line of shrubbery blocking off the opposite direction. Unless the intruder had the ability to jump a hedge several feet taller than I am, he must have gone toward the back of the house."

Olive rested her elbows on the table as she held her cup between her hands. "I wonder if he went to the little shed to wait out the storm. It's about halfway down the lawn behind the shrubbery." She described what she had seen that morning as Hendricks went about his work.

Jasper said, "I did ask Mrs. Lum if there are any homes nearby. The nearest is over five miles away."

Olive studied him over the rim of her cup. "Careful, or you'll completely smash your careless man-about-town persona."

"Come now, I've never fooled you for a moment. You know it's all a ruse."

"I do. What I can't figure out is why."

Jasper's tone shifted. "It's so much easier to pretend not to care, old bean. One is never in danger of feeling anything too . . . uncomfortable." His words were quiet, and his usual mocking, half-joking tone was gone. Olive's heart began to beat quickly, and she didn't want to examine the reason why. Before she could say anything, Jasper picked up his cup and waved it around the room, his voice taking on its usual light tone. "Besides, an unidentified intruder at a quiet country house? How could one *not* be interested in finding out more?"

Mrs. Lum entered to remove their plates. Jasper said to her, "That was a delicious breakfast. Thank you, Mrs. Lum."

Her sour expression faded. Olive added her praise as well, but Mrs. Lum was clearly more interested in Jasper's words than Olive's. Mrs. Lum had several questions for Jasper. *More coffee? Another rack of toast? Perhaps the gentleman would like some kippers?*

Olive hid her smile behind her napkin. He'd always had a way with females. There was something about his teasing, relaxed nature that made people—women especially—long to coax his smile wider or hear him lavish compliments on them. It was the same at Parkview Hall. When he visited, Cook baked him special treats for tea, and all the housemaids tittered anytime he walked by. If he favored them with a wink, they nearly fainted. If Jasper's charm meant excellent meals and ameliorated the bad feelings belowstairs, Olive was glad.

As they left the dining room to begin inventorying the paintings in the morning room, Olive said, "Thank goodness I have such a charming assistant. I expect Mrs. Lum will outdo herself with lunch to impress you."

"One tries to be as useful as possible. And it was a delicious breakfast."

"I agree. I'm just glad you were there to impress on Mrs. Lum how much you enjoyed it. Perhaps it will remove some of the resentment they feel toward us—and by *us,* I mean you specifically and me by extension."

They worked steadily through the morning, then stopped for a brief lunch, which was excellent as Olive had predicted. Carter had a tray in his room, which suited Olive and Jasper. They ate more of Mrs. Lum's scrumptious fresh bread, this time with ham slices between it, and washed it down with tea. They were back at work again in half an hour, working their way through the inventory of each room on the ground floor. Olive had made her notes in longhand, and Jasper had carted the typewriter from room to room, setting up and clacking away, transferring Olive's scribbles to neatly typed lists.

It was nearly teatime when Olive collapsed onto a wooden chair in the library, their last room on the ground floor, as Jasper finished typing her final notes. The typewriter bell rang, and he threw back the carriage. He banged out one more sentence, then rolled the paper out and added it to the stack beside him with a flourish. "There you are, my dear. Fini."

"Thank you, Jasper. An excellent day's work. I think we deserve some refreshments. Perhaps we can have it in the small sitting room."

"Jolly good idea."

Mrs. Lum poked her head through the doorway. She looked almost friendly as she asked, "Will you be wanting tea in here?"

Jasper said, "Tea would be marvelous, Mrs. Lum."

A pink blush stained her cheeks as she said, "It'll be right up, Mr. Rimington."

"Thank you, Mrs. Lum. We thought we'd have it in the small sitting room."

She nodded her approval. "That's a right lovely room. I don't know why Mr. Carter prefers the drawing room, what with it so cramped in there. I'll bring the tea along to the small sitting room shortly."

"Thank you, Mrs. Lum," Olive called, but Mrs. Lum had already shut the door. "Well, she's thawed completely—at least toward you." Olive took the papers with them as they went along to the small sitting room. "Perhaps by the time we leave, she'll smile at me."

Jasper held the door for her. "She's probably just keeping her distance. You're rather intimidating."

"Me?"

"Yes."

"Why?"

"You're a beautiful young woman from London. That combination often results in someone with a supercilious attitude and demanding demeanor. Of course, that doesn't describe you. You're refreshingly unaffected."

That funny heartbeat thing was back. A few years ago she would have brushed off his comment, saying something like, "Don't be a goose, Jasper. It's bad manners to be unkind," but the little hitch of her heartbeat had thrown her off her normal stride.

Before she could say anything, Jasper continued. "I'm sure Mrs. Lum is keeping her guard up in case you turn out to be a young woman of the difficult variety. She'll come around."

In the small sitting room, late afternoon sun streamed in

through the long windows, giving the room a cozy glow. Olive said, "Oh, it's even nicer in here when it's not so overcast."

"Olive."

She turned quickly at Jasper's serious tone. He nodded to the wall behind her. "The painting's gone."

The space between the bookcases was bare. The modern painting of the glamorous woman in the fur was missing.

25

J asper gathered playing cards into a stack. He cut the deck with a deft movement. As he shuffled them, the cards fell into place with a soft *thrum*. "Another game?"

"No. I can't concentrate." Olive stood and moved away from the card table that was wedged among the furnishings of the drawing room. She poked the blazing fire more because she wanted something to do than because it needed attention. She and Jasper were waiting while the police finished in the small sitting room. Despite Carter's disparaging comments about the police's competence, they'd conducted what seemed to Olive to be a thorough investigation, fingerprinting the French doors as well as all the surfaces in the room. Then the constable had interviewed everyone in the house.

Olive replaced the poker and dropped into Carter's cushy chair. "Who do you think took the painting?"

"No idea, although I'm sure the first suggestion will be a passing burglar, especially since there was an intruder last evening."

"A random burglar is the easiest answer." Olive ran her

finger along a seam of the chair. "Mr. Carter certainly seemed shocked when we informed him the painting was gone." Olive had expected Carter to be irritated or angry when they brought him the news that the painting was missing, but he hadn't reacted in that way. He'd looked absolutely floored.

Jasper dealt out a hand of Patience. "The poor chap did look rather like a trout, standing there opening and closing his mouth."

Olive tilted her head. "I think I heard something." A cadence of footsteps sounded on the other side of the door. She shot out of the chair, threaded her way through the furnishings, and cracked the door an inch.

In the entry, Carter was opening the door for the police sergeant.

Jasper's breath tickled the back of Olive's neck as he said in a low voice, "You're not going to eavesdrop, are you?"

Olive did her best to ignore the rather delightful shiver that ran through her. "Of course I am," she whispered back. "We were sent here to inventory the art, and a piece is missing. I want to find out everything I can. If you're going to be judgmental, then you can go back to your card game."

"The game of Patience pales in comparison to a good round of eavesdropping."

"Then you'd better come closer—and stop asking distracting questions."

Olive shifted to the side so Jasper could step up to the door. He was taller than her and could easily lean in and listen, his head above hers.

"My questions are distracting, are they?"

"Yes, they are." And his presence so close to her was unsettling, but in a fizzy Champagne sort of way. The scent of citrus and cinnamon, Jasper's shaving lotion, enveloped her. "Now shush." She leaned her ear against the seam of space between the door and the frame. She focused on the words being spoken, not the way Jasper's tie, which was inches from her nose, angled to the side as he leaned, or how the fabric of his shirt shifted with his breathing.

She closed her eyes in an effort to block out the view and concentrated on the words of the police sergeant.

". . . assure you, we'll do everything we can to find the painting. I'll check about the village, but—"

"No need for that." Carter cut in, his words quick. "We don't want to spread the news far and wide until we're sure we need to. I mean, it might've been someone in the local area."

"I think that's unlikely, sir. We haven't had any reports of tramps or prowlers, except the intruder the young lady and gentleman mentioned. They scared off the chap last night. I doubt someone would return again the next day and take a picture—and in broad daylight too. It's hard to imagine a thief would take one painting without anything else. After all, there were two nice big silver candlesticks on the table near the painting, not to mention that fancy clock. None of those things were touched, and the locks were intact. No one forced their way in."

"You think someone *here* took the painting?"

"Seems the most likely possibility. My constable had a look around the old stable in case someone stashed it there out of sight until they could cart it away, but there was nothing there."

The stables had been converted to a garage, and that's where Jasper's motor was parked.

The sergeant continued, "No recent tire tracks on the drive either, except for the ones we made on our way in. No, it's most likely an inside job. Someone took the picture and walked out to meet an accomplice—somewhere on the grounds or along the lane, most likely. Then the accomplice beetled off to London, and Bob's your uncle."

As Carter sputtered a protest, Jasper murmured, "Mr. Carter seems to have severely underestimated the interest of the local constabulary."

"And their intelligence," Olive added.

The police sergeant said to Carter, "What can you tell me about Hendricks?"

"Hendricks?"

"Yes. Seemed a bit nervy."

"He's been employed by the Blakely family for over two decades. You're new to the village, aren't you, Sergeant?"

"Assigned here last summer, sir." The sergeant's tone was mild. He continued speaking before Carter could go on. "I'll keep an eye on Hendricks. It may be the toff or the lady you have visiting who stole the picture, but that doesn't seem likely. They're still here. If they'd taken it, I think they'd have hopped in their motor and left, quick-like. No, I'm confident our best course of action is to send this up the chain of command. I'll ring my superior. He can pass the information along to London. They'll alert the antique shops and pawn—"

"No. As I said, no need for that. Best keep it quiet."

"But sir, it's unlikely that the picture is still in this area. Your best chance of recovering it is to get the word out."

"That's exactly what we *don't* want to happen. Let me have a quiet word with Mr. Blakely. I'll let you know how he wants to handle it. Don't do anything until I contact you. I'll ring you first thing in the morning, after I've spoken to Mr. Blakely."

"But we're letting time slip away. The longer it goes—"

"As I said, not a word of this goes farther until tomorrow morning." Carter's tone was commanding.

There was a pause. Olive opened her eyes and shifted so she

could see out the opening. The police sergeant scratched his ear. His expression was doubtful. "I suppose I could delay informing my superior until tomorrow morning, seeing as how you're not the actual owner of the picture and you want to speak to him."

Carter clapped his hand on the sergeant's shoulder. "Good man." Carter maneuvered him outside. "Excellent work this evening. Very—um—extensive. I'll be in touch in the morning."

Olive and Jasper backed away from the door, bumping into each other. They gripped each other's arms to steady themselves, then zigzagged back through the furnishings.

By the time Carter joined them in the drawing room a moment later, Olive was seated on the couch, and Jasper was standing by the fire, his hands clasped behind him. Olive tried to discreetly draw in a deep breath to calm her racing heart. Nothing like a little eavesdropping to get the heart racing—or being so near a man, she thought as she glanced at Jasper. Carter went directly to the drinks cart. "What an ordeal." He poured himself a whiskey, then looked toward Jasper with raised eyebrows. "Care to join me? Need a pick-me-up?"

"No, I find I'm feeling quite perky this evening already," Jasper said with a look at Olive that made her heart flutter.

Carter took a swig of his drink. "Quite shocking, the whole thing." The crystal stopper clattered against the decanter as he replaced it. He collapsed into his armchair by the fire and took a long drink.

Olive waited a moment. She expected him to set down his glass and go to the telephone in the hallway, but he only shifted his hips and settled deeper into the cushion.

"You are going to contact Sebastian, aren't you?" Olive asked.

"Sebastian's never home in the evening. He'll be at a play or a dinner party, something of that sort." Carter rubbed his palm across his forehead, smoothing down his hair. "No, it will wait until morning." Carter took another sip of his drink, then his tone became hearty. "Well, enough of this nonsense. Let's speak of something else." They made stilted conversation for a little while, then Olive made her excuses and retired for the evening.

Jasper caught up with her on the stairs. She waited until they were on the landing, then said, "I can't believe Mr. Carter has put off ringing Sebastian."

"I'm sure Mr. Carter doesn't like the idea of word getting back to Sebastian that someone broke into the house yesterday and he did nothing about it."

They reached the top of the stairs, and Olive paused, her hand on the newel post. "I think I know where the painting might be."

"And you're going to look for it right now."

"Of course. Well, after I change into sturdier shoes. I think it's in the little shed that I saw this morning. It's definitely worth a look. Are you coming?"

"Wouldn't miss it. You know how I love midnight strolls around the countryside."

"Glad to hear it. Meet you back here in a few moments."

When Olive returned to the top of the stairs, Jasper was trotting up them. "Where have you been?"

Jasper removed a key from his waistcoat pocket. "A spot of pilfering in the kitchen while Mrs. Lum was speaking to Mr. Carter in the drawing room. Can't have us locked out."

"Good thinking. How will you get it back?"

"That's a problem for later. I'll think of something." Jasper gave an approving nod at the torch in her hand. "Did you come prepared, or did you find that somewhere around here?"

"I brought it with me. I've learned there are a few essentials a girl needs on hand."

"I would think that would run more along the lines of lipstick and powder."

"A *working* girl."

"I see. Shows how out-of-touch I am. Well, topping idea. We won't have to use my lighter to see the way."

As they descended the stairs, Olive said, "I think we should go out the French doors in the small sitting room."

"Retrace the intruder's steps? Unlike our village police chap, you think the intruder and the theft of the painting are connected."

"It seems the logical place to start."

"I agree. The police didn't seal off the room, so I don't see why we can't do it."

They didn't switch on any lights when they entered the small sitting room. Olive paused for a second, remembering the blinding beam of light that had flashed across her face. But tonight, the air had a trace of mustiness instead of the scent of fresh air. No movement came from within the room, and Olive navigated across it, managing to avoid the sofas and chairs. She pushed back the drape, which had been pulled in front of the French doors. Jasper swung one open. "Allow me."

The thick hedge towered to Olive's left, a blocky chunk of darkness against the trees and sky. The cool air traced over Olive's bare arms, a refreshing change from the rather dank atmosphere of Hawthorne House. They set off across the lawn, moving toward the back of the house. The sky was clear, and light from the stars allowed them to pick their way through the hedges and ornamental shrubbery. Olive sidestepped a low Boxwood. "No need for the torch here."

"I agree. Best to leave it switched off."

They made their way across the expanse of lawn that ran down to the belt of trees. Olive glanced back at the house a few times, but no lights were on in the back windows. As she swept her gaze along the rows of blank unlit windows, Olive again felt that pressing ominous sensation that had come over her when she looked out over the vast emptiness behind the house. She'd taken a few sideways steps as she looked over her shoulder, but now she turned her back to Hawthorne House and quickened her steps as they closed in on the shed.

"You should have worn a hat," Olive said. "Your fair hair is shining like a beacon in the middle of the Channel."

"Unfortunately, I left my burglar kit in London. Next time, let me know before we depart, and I'll have Grigsby pack it in my luggage."

"Sorry. I don't mean to be critical. I'm a little jittery." The tall shrubbery enclosed two sides of the shed, shielding it from the house. They walked to a rough wooden door on the far side with a metal lock on the latch. Olive asked, "Can you pick it?"

"Why would you think I'd be able to do that?"

"You know how to touch-type. Perhaps lock-picking is another of your skills?"

"While I'm flattered you think I'm a man of many talents, sadly, they don't extend to lock-picking."

"Pity."

Olive switched on the torch, shielding the light with her hand so it wouldn't blind them.

"Oh, I say. We are in luck." Jasper flicked the lock around and removed it from the latch. "It wasn't fastened. It was only for show."

"Hendricks must feel that there's no need to lock up. It is rather deserted around here."

"Yes. Probably saves him carrying around a key." Jasper opened the door, and Olive aimed the light inside. Gardening tools of all sizes ranged around the walls. Pots and hand tools sat on a rough wooden counter, which was dotted with traces of soil. Several burlap sacks sagged in one corner. A few had crumpled over onto the hard-packed earthen floor, and a wheelbarrow was propped up against another section of the wall.

A cursory examination was all it took to see the painting was not in the shed. Olive traced the light over the pile of burlap sacks, which had soft bulging contours. "No painting here. I was completely wrong."

"It was a good idea to look, though."

In the corner, a single empty burlap sack was draped over a box-like shape. Olive stepped into the shed and cautiously lifted an edge of the burlap, expecting to see pots or gardening tools or —worse—a rodent nest. But there was only a crate under the sack. "Jasper, look at this." He peered over her shoulder as she trained the torch on several expensive leather books. The gold lettering on their spines glittered under the bright stream of light.

Olive handed the torch to Jasper and picked up the one on top. "It's *Pride and Prejudice*. And *Northanger Abbey* as well." She stood up, the books in her hands. "Mr. Hendricks is stealing books from Hawthorne House?"

A voice behind them said, "No. I'm reading them."

Startled, Olive dropped one of the books. She spun around as Jasper cut the light toward the door. Mr. Hendricks stood there, squinting, one hand thrown up to block the light. "I didn't mean any harm."

Olive picked up the book—a copy of *Pride and Prejudice*—and brushed off the cover. "You enjoy reading Jane Austen?"

Jasper lowered the torch so it wasn't in Hendricks' eyes. He stepped inside the shed and removed his flat cap. "Oh yes, miss. Her books are a right treat, they are." He twisted the fabric of his cap. "And I'll return it. I promise you, I will." Hendricks looked down at the packed ground. "I would like to finish it, if I may." His Adam's apple worked up and down, then he spoke quickly. "I want to find out what happens between Miss Elizabeth Bennet and Mr. Darcy."

"Completely understandable," Jasper said. "Excellent choice of reading material, old boy. How did you come upon it?"

"There was an old copy of *Northanger Abbey* in my quarters." He loosened his grip on his cap long enough to gesture in the direction of the converted stables. "There's a bookshelf with stacks of books. I tend to read in the evenings. *Robinson Crusoe* and *Sherlock Holmes.* I like a good yarn."

"Everyone enjoys a good story."

Hendricks' shoulders relaxed a bit at Jasper's words, but his grip on his cap remained tight. "There was one book in my quarters that I hadn't read. I finally picked it up. It was *Northanger Abbey*—not that one there, miss. A different copy." A smile briefly crossed his face. "Well, it was a corker. And once I finished it, I decided to look around the house to see if there were any more by this Miss Austen."

"And you're enjoying *Pride and Prejudice* as much as *Northanger Abbey*?" Olive asked.

"Oh yes, miss. I'd hate to not know how it ended."

"I can assure you that you're going to enjoy the ending," Olive said. "I certainly won't take it away from you."

Hendricks looked at Jasper, who said, "I'd never interrupt a man's reading. That would be uncivilized."

Relief flooded Hendricks' face. "Thank you, Mr. Rimington, Miss Belgrave."

"Perhaps you were looking for reading material last evening and we interrupted you?" Olive asked.

"No, it's the other way around. I'd—um—borrowed the copy of *Northanger Abbey* earlier that afternoon."

Olive thought of the square bulge in Hendricks' pocket and the way he'd tried to cover it with his hand when Carter appeared in the door behind him.

Hendricks dipped his head toward the expensive volume in Olive's hand. "The copy at Hawthorne House has pictures, you see. I wanted to take a look at them. The book in my quarters is only words. I looked through the one with pictures yesterday afternoon and was returning it when you came into the small sitting room. I'm very sorry if I startled you, Miss Belgrave. I intended to slip in, put the book back on the shelf, and be gone in only a moment."

"Did you see anyone skulking around the grounds last evening?" Jasper asked.

"No, sir. And I would know if someone had been around. With all the rain, they'd have left tracks in the mud. I was all over the grounds this morning and didn't see anything."

"And what about today?" Olive asked.

"No one, miss. And I was out all day, cleaning out the leaves from the drain spouts, except when I had my tea. I have my cuppa out here and have a bit of a read."

Olive handed the books to Hendricks. "Well, you don't have to worry about us telling your secret. Enjoy your reading, Mr. Hendricks."

27

Olive

7 November, 1923

Hawthorne House

The next morning, Olive again found Jasper in the dining room before her.

"Good morning, Olive, old bean," Jasper said. "Sleep well?"

Olive had thought she'd have a difficult time getting to sleep after their encounter with Hendricks, but she'd dropped off to sleep almost immediately. "Surprisingly, yes."

"I find a brisk walk outdoors often produces that effect."

Tromping around the grounds coupled with the heightened atmosphere of trying to keep their activities secret must have been more of a strain than she realized. "And you?" Olive inquired. "How was the rest of your evening?"

"Slept like a babe." Jasper poured himself a cup of coffee, then one for Olive as she took a seat across from him with her plate. "What are your plans for today? Other ideas on where the painting might be stashed?"

"No. And considering my brilliant thought turned out to be completely wrong, I think we should focus on the inventory."

"What rooms are on the agenda for today?"

"Let's move up to the second floor."

"Jolly good. I'll bring the typewriter." Jasper took a sip of his coffee and looked across the room. "Perhaps I should consider an attempt to parlay touch-typing into a regular activity. I could place an advertisement." He swept his palm across the air as if he were reading a sign. "Have typewriter, will travel."

Olive spread marmalade across her toast. "Become a secretary-typist for hire? I'm sure the society ladies would mow each other down to hire you." She grinned at him. "I do realize you're teasing me. You can't quite hide the glint in your eye."

"True. I only type for you, my dear."

"And the War Office."

"In a pinch." Jasper put down his cup. "All right. On to the next floor."

"And once we're done there, the inventory will be complete."

Jasper paused, his hands on the back of his chair as he pushed it under the table. "Don't forget—there are still the attics."

"Oh, you're right." Olive suppressed a sigh. "I hadn't thought of those. I'll have to check with Sebastian and see if he wants them inventoried as well. Has Mr. Carter made an appearance this morning? Perhaps I can speak to Sebastian when Mr. Carter rings him about the missing painting."

"No sign of him. Late riser, remember."

"Yes, but one would think he'd want to report the news of the theft first thing."

"One would think, but it's apparent Mr. Carter wants to put it off as long as possible. If you'll excuse me, I'll gather the typewriter, carbons, and paper."

"I'll meet you upstairs as soon as I finish here."

The bedrooms had a more limited number of paintings, and they moved through them at a quick pace. Olive was writing down the dimensions of a portrait of a young boy on a pony when the noise of a throat clearing sounded behind her. Mrs. Lum stood in the doorway, a frown replacing her usual sour expression. "Begging your pardon," she said hesitantly.

The rapid cadence of the typewriter keys broke off. Jasper said, "Hello, Mrs. Lum. How can we help you?"

"The police sergeant has rung up and needs to speak to Mr. Carter, so I went along to Mr. Carter's room, but it's a tip. It usually is a right mess—he doesn't like me to clean in there. Quite particular he is, but . . ."

Olive had been double-checking a measurement, but she looked up at Mrs. Lum's tone. "You're worried."

Mrs. Lum's shoulders dropped. "Yes, miss. I don't know what to do, what with the police ringing up and Mr. Carter nowhere to be found."

Jasper pushed back his chair. "Shall I have a look?"

"Oh, yes. Please do. The room at the end of the hall, there."

Olive capped her pen and followed Jasper and Mrs. Lum to the open door. Carter had occupied a spacious room with ornate Jacobean furnishings and rich damask wall coverings. "Goodness." Olive paused on the threshold. Mrs. Lum was correct. The room was a mess, with the sheets in a tangled pile and several drawers hanging open.

Jasper opened the wardrobe and glanced at the bureau. "I believe Mr. Carter has done a bunk."

"What?" Mrs. Lum exclaimed and went into the room. "You think he's left?"

Jasper pulled open one of the wardrobe doors. "There's no clothing in here and no shaving kit. I don't see any luggage. Unless he stored it somewhere else?"

Mrs. Lum's gaze traveled to the top of the wardrobe. "No, he kept his suitcase up there, and it's gone. I didn't notice it earlier. I was only looking at the mess. But how could he have left without anyone knowing?"

"Probably during the night," Jasper said. "I'll check the stables and see if one of the motors is gone."

"And I'll call Sebastian," Olive said.

"What about the police?" Mrs. Lum asked.

"I'd be happy to contact them as well if you'd like, Mrs. Lum."

She smiled at Olive. "Oh yes. Thank you, miss. I don't like dealing with them. Talking to them makes me nervous, it does."

Olive assured her she didn't mind—and if it got her on the housekeeper's good side, all the better. After all, she'd dealt with the police rather often, but she didn't mention that to Mrs. Lum. She didn't want to break the fragile bond that seemed to have formed between them.

As Olive and Jasper trotted down the stairs, Olive said, "Well, that explains who took the painting."

"Yes. The local bobby was correct. It was an inside job."

"Mr. Carter didn't seem the most conscientious fellow. I can't say I'm actually surprised by the outcome."

"Neither am I. I'll just toddle along and have a look in the stables to confirm whether or not any of the motors are missing.

I suppose he might've set out on foot and had someone pick him up on the lane as the good sergeant speculated yesterday."

They parted at the base of the stairs. Olive rounded the corner and went along the hall to the small telephone table. Once she reached the local police station, she explained the situation, then asked the operator to connect her to Blakely's home in London. Sebastian's man answered and informed her that Sebastian was not available.

"Please have him call Olive Belgrave at Hawthorne House as soon as possible. I have important information he needs to know."

"I will pass on the message as soon as he returns home, miss," the man replied in a sonorous tone that wouldn't have been out of place announcing names at Court.

Olive replaced the earpiece and sat there a moment, lost in thought. She did hope that Sebastian wouldn't blame her for the loss of his painting. Had her presence and attention to the paintings brought about the theft? Had Carter been planning it all along? Or was it a spur-of-the-moment action? Did her arrival make Carter realize the paintings would be under more scrutiny, and he'd seized his chance to take one?

Olive stood, shaking off her guilty feelings. Whether or not a man decided to rob a house wasn't her fault. She may have hurried Carter along, but he hadn't stolen the painting simply because she'd appeared on the scene. She was walking down the hall, lost in her own thoughts, when something made her stop. "No, surely not," she muttered. She must have imagined it. She retraced her steps to the open door of the small sitting room.

The painting of the woman in the white fur hung on the wall between the two bookcases.

28

Zoe

Present Day

Zoe finished reading the last page of the report. "That's it?"

Jack had caught up with the other pages and was reading over Zoe's shoulder. His gaze tracked along the last lines, then he swiveled toward Zoe, the iron legs of the café chair screeching on the concrete. "There's no more? No summary, no wrap-up?"

"No." Zoe shook the paper. "Nothing like that. This is the last page." She fell back against the chair. The sidewalk café was now buzzing with activity. The tables around them were full, but no one turned a head at Zoe's frustrated outburst. "The painting went missing for a few hours, then was put back? Why take it and put it back almost immediately?"

"Could it have been copied?"

"I wouldn't think so. It was done in oils. It would take time to dry. Oh, here comes the waiter again. I've never had such attentive service." She glanced at a nearby table where plates were being positioned in front of diners with a flourish. The restaurant had been empty earlier in the afternoon when Jack had first arrived, but it was gradually filling with customers as evening approached. "Let's order some food. My head hurts. Maybe eating will help."

"Sure. Let's get something to eat. The food looks good, and if we leave here and go to another restaurant, we'll just have to wait for a table." Jack asked for menus, and they decided on meze, a selection of small plates, so they could sample lots of different foods. Zoe skimmed back over the pages and double-checked that she hadn't overlooked a page and accidentally left it in her messenger bag while they waited, but she didn't turn up any more pages. Their food arrived—olives, skewers of grilled lamb, fresh pita bread, cheese, stuffed peppers, and meatballs—and they ate without speaking, savoring the different flavors and textures.

After they'd devoured the sampling of Greek food, Zoe waved her fork at the last bite of saganaki, fried feta drizzled with honey. "Split it with me?"

Jack said, "No. You go ahead. I want to look at this again." Jack reached for the pages of Olive's report.

Zoe swirled the wedge of cheese through the golden trails of honey. "Why have we never thought of drizzling honey over cheese? It's delicious."

"No idea," Jack said, but Zoe doubted he'd really taken in what she'd said. His head was bent over the last page of Olive's report as he reread it.

Zoe put down her fork and sat back with a satisfied sigh. She ordered coffee for them, then flicked her fingers along the stacked pages of Olive's report. "It has a narrative style to it. It's as if Olive is telling a story. She wouldn't just end it there." Zoe tapped the last line of the page Jack held. "There's no conclusion."

"I agree." He handed her the paper. "Look at the last line again. The copy isn't the highest quality. It's a bit blurry, but look, there, after the last word on the page. That could be a period at the end of the sentence . . . or it could be a comma."

Zoe angled the paper to the light, holding it so it was outside of the shadow of the umbrella. The setting sun was bright enough that it reflected off the white paper, making her squint. It also showed a dot of ink with a faint line, what could be the faded tail on a comma, after the last word. She skimmed up the page, checking the other commas. "Yes, you're right. Look at this comma near the top of the page. It's exactly the same. It's only because it's in the middle of a sentence and surrounded by lower case letters that I read it as a comma, not a period." Zoe dropped the paper to her lap. "This isn't the last page of Olive's report. There's more."

The waiter cleared their plates, and they fell silent as he worked, but once he moved away, Zoe hunched forward. "Do you think Ferris Thompson kept the last couple of pages of Olive's report? Did we miss them?"

Jack looked up from the credit card bill. "It's a possibility. But why would Thompson separate some of the pages?"

"I don't know. They were the most valuable?" Zoe tucked the last page in with the rest of the report and tapped the edges on the table to align them. "Thompson should have arrived in New York yesterday. If he kept any pages back, he should have handed them over to Mr. Best's office already."

"You're going to call Mr. Best's office? If you contact him, you'll have to let him know that *you* know he hired you as well as someone else to go after the pages."

"Oh, I don't think I should call him. Harrington has been the point of contact. Harrington should be the one to reach out to Mr. Best." Zoe picked up her phone and sent a text to Harrington, explaining what they needed to know. "I don't think Mr. Best will take my call. I haven't had any interactions with him. I imagine Mr. Best will be happy to talk to Harrington, though. And if Mr. Best will be straight with anyone, it will be Harrington."

They left the restaurant and made their way back to the hotel. Jack reached for her hand. "You're quiet."

"There is one other person who might have the last pages."

Jack's steps slowed. "Mallory? You think the rest of Olive's report could still be in the houseboat?"

"What if Mallory didn't find all the pages?"

"Her place was a mess."

"Right. What if she looked at that page we have and thought that was the last one, like we did?"

"It's possible."

Zoe took out her phone. Jack looked doubtful. As she dialed, she said, "It's a long shot, but I have to give it a try." The phone rang and rang. Zoe shook her head at Jack and mouthed *no answer*.

"Not surprising."

"Well, we didn't part the best of friends." Zoe shifted the phone to speak into it as the call went to voicemail. "Mallory, this is Zoe Andrews. I know you probably don't want to hear from me, but after we left, Jack and I were able to track down the pages of the report that were stolen from your houseboat. But I think there's at least one page—maybe more—missing. Perhaps they were separated from the others and are still in your houseboat. If you can locate any more pages, I'll pay for them. Give me a call back."

Zoe hit the End button. "Well, I hope that will at least get her attention."

Zoe awoke with a jerk. It took a second for it to register that she was in the hotel in Athens and it was her phone on the nightstand that was ringing, its shrill tone cutting through the darkness like a fire alarm. She grabbed her phone, and Jack propped himself up on an elbow. "Who's calling?"

"Unknown number."

Jack collapsed back onto the pillow. "Send it to voicemail."

"Can't. I have a message out to Mallory, remember?"

Jack rolled over as Zoe answered.

She expected to hear Mallory, but it was a male voice on the line. "I found them—those extra pages you want. Had to turn the place upside down, but I have them. Same price as before."

"Rolf?"

"Yes, of course it's Rolf. Who else would shift through all Mallory's junk? Not Mallory, that's for sure."

"So you found more pages."

The bed creaked as Jack rolled back toward her.

"That's right."

Zoe pushed her hair out of her face. "What do they look like?"

"Old. All yellow, and the ink is faded."

"Typed or handwritten?"

"Typed."

"Great—"

"And you'll pay for them—the same amount."

"That's fine, but I need—"

"Be here tomorrow at seven. You can get them then."

"Tomorrow?" Zoe struggled into a sitting position. "But we're not in Amsterdam at the moment."

"Don't matter to me where you are. Either you're here by tomorrow night, or I start asking around on the internet. I'm sure someone else will be interested."

Zoe looked at Jack as she said, "Okay. I'll be there."

Rolf said, "Good."

"Wait. Don't hang up. Before I travel back to Amsterdam, I need proof that you actually found more pages."

"I'm not going to send you photos of the pages."

"No, of course not. Just send a photo of a few lines—" A dial tone buzzed in Zoe's ear. "He hung up on me!"

"Maybe he doesn't have them after all." Jack's voice was muffled because his head was burrowed into his pillow. "He must have heard the message you left for Mallory and saw an opportunity to take some money off you."

Zoe's phone pinged. "He texted an address and an image." She clicked through to it. A type-written page had been laid out on a table. Another sheet of blank paper covered everything on the sheet except for the first line of text: *which, as you can imagine, was rather a shock!*

Zoe shook Jack's shoulder. "Jack, I think he *did* find it. The line begins with a lowercase word. The paper looks old, and the phrasing sounds like Olive's."

Jack shifted to a sitting position. She looked up, expecting him to be hunched over her shoulder, but the blue glow of his phone lit up his face as he tapped away on it.

"What are you doing?"

"Booking us a flight to Amsterdam tomorrow. Have to be there by seven, you say?"

Zoe leaned over and kissed him on the cheek. "You're awesome. You know that, right?"

"There'll be time for that later, after I've got us checked in."

The steep marble steps to the entrance to the Acropolis were still in shadow early the next morning. Zoe zipped up her jacket against the cool and breezy air. They'd gotten an early start and were packed and checked out of their room. Their bags were back at the hotel, stored away by the concierge, waiting for their return and the taxi they'd booked for eleven o'clock to take them to the airport. They had a few hours in Athens before they had to leave, and they'd decided to make the most of them.

After a quick breakfast, they'd made the trek up the hill to the Acropolis, stopping at Mars Hill. Stepping carefully over the smooth stones, they'd had an amazing view and were able to see down into the Agora, the hub of ancient Athens, which was quiet with only a few tourists moving among the ruins.

"Impressive," Jack said a little later as they approached the Doric columns and the carved triangular pediment of the Propylaea, the entry to the Acropolis.

"And we're not even inside yet." Zoe snapped photos of the gate, which was flanked by the Temple of Athena Nike and a square tower-like structure.

Jack flipped pages in his pocket guide. "That's the Monument of Agrippa, but it sounds as if it was more of a rotating display for whoever was in charge." He skimmed the page. "Originally, there was a bronze statue of a chariot, then it was replaced with a statue of Antony and Cleopatra. When Agrippa took over, he switched that out with a statue of himself."

"And it's empty now." Zoe put her phone away. "Almost as if it's a statement—you can't hold onto power. Time goes on. Leaders fade. Everything changes."

"Well, unless you build on the scale of the Athenians," Jack said as they moved between the towering Doric columns and into the open area of the hilltop where the Parthenon rose in front of them, the west side shrouded in shadows and scaffolding. They crossed the stony ground to the east side, which was free of scaffolding. The stones glowed golden in the morning sun. It looked both massively impressive and fragile. The sturdy columns looked as if they'd stand for another thousand years, but the gaps in the pediment and the pieces of column sections and hunks of marble scattered around the base showed the structure wasn't impervious.

Only a smattering of tourists moved around the flat mesa-like hill. Zoe and Jack circled the Parthenon, then ambled around the limestone plateau to see the elegant caryatids, columns that were sculptures of women. "Copies," Jack said. "The originals are in the Acropolis museum, except for one, which Lord Elgin carted off to England."

"Along with a good portion of the pediment from the Parthenon," Zoe said. "I wish we could go to the Acropolis museum, but we won't have time before our flight." Jack had found them a flight that departed in the early afternoon.

"We'll just have to come back." Jack checked his watch. "We do have time to look at the views." From under the Greek flag, they spotted the Temple of Olympian Zeus with its tumbled column, then they moved around to the south side and looked down onto the ruins of the Theater of Dionysus, a semicircle of stone seating rising in an open-air amphitheater around the stage. Jack tucked the guidebook into his pocket. "Sophocles' plays were performed there. It was originally grass, but the Romans added stone seating for about 17,000 people. Want to take a closer look? It's included in our Acropolis ticket."

"Yes, let's."

As they made their way back across the stony ground of the hilltop, Zoe's phone buzzed. "It's a text from Ava," Zoe said, then read the message aloud. *"Keeping you up-to-date because I know watching the news is the last thing on your mind right now."* Zoe skimmed the news article Ava had attached, then said to Jack, "Vokos has gone to the media."

Zoe hit the Play button on the video of Vokos that accompanied the story. His signature smile was missing as he looked into the camera and said, "My grandmother bought this painting in the twenties. It's very dear to our family. The thought that there's a fake out there—I have impeccable provenance for *my* painting —pains me greatly. My grandmother would be so disturbed. She loved *Woman in a White Fur*. It held a special place in her heart. It was the first painting she bought, the first of what became an impressive collection. You see why I must speak out. All this coverage of a theft! It's nothing but a fake. *My* painting is the real one, and anyone who says otherwise must answer to me."

The video shifted to footage of the Janus Gallery as a reporter said, "Mr. Vokos' statements call into question the ownership of the famous painting. The Blakely estate maintains they own the original Tamara de Lempicka. Mr. Vokos says his family wasn't aware of another painting of *Woman in a White Fur* until recent reports of its theft from a gallery in London."

Vokos appeared on the screen again. "This painting that was stolen in England—where has it been all these years? In a vault, they say! Well, mine has been on display in my home for decades for any visitor to see."

Zoe closed the video, and they made their way down from the high plateau, taking a path that branched off the main walkway to a dirt trail that rounded the south side of the hill and cut between tall grass and wildflowers. "Interesting that Vokos would go to the media," Zoe said as they paced along. The sharp drop of the cliffside hid the Parthenon from their view.

"Vokos is setting the narrative. He wants to control the story."

"He's certainly managed to raise questions about the Blakely family's painting. I hope Rolf comes through with the rest of Olive's reports. Right now, it seems it's the only thing that can tell us what really happened with *Woman in a White Fur*. Oh, now this is interesting."

They'd woven their way through ropes set up to direct foot traffic around the theater and emerged behind the stage. Rows of marble blocks rose above them in a half circle. "Not so different from stadium seating today," Zoe said. Two children were dodging in and out of the rows, their giggles echoing around the amphitheater. Their parents climbed more slowly behind them.

"Unless you're in one of the special seats." Jack nodded to a grouping of marble seats with curved backs. Some had scroll-like details carved into their edges.

"I bet those were pricey."

"Or reserved for government leaders," Jack said with a smile as they walked up through the rows of "cheap seats" to a higher point.

Zoe's phone rang, and she paused to fish it out of her pocket again. "It's Harrington."

"Busy morning in art recovery," Jack said and moved off to explore more of the theater on his own while she took the call.

"Zoe, good morning. I spoke to Mr. Best."

"So soon? I didn't expect to hear anything until later today."

"He's traveling—in Hong Kong, in fact. I left him a message last night after I heard from you. He picked it up a few hours ago, which was morning for him. He admitted he'd hired a private detective to look for details about the provenance of the painting. He's one to cover his bets."

"He is thinking of investing a lot of money in the painting."

"Very true. But he's received nothing regarding the provenance of the painting. The private detective returned empty-handed."

"Then Rolf may actually have the rest of Olive's report."

"Rolf?"

Zoe summarized how she'd reached out to Mallory, but that it was Rolf who'd contacted her with the claim of finding the last pages. "I'll let you know what happens in Amsterdam."

"Excellent. You'll be reimbursed for the expense of the flight, of course."

"Thanks. How are things where you are?"

"I think we'll wrap up here today."

"Good luck with it, then," Zoe said, and they said goodbye.

She glanced around for Jack. He was making his way toward her. "It must be time for us to head for the airport if you're folding the Acropolis map."

"Yes, we'd better go. We can take this path here down to the Dionysiou Arepagitou—that's a pedestrian zone. We take that to the Acropolis Museum. We can catch a taxi near there and go back to our hotel. Ready?"

Zoe surveyed the ruin of the theater, the sheer cliff face, and the small corner of the Parthenon that showed white against the clear blue sky. "Not really. There's so much of Athens we haven't experienced, but I need to see what Rolf has found." Zoe turned away from the incredible view. "On to the airport."

29

It was drizzling when Zoe and Jack landed in Amsterdam. Raindrops tracked down the windows of the taxi as their driver navigated through congested streets. Zoe had booked a room for them at the same hotel they'd checked out of a few days before.

Jack looked at his watch as they drew up to the familiar awning over the hotel's entrance. "Plenty of time to check in and drop our bags before we leave to meet Rolf."

"Good." Chilly air enveloped Zoe when she opened the car door, and she pulled her coat collar closer around her throat. She grabbed her bag from the trunk and darted through the rain to the awning, where she waited for Jack as he paid the driver. The thick layer of dark clouds imbued the day with the feeling of twilight, even though it was still afternoon. It was hard to believe they'd been in sunny, blustery Athens only a few hours earlier.

Jack ducked under the awning. "Quite a change," he said as the doorman held the door.

"I was just thinking that. Let's get another taxi after we drop off our bags. We'll be drenched if we don't, even though it's not far—" Zoe broke off as a woman flew across the lobby toward them.

"Finally! I've been waiting and *waiting.*"

It took Zoe a second to recognize her. "Farina!" Zoe bit back the words *you look terrible.* "What's happened?" The change in Farina's appearance was startling. She wore faded leggings and a wrinkled rain jacket that had a stain on the collar. Her swath of pale white hair, limp and oily at the roots, hung over her face.

Farina shoved her sagging hair behind her ear, showing her nearly makeup-free face. She only had on a bit of lipstick that had worn away except for around the edges of her lips. Without mascara, her pale lashes were barely distinguishable, and her eyes looked smaller. "They wouldn't tell me anything at the reception desk, so I've been waiting here, hoping to catch you."

Jack motioned that he'd be at the reception desk. Zoe nodded in agreement. They didn't have much time, and Farina was distraught. They couldn't just walk away from her, but they couldn't miss their meeting with Rolf either. Zoe drew Farina to a bench in a quiet corner of the lobby. "We left Amsterdam for a few days. Why didn't you call me?"

"I had to speak to you in person. I thought you'd gone on an overnight trip to see Haarlem or Delft. Lots of tourists take short trips like that. I've been in and out of the lobby, hoping to catch you. I didn't know what else to do. I couldn't leave a message with a little secretary—not about this."

Zoe knew Ava wouldn't like the designation of *a little secretary.* "Ava is Mr. Harrington's direct assistant. She's very discreet. You can trust her with any—"

"No! I can't—not with this." Farina leaned forward, her voice lowered. "I know who—" She broke off as Jack joined them.

"We're checked in. They'll see to our luggage." Jack steered Zoe's rolling suitcase toward a bellboy who'd followed him.

Jack took in Farina's distraught expression and sent Zoe a questioning glance. Zoe lifted a shoulder to indicate she didn't know what was going on and turned back to Farina. "Jack and I have an appointment that we can't miss, but I do want to hear what you have to say. Let's meet in a few hours. Can you do that?"

Farina's bare face went splotchy with anger. "No! You don't understand. This is important. I know who has the paintings— all of them. We can get them back—well, you can."

"You know or you *suspect* you know?" Zoe asked, thinking of Farina's insistence the last time they met that Pieter had the paintings.

Farina looked away for a moment as she dragged her fingers through her droopy bangs, then she focused on Zoe. "Look, I wasn't completely honest with you before. Pieter has the paintings, mine and the Tamara de Lempicka. I know he does. I'm sure of it."

Jack sent Zoe a glance full of doubt, and she knew he was thinking the same thing she was—that Farina was a little obsessed. "Farina, I can tell you're very concerned about this, but there's been a new development regarding the paintings. Another person has come forward—"

Farina grabbed Zoe's arm and said in a fierce whisper, "I know Pieter has them because I hired him to steal them."

"Oh." Zoe exchanged a glance with Jack, who looked at his watch and said, "We have about ten minutes."

Zoe turned back to Farina. "We don't have long, but we do want to hear what you have to say." Jack pulled over a chair and sat down with them.

"It won't take long."

"You hired Pieter to steal the paintings?" Zoe repeated the words just to make sure she'd heard Farina correctly.

Farina blew out a deep breath. "Yes, and it's such a relief to tell someone." Her shoulders relaxed. "It was a crazy idea. I knew that, but I thought it might just be the thing to help me break out."

Jack leaned forward. "Break out?"

Farina made little circles with one hand. "You know, get some publicity. You only need a couple of social media posts from someone influential. Or if you catch the eye of a prominent collector, your career can take off. It can make all the difference in the world. It's extremely difficult to break through all the noise. I asked Pieter to help me. I thought I could trust him." Her expression darkened. "Turns out I was wrong."

"What happened?" Zoe asked.

Farina shifted on the bench, recrossing her legs and rearranging the folds of her coat. "It was all supposed to be very simple. I knew the security at the Janus Gallery wasn't . . . impenetrable, shall we say. I knew there was a weakness, the back window in the women's restroom. I'd stopped by the gallery one afternoon to look around and went to a little café nearby for a coffee afterward. I was in line behind two of the employees, who were talking about the sticky window that they couldn't get to fasten completely closed and how the owner would have 'a cow' if he knew they had left it unlocked so they could take a smoke break without going outside."

Farina caught Jack's disapproving gaze. "Very lax, I know."

"So you decided to take advantage of it," Jack said.

"Not me. Pieter. He was supposed to get in, take my paintings along with *Woman in a White Fur*, and disappear—*but only for one day*." Her hand tightened into a fist, and she banged it on her knee as she said each word. "The next day everything was supposed to turn up." She swooshed her hand through the air like a magician pulling a rabbit out of a hat. "It would be just enough time to cause a . . . well . . ."

"A media sensation?" Zoe supplied.

"Yes." Farina crossed her arms tight across her chest. "Pieter was to leave England immediately and come back here. He was supposed to leave all the paintings in a bin bag in a warehouse and anonymously notify the police. But the next day nothing happened." She closed her eyes and sighed again, a long breathy exhale. "There was a media sensation, all right. And Pieter had seen the reports. Once he saw what *Woman in a White Fur* was valued at, he decided he'd keep it along with my paintings."

"So the story about him being a relative of your friend . . .?"

Farina's shock of bangs fell forward over one eye as she ducked her head. "I did make that up. But Pieter is—or was—a longtime friend. I needed a reason to explain why I hadn't gone to the police."

She flicked her head to the side, tossing her hair out of her eyes as she scooted closer to Zoe. "Pieter won't speak to me, but you can convince him to give up the paintings. By now he's got to have realized his plan is hopeless."

"I don't know about that." Farina's expression was so hopeful that Zoe felt she had to tamp down Farina's confidence in her. "If he's blinded by the thought of making a lot of cash from them, he may not be interested in giving them up."

"Please, will you at least try? He won't take my calls, and when I tried to talk to him face-to-face, he wouldn't listen to a word I said. He just walked away. But he has to answer the phone at work." Farina had taken her phone from her pocket and was pulling up her contact list. "I know he's there now. He works Friday afternoons. You'll try, won't you? It's what you do, right? Recover paintings?"

Zoe blew out a breath as questions swirled in her mind. Was Farina telling the truth now? That didn't even take into account all the questions about Vokos and how he'd come to have a painting so similar to the one in the Blakely collection. Farina widened her eyes, and her face transformed into a pleading expression.

Zoe checked the time. "I suppose it can't hurt. We still have a few minutes before we have to leave." She couldn't imagine that it would take more than a few seconds for Pieter to either ignore the call or hang up on her. Zoe glanced at Jack.

He said, "I'll get us a taxi while you do that."

Zoe dialed as Farina read out Pieter's number. When a masculine voice came on the line after two rings, it startled her. "Pieter?"

"Ja, who's this?"

She ignored his question. "I have it on good authority you have some—um . . ." She had to pick her words carefully so she didn't spook him. "Some valuable items, let's say. Artistic things that you're interested in, um, transferring to someone else."

His voice was cautious. "That might be the case, but only for the right price."

"Excellent." Zoe sat up straight and inched away from Farina, who'd scooted over to the end of the bench and was trying to hear the conversation through the phone.

"Who is this again?" Pieter asked, "And how did you get this number?"

"A friend gave it to me. I want to help you."

"Help me?"

"Yes. We both know what you have is valuable. In fact, it's so valuable that it's practically worthless."

Anger flicked through in his tone. "That's sh—"

Zoe talked over him. "What you have is recognizable. With

all the news coverage of the—um, your little indiscretion—no one will touch what you have. No reputable dealer, that is. And how will you find a *disreputable* dealer? Anyone you talk to about selling your merchandise, if they're law-abiding citizens—and most people draw the line at accepting stolen goods worth millions of dollars—the first thing they'll do is call the police. You don't want that, do you?"

Silence stretched out on the line, and Zoe clamped her lips together, letting her words sink in a moment. Farina made a circular motion with her hand, a *get on with it* motion, but Zoe waited a few more beats. Jack came back from speaking with the doorman.

Zoe nodded at him, then said, "Let me tell you about a man I met recently. He'd—um, *relocated* two items—very famous items —from a museum to his house. He thought he could sell them. He couldn't. He didn't have connections. So they sat in his house for months until I tracked them down. Now he's in jail."

"Who are you?"

"Zoe Andrews. The man's name is Bobby Greer. Look him up. It's all online. You've got two choices. Either destroy the paintings"—Farina shook her head in a jerky motion as she reached for the phone. Zoe leaned away, out of range of her hand—"or you get rid of them. Now I think you're a person of taste and refinement. You don't want to destroy a famous painting. You'd be better off giving it up. A whole lot less of a headache for you."

"And you can help me with that." Sarcasm layered Pieter's words.

"Yes. I can. This is the sort of thing I do. We can arrange for me to take the items off your hands."

"And you'll just take them and not tell the police?"

"Of course, I'll have to share details about my suspicions, but

I have no proof you have anything, only ideas. The police don't get too excited about ideas—believe me, I know. And if you don't have the items in your possession, then there's nothing to tie you to them." Zoe glossed over the fact that there might be evidence at the gallery that would link him to the crime. If he were smart, there wouldn't be, but she wasn't about to point out a possible flaw in her argument. And she knew the police wouldn't be as concerned about art theft as other crimes like homicide, but she didn't mention that either. More likely, the police would be happy to do a cursory investigation and close the file, but she wasn't about to mention that to Pieter.

"Let's set up a place to meet," Zoe said.

His breath, huffy and short-winded, came down the line. "No. You just want them for yourself."

Zoe laughed. "Hardly. You really should do an internet search for the name Bobby Greer. You'll see I'm telling the truth."

"Don't call me again." His voice was sharp.

"Don't be hasty." Zoe made her tone as smooth and calm as she could. "Think it over. Wouldn't it be nice to get rid of them? No worry weighing you down? No looking over your shoulder? No—" The dial tone buzzed in her ear. She slipped her phone into her messenger bag. "He hung up on me."

Farina reached for her phone. "I'll call him. He's always been stubborn—idiotically stubborn."

Zoe put her hand on Farina's wrist. "Don't. That's the worst thing you could do. Give him a little time. Let him stew a bit."

"But what if he destroys them?"

"Do you think he will?"

Farina let out a sigh and closed her eyes. "No, not really."

"Good. Then promise me you won't contact him. I'll call him in the morning. I'll get in touch with you and tell you how it went. It's not unusual for these things to take time—days, even. So just back off for a bit. I know it's hard. I don't like to wait either, but it's the best thing to do now."

Farina studied Zoe's face for a moment, then put her phone away.

"You promise you won't call him?" Zoe asked.

She gave a jerky nod. "Yes, okay."

A few moments later, Zoe and Jack climbed into the taxi as Farina jogged across the street to the nearby tram stop. Jack slammed the car door. "Do you think she'll keep her promise?"

"I have no idea. I hope so. I'd have a terrible time backing off. I hope she has more willpower than I do."

Jack grinned at her. "It was quite entertaining to watch you advising patience."

Zoe groaned. "I know. I couldn't believe those words were coming out of my mouth either, but it's true. Look at Harrington —he's been waiting for days to finish the job he's on."

"And look at you. You waited for months to find the Picasso and the Canaletto. You're more patient than you think."

"Only when I have no other choice," Zoe said with a grin. "How much farther to the restaurant where we're meeting Rolf? I'm ready to see those last pages of Olive's report."

Jack made a show of checking his watch. "I'd say about . . . now." The taxi cruised to a stop at the curb near the Rembrandtplein.

Zoe reached for the door handle. "That's the kind of wait I like—a short one."

30

"It should be along this street here," Jack said as they hurried through the rain to one of the streets that branched off the Rembrandtplein, a wide tree-lined boulevard. Restaurants filled one side of the boulevard, their open-air patios deserted. They dodged through the tables with furled umbrellas and into the gastropub Rolf had sent them to. They snagged the last open table. It was off to one side of the packed room, which pulsed with conversation and pop music.

Zoe scanned the room. "I don't see Rolf anywhere." A waitress arrived and was just pulling out her pad to take their order when Rolf appeared behind her shoulder. He said something to her in Dutch, and she left with a shrug.

Rolf wore the waitstaff's uniform of black T-shirt and jeans with an apron tied around his waist. He grabbed an empty chair, pulled it to the end of their table, and took a seat.

He hunched forward and braced his crossed arms on the scarred wood tabletop, which was spotted with crumbs and wet rings of condensation left from the glasses that had just been cleared away. There was no aroma of weed about Rolf today. His gaze was clear and sharp as he surveyed them. Over the noise of the conversation and music, he asked, "You have the money?"

Zoe nodded. "As long as you have the papers."

"I do." Rolf pulled a crumpled envelope from his apron pocket and put it on the table, his hand positioned over it.

Zoe took out the envelope that contained the money, which she had buried deep in her messenger bag. She held it below the edge of the table at an angle that only Rolf could see. She lifted the flap of the envelope and fanned her thumb across the bank notes, then put it back in her bag and held it close to her body. "Does Mallory know you found the other pages of Olive's report and that you're selling them to me?"

"Nah. I didn't want to get her hopes up in case you didn't come through." He reached for her bag, but she tucked it close to her body, crossing her arms over it.

"First, let me see what you brought."

"It's good." A fake smile split Rolf's face. "You can trust me."

She gestured with her chin. "I'm sure I can, but why don't you prove it to me?"

Rolf's smile vanished. "You hand over the money first."

Jack leaned forward, locking his gaze with Rolf's. "Show her what's in the envelope. That's not that hard, is it?"

After a long moment, Rolf broke eye contact with Jack and opened the envelope. He flung the contents on the table. Zoe snatched them up out of the patchy circles of condensation. It only took a quick scan to see the pages looked like they were from Olive's original report. The papers themselves were yellowed and fragile. The typed letters were faded, and the top line on the first page was exactly what Rolf had sent in his photo.

"Well?"

Zoe opened her bag and took out the thick envelope of money.

Rolf's fake smile was back as he snatched the money from her hand. "Pleasure doing business with you." He shoved his chair back and left it in the middle of the aisle as he strode out of the restaurant.

Zoe blotted the wet marks on the aged paper with a napkin from a dispenser on the table. "I wonder if Mallory even knows that he found them. I can see him taking these papers and selling them to us without ever letting her know."

Jack reached over to push the empty chair out of the way of a passing customer. "I think if she didn't know, she will soon. Take a look over there."

Zoe followed the direction of Jack's gaze. Mallory was crossing the grassy boulevard that stretched in front of the restaurant, juggling her umbrella as she untied the strings of a half apron as she walked. Rolf jogged up to her, caught her by the waist, and swung her around in a circle. He set her on her feet and pulled the fat envelope out of his pocket. They both bent over it for a moment, then she flung her arms around his shoulders and kissed him. They paced off, arms wrapped around each other, the umbrella sheltering both of them.

Zoe shook her head as she wiped down the table with a fresh napkin. "That would have been touching if they weren't both thieves."

Jack grinned. "They're amateurs. I don't think they'll make a career out of it. More than likely, they're off to the first coffee shop they can find to splurge." Jack came around to her side of the table. "What does Olive's report say?"

Zoe put the pages down so they could read the final pages at the same time. "Let's find out."

Olive

7 November, 1923

Hawthorne House

Jasper strolled into the small sitting room, his hands in his pockets. "One of the estate motors is gone. I had a chat with Hendricks, and he said it was there last evening—" Jasper halted beside Olive, his gazed fixed on the painting. "I say, you found it. Good show."

Olive couldn't help but laugh. "Not really. I had nothing to do with it. I just happened to notice it as I walked down the hall. I'm glad it's back, of course, but it's decidedly odd."

"Indeed. It was hanging there on the wall?" Jasper used a knuckle to lift the edge of the painting and look at how it was attached to the wall.

"Yes. It looks as if it has never been moved, doesn't it? Almost makes me think I'm going barmy."

"You're not mad, old bean. I can attest it wasn't here yesterday."

Olive turned to Jasper. "But if Mr. Carter didn't make off with the painting, why did he leave?"

"And where was the painting yesterday?"

A new masculine voice sounded behind them. "You mean I've come all the way from London for no reason?"

"Sebastian!" Olive went across the room to shake his hand. Sebastian had a thin build and a rather sickly appearance that reminded Olive of a skeleton because the skin of his face seemed to stretch so tautly over the bone structure of his skull.

"I rang London this morning. I spoke to your man, but he said you weren't available."

"I was on my way to visit a friend nearby and decided to drop in and see how the inventory was coming along." Despite his rather cadaver-like appearance, Sebastian had a busy social life. As far as Olive could tell, he wasn't actually ill, just pasty and anemic. "It sounds as if something interesting has been happening here." Sebastian surveyed *Woman in a White Fur*. "The painting has been missing, has it? You'd better tell me about it."

While Olive told him how the painting had disappeared, Sebastian peered at the canvas, his nose inches from the painting. When she finished, Sebastian said, "Jasper, may I prevail on you to give me a hand? I'd like to take this down and examine the back. I could manage on my own, but since you're here..."

"Of course, old boy. It's a stunning painting. Wouldn't want to take any risks and damage it. But perhaps we shouldn't handle it without gloves."

"Ah, yes. Fingerprints. Good point." Sebastian hadn't removed his coat, and he took his gloves from his pockets. Jasper picked up a blanket from the back of one of the sofas and covered his hands before they took the painting down from the wall. They propped it up in one of the chairs, then Sebastian studied the back as Jasper brushed down his jacket where he'd bumped against the dusty wall. After a few moments, Sebastian stepped back. "Whatever its travels yesterday, it's undamaged and in order. It looks exactly as it did when I purchased it before the War."

"That's good news," Olive said.

Sebastian nodded to Jasper, and they returned the painting to the wall.

Jasper again brushed at his suit coat. "All's well that ends well."

"Indeed," Sebastian said, but he didn't sound satisfied, which Olive completely understood.

She felt the same way.

"Why was the painting removed then returned? And why has Mr. Carter left?"

Jasper said, "Perhaps Mr. Carter didn't realize the painting had been returned, and he was worried about your reaction, Sebastian."

"Leonard's scampered, has he?" Sebastian asked.

"You look genuinely surprised," Olive said.

"I am." Sebastian's manner turned contemplative. "Well, I suppose his reasons will become apparent in time."

Olive glanced at Jasper. "You don't think it might be because of the missing painting?"

Sebastian shook his head. "I doubt that. I've always given Leonard a lot of leeway. Look at the drawing room. I asked Leonard to take care of removing the extra pieces of furniture months ago, and he hasn't even made a start on hiring someone to shift it. Of course, it's difficult when one hires a family member—even a distant one. One can't fire a relative, even if that relative is several times removed. I can't imagine he'd take to his heels simply because something went missing."

Olive was surprised at his words. Sebastian didn't seem the least bit sentimental, but apparently he kept his distant cousin on in the capacity of an estate manager simply because Carter was a relative.

Sebastian glanced at the painting one more time, then turned away from it. "So how is the inventory coming along?"

"It's nearly complete. We're working on the second floor. Do you want me to check the attic as well?"

"There shouldn't be much up there, but take a quick look, if you don't mind."

"Of course. Jasper has typed the reports for me, so we should have everything ready for you later today."

"Excellent, Olive. I knew I could count on you to sort it out."

As they worked their way through the last rooms upstairs, Olive's mind was more occupied with questions concerning Carter than the descriptions of the paintings and their measurements. As they finished in the final room, a little-used guest room with only three small botanical prints, she gave her notes to Jasper and sat down in a chair to wait as he typed them. When he rolled the paper out of the typewriter and added it to the thick stack, she said, "I can't help wondering if Mr. Carter planned to take the painting, then got cold feet when the theft was discovered."

"So he returned the painting and did a bunk?" Jasper said. "It's possible."

The door opened, and Mrs. Lum arrived with a tea tray. "What a turn of events, that painting showing up again."

"It certainly surprised us," Olive said as Mrs. Lum put down the tray. She was clearly bursting to talk about it. Olive thought it must be lonely for her, working in Hawthorne House with no other women around. Olive reached for the teapot. "Care to join us for a cup of tea?"

"Oh, no. I couldn't. Wouldn't be right to sit down with you."

Jasper grinned at her. "We won't tell."

She flushed all the way up to the tips of her ears under her escaping wiry curls. "Thank you, sir, but I have to get back to the kitchen. I have bread in the oven." She moved away, then paused at the door. "I don't understand it, myself. That picture isn't pretty like a nice view of the hills or the ocean, is it? But to each his own, as they say. I don't pretend to understand these things. After all, there was the foreign gentleman who telephoned about it too. The picture must be art if foreigners are ringing up, inquiring about it."

Olive put down the teapot. "A foreign gentleman telephoned about it?"

"Yes. It must have been . . . oh, several months ago. I'd forgotten all about it until today. Rude, he was. Wouldn't give his name so I could pass on a message."

"And he was interested in the painting?" Olive stirred her tea.

"He said he wanted to speak to the owner about acquiring it, but when I said I'd inform Mr. Carter, who would pass on the message, the gentleman became . . . well, huffy and rang off."

Jasper asked, "What sort of accent did he have?"

"Foreign."

"Yes, but perhaps you detected a trace of what country he might be from?" Jasper suggested. "American? Or did he sound more continental?"

"Not American," Mrs. Lum said decisively. "Somewhere in Europe, I suppose. I really couldn't say. I must check on my bread."

Olive held out a plate to Jasper. "That's rather intriguing. I wonder if Sebastian knows about the foreign gentleman."

Jasper reached for a biscuit. "I bet Carter didn't tell him. Perhaps, as you speculated, Carter had arranged to *sell* the painting to this foreign gentleman, but decided it was too risky with our arrival."

"Before we popped in, Mr. Carter had the run of Hawthorne House. No one used the small sitting room. Carter could have taken the painting, sold it off, and the theft might not have been discovered for months." Olive sipped her tea, her thoughts spinning. "But why would Carter remove the painting while we were still here? Why not wait until we'd left?"

"He asked you if we were finished in the small sitting room, remember? Perhaps he was on a deadline and assumed we wouldn't go back into the room."

"It does explain his reluctance to call the police and to contact Sebastian. But then why did Mr. Carter abandon his plan?"

Jasper gestured with his cup. "As you said earlier, cold feet. It became too risky."

"I suppose so." Olive returned her cup and saucer to the tray. "Ready to get on with the inventory?"

"Yes, on to the attics."

They climbed the narrow flight of plain white-painted treads to the attic's full-size walk-in door. Olive pushed it back, expecting to see a gloomy room jammed with furniture—something akin to the drawing room but on a larger scale. However, most of the attic area was open, and a hint of a pine aroma hung in the air. Wooden floorboards stretched from one end of the open room to the other. Rows of dormer windows on each side let in plenty of daylight. A smattering of worn trunks, some wooden crates, and a few pieces of furniture were stacked along the walls, but it wasn't anywhere near the plethora of items that Olive had expected.

Jasper, typewriter under one arm, surveyed the space. "Surprisingly pleasant up here."

"Probably a result of the flights of stairs between the ground floor and here."

Jasper said, "Yes. Much easier to chuck something into the drawing room than heave it up several flights of stairs."

Olive moved around the attic, checking behind steamer trunks and ragged chairs. "Only a few paintings." Olive made notes on the three paintings that were stacked against the wall. She handed her notes off to Jasper, who had set up his typewriter on a rickety table and was pulling a scarred straight-backed chair into place in front of it.

While he typed, Olive wandered around the room. As she neared a bureau that would have been quite nice if it had been refinished, her foot slipped. There was a slick spot on the floor —paint, she realized, as she tracked some of it away on the sole of her shoe when she stepped back.

She leaned closer. A thin line of rich purple merged into iridescent white. The colors ran in a single narrow strip with a sharp edge on one side. The other side was blurred and wavy.

"Jasper, come look at this."

The typewriter bell dinged, and Jasper spooled the paper out. He came and peered over Olive's shoulder, then let out a low whistle, his gaze meeting Olive's. "Those colors look familiar."

"I thought so too." She pointed to the place where the sole of her shoe had smeared the line. "Fresh too." She scanned the attic. "If someone set a wet oil painting down on the floor and propped it up against this bureau, it could leave a mark like that on the floorboards."

Jasper leaned close to the bureau. "Yes, there are a few daubs of white and purple paint here as well."

Olive turned to Jasper, her hands on her hips. "I wonder if Mr. Carter was artistic."

"You think he made a copy of *Woman in a White Fur*."

"I think someone did. We haven't seen anyone else around

except Mr. Carter, Mrs. Lum, and Mr. Hendricks, but someone could have stayed up here out of sight."

Jasper pivoted, his gaze running over the discarded furniture. "There's no evidence that anyone has been staying up here, but I suppose someone could have slept on blankets on the floor."

"Let's have a more careful look around."

They went over the room a second time and didn't find any evidence of a bedroll or makeshift bed, but Jasper discovered an easel, and Olive found squashed tubes of oil paint in the drawers of the old bureau along with a jar of turpentine and several paint-stained rags. Olive pushed the drawer shut, closing off the potent turpentine smell. "That's where the pine aroma is coming from."

Jasper returned from examining the far corners of the attic. "It doesn't look as if Mr. Carter invited someone else in to live in the attic. Mr. Carter is the most likely candidate for the person who was painting up here."

"I agree," Olive said. "But there's still another question—is the painting downstairs an original or a copy?"

The easel began to slip, and Jasper repositioned it against the bureau. "It takes quite a while for an oil painting to dry."

"But Mr. Carter has had free run of the house for years. Until our arrival, it doesn't sound as if anyone used the small sitting room. He could have had both the original and a copy up here, and no one would have noticed. He'd need a canvas, though." Olive said. "I wonder if he made his own?" She waved her hand, dismissing the thought almost immediately. "No, he'd find an easier way."

"It would be rather a lot of work for him to go to—making a wooden frame and stretching the canvas . . . especially when he was surrounded by artwork." Jasper looked at the stack of paintings leaning against the wall.

Olive bounced on her toes. "Oh! The inventory. The original one from before the war." She dashed across the wooden floorboards and retrieved the paperwork, paging through the older inventory that Sebastian had given her before she arrived at Hawthorne House. She'd been putting a tick beside each painting as they re-inventoried Sebastian's collection. She skimmed down the row of checks, then pointed to a blank space. "This one. It's the only one we haven't found. *Summer landscape with flowers* is the description. It measures thirteen and three-quarters inches by ten and a half."

Jasper flipped through the freshly typed inventory. "Let me check the entry for *Woman in a White Fur* . . ." He grinned. "It's the same size."

Olive took the tape measure from her pocket and laid it on the floor next to the line of paint. "Thirteen and three-quarters inches. Just the same as the painting from the old inventory that we haven't found."

"Oh, I think we know where it is. It has a fresh coat of purple and white over it, and I bet Carter is on his way to deliver it to one unspecified foreign gentleman."

Olive stood and slipped the tape measure into her pocket. "I'd better find Sebastian and give him the news. I hope the good news that he's lost a minor landscape outweighs the fact that it seems Mr. Carter made a copy of one of his favorite paintings."

"As long as his *Woman in a White Fur* is the original, I think he'll be quite happy."

As they bumped down the drive the next morning, Jasper's

motor rattled and shuttered with every dip in the road. "Well done, old bean. You inventoried an art collection and uncovered a forgery."

"We did."

"I'm only a lowly assistant, remember."

"You're much more than an assistant, Jasper."

"I should hope so. Who else can you count on to traipse about the countryside in the dark of night?"

"Only you, Jasper."

He nodded. "That's correct."

"I'm glad we sorted out that Mr. Carter made a copy of *Woman in a White Fur*, but I do hate to leave without knowing *exactly* what happened."

"We have most of the answers. Mr. Carter was an artist and had the skill to copy the painting."

Sebastian had confirmed that Carter had shown artistic talent in his youth and had studied art at university. Carter had dabbled in painting, but he'd had more success in copying other artists than with his original artwork, so he'd abandoned a career in art—at least for a while. Sebastian had contacted the local police, who'd spread word to London and Scotland Yard, but there had been no sightings of him yet.

Thankfully, Sebastian had reacted as Jasper predicted. Sebastian's main concern was for his painting, *Woman in a White Fur*. He'd even thanked Olive for exposing Carter's actions. "You've rousted the man out of my life. I predict he'll take his forgery and pawn it off on some unsuspecting boob, then he'll lose all the blunt in some glamorous location like Monte Carlo. That's where the police should look for him—in the play-grounds of the wealthy. Of course, I doubt they'll find him. He's the sort who will live by sponging off others. He'll hopscotch from one wealthy widow to another so quickly that I'm sure he'll stay out of the police's crosshairs."

The car bounced in and out of a rut, and Olive clamped her hat to her head to keep it from slipping over her eyes. "I know we worked out what happened here at Hawthorne House, but what about who Mr. Carter was going to sell his copy to? Aren't you curious?"

"Of course I'd like to know, but sometimes we don't get all the answers."

"I suppose you're right. I do hope that someday it's all sorted out."

Jasper slowed to maneuver the motor through the hedgerow that bounded the grounds of the estate. "These things have a way of working themselves out. It might take years, but I'm sure the forgery will eventually come to light. Someone will figure out there are two paintings of *Woman in a White Fur*."

Olive gripped the seat as Jasper turned onto the road and they accelerated away from Hawthorne House. "Then the issue will be figuring out which is the original and which is the forgery."

31

Zoe
Present Day

Zoe put down the last page of Olive's report—and she knew it was the last page because the text stopped halfway down, and Olive had signed her name under the last typewritten line. "Well, now we know where *Woman in a White Fur* was when it went missing in nineteen twenty-three—the attic of Hawthorne House. We just don't know where it is *now*."

"It sounds as if Pieter has it," Jack said, "according to your conversation with him."

"Yes, I think he probably does have it." Zoe returned the pages to the envelope and put it deep in her messenger bag. "I think a visit to Lux is in order."

"Thinking of a little more B and E after the store closes to see if Pieter hid the paintings there? That's how these things go. You get a taste for it, the adrenaline rush, and then—"

"Just a little observation. I want to see what Pieter does when he leaves work."

"You want to follow him home, see where he lives."

"Possibly."

"And *then* do a little B and E."

"No. I promised. No more of that sort of thing. I just want to see how he looks and where he goes. Check up on him."

"Just keep an eye on him. Right. Got it."

The rain had stopped, but a layer of nearly translucent clouds veiled the sky as they walked to the Nine Little Streets area of Amsterdam. Pieter was still at work in Lux. It was easy to spot his ginger hair through the shop's window. Zoe and Jack found a restaurant down the street and had no trouble getting a table on the damp outdoor patio where they could keep the store in view. They ordered a dinner of steak and Vlaamse Frites.

Zoe savored the crisply fried strips of potatoes, then asked, "What do you think about Farina's story?"

Jack paused, his knife and fork poised over his steak. "You don't think she's telling the truth? That's quite a story to invent."

"I know, but Farina is the type of person who likes drama and . . . flamboyance."

"You think she's exaggerating?"

"No, I don't think so." Zoe took a sip of her drink, her gaze fixed on the shop down the street. "But I don't completely trust her." Zoe put down her glass. "Pieter is leaving."

Jack didn't turn around. "Closing up?" He signaled for the check.

"No. There must be somebody else doing that tonight. He's just walking down the street."

"Might be a smoke break. You go ahead. I'll catch up."

Zoe settled her messenger bag over her shoulder and set off at a slow pace. There was plenty of foot traffic and she wasn't worried about Pieter noticing her, but she still left plenty of space between them as she trailed him to the canal. He turned left and paced along the water at a good clip until he came to a bar. Zoe walked by the bar and got in line at a stroopwafel stall where she could keep an eye on the bar. It was in a building that had been updated. Four large plate-glass windows lined the street. The interior was done up in a modern aesthetic with chrome bar stools and white walls. The only color came from the row of televisions across the back wall, flashing news and sports.

Zoe texted Jack her location, and he joined her a few moments later. "I got a quick look as I went by," he said. "Pieter's at the bar, having a drink by himself."

Zoe handed him a paper-wrapped stroopwafel. "Dessert."

"Thanks."

"Let's go over to that bench under the trees that faces the canal." Zoe took a seat and watched one of the low glass-enclosed water tour boats cruise by. "Can you see him?"

Jack was turned toward her, his arm propped up along the back of the bench as he looked over her shoulder. "Yes. He's still at the bar, watching the televisions." They finished their stroopwafel while Pieter sipped his drink. "He doesn't look too worried or seem to be in a hurry," Jack reported. He crumpled his paper wrapper and reached for hers. "I'll throw them away."

While he went in search of a trashcan, Zoe slid over and took up his position on the bench, angled so she could watch Pieter. He was chatting with the bartender, but then his head whipped up, and he focused all his attention on one of the televisions.

The bartender moved away, but Pieter remained completely still, his gaze riveted on the TV.

Zoe squished down so she could see what he was watching. An image of *Woman in a White Fur* filled the screen, then a photo of Vokos replaced it. After a few minutes the video switched to another story. The moment the video ended, Pieter tossed some money on the bar and stood, leaving his half-full glass. He surged out of the door and was striding down the street by the time Jack returned. Zoe said, "Pieter's on the move," as Jack fell into step with her.

"He's almost jogging," Jack said as they raced along, threading through pedestrians to keep Pieter's bright head in sight. "Maybe he's late for something?"

Zoe shook her head. "I don't think so. A news report about the de Lempicka painting came on, and he flew out of there the moment it ended."

"Interesting." They had to drop back when Pieter left the bustling tourist area around the canals. The streets were pleasant and wide, each side lined with parked cars and bicycle racks below rows of modern multistory apartments. After several blocks, Pieter trotted up the steps to the double glass doors of one of the apartment buildings, punched in a code, and disappeared inside.

They crossed to the opposite side of the street, still keeping well back. The trees that lined the street along with the rows of parked cars provided some cover, but Zoe still felt exposed in the quiet residential area.

Jack looked at Zoe. "Now what?"

"I don't know. We can't stay here. If he comes out, he'll see us right away."

"Let's walk past his building to the street at the other end." Jack moved so he was on the side by the apartment. The block dead-ended into a busy four-lane road with a tram stop. They could just see the door to Pieter's apartment building, and they lingered on the corner for a bit with Jack's head bent over his map as if they were lost tourists.

After two helpful Dutch citizens offered to help them find their destination, Zoe said, "This isn't doing us any good. We might as well head back to our hotel. It'll be dark soon. We can't stand around here all night. At least we know where he lives now."

"We *think* it's where he lives. He might be visiting someone."

"Good point."

Jack changed out his map for his phone. "We might be able to find out, though. What did Farina say his last name was?"

Zoe stared at the sidewalk for a moment, then looked up. "Ecker. That was it. Pieter Ecker."

He checked the street sign and began tapping on his phone. After a few seconds, he said, "The internet comes through again. There are a couple of links to Pieter with this street address, so I'd say this is probably where he lives."

Zoe grabbed Jack's arm and pulled him around the corner of the building, out of sight of the apartment. "Pieter just came out again, and he has a long narrow tube like the kind you use to carry rolled blueprints—or paintings."

"That news story must've spooked him."

Zoe inched around the building to keep an eye on Pieter, who headed in the opposite direction from them. He threaded his arm through a strap attached to the tube and adjusted it so the tube rested on his back, then he bent over one of the bike racks.

"Oh no." Zoe gripped Jack's arm. "He's getting on a bicycle. We'll never be able to keep up with him."

Jack scanned the street and zeroed in on a hotel. "There are two taxis in front of that hotel. I'm on it."

Jack sprinted away while Zoe kept an eye on Pieter. He settled on the bike and pedaled down the street away from her.

A taxi cruised to stop beside her. Jack swung open the door.

The driver asked, "Where to now?"

Zoe slammed the door. "Down the street. Follow that—um—bike." She leaned back against the seat. "Now's there something I never thought I'd say."

32

A s the taxi cruised through the streets, Jack leaned forward. "Don't get too close."

The taxi driver gave them a curious glance in the rearview mirror but eased off the gas. After a couple of blocks, they reached the busy tourist area. Their driver didn't have trouble following Pieter because he stayed on the road that followed the canal.

The driver said, "You know bikes can go places cars can't. I may not be able to follow him."

"Then let's just hope he stays on the main roads. If he turns off to a pedestrian area, we'll get out." Zoe gripped the back of the seat and pulled herself up straighter so she could have a better view ahead of them.

Jack followed her gaze. "What is it?"

"I think we might not be the only ones following Pieter. I can just see a woman with whitish blonde hair on a bike weaving along not too far behind him."

"Farina?"

"Looks like it. Although I didn't see her on the street where Pieter lived."

"If it's her, she must've been lingering somewhere, watching him like we were. I'm getting rusty if I missed her."

"She could have been in another building," Zoe pointed out.

Pieter stayed on the main road, following the curve of the canal, then he turned and navigated around the trams, cars, and pedestrians in the Leidseplein, a large square with restaurants and hotels. All the while, the blonde woman pedaled a few yards behind him.

As their taxi turned toward the Leidseplein, Zoe caught a glimpse of the woman's profile. "It *is* Farina."

Their driver edged through a light at the last moment and followed Pieter over another canal bridge. The entrance to Vondelpark was congested, and they had to wait at a red light. Pieter and Farina disappeared into a phalanx of bike riders beyond the red light. The light changed, and Zoe scanned the throngs of people biking as they surged forward. "I don't see either Pieter or Farina now."

Jack pointed. "There. Pieter's heading for the Rijksmuseum. I don't see Farina, though."

The driver switched lanes, shaking his head. "I can't go in there—"

"We'll get out here." Zoe was already swinging the car door open as they coasted to a stop. Jack handed the driver some euros, and they scrambled out.

They jogged through the arched tunnel that cut through the museum. The Rijksmuseum was still open, and late evening museumgoers were milling around the doors. They threaded through the clusters of people, then lengthened their strides as they cleared the other end of the tunnel, coming out into the twilight. Their pace slowed to a jog, then they both stopped as they neared the shallow reflecting pool. "So many people!" Zoe said. "How will we ever find them again?"

"Look for people with bikes. That hardly narrows it down in Amsterdam, but it's something," Jack said as they skirted around the reflecting pool. The Museumplein stretched out in front of them. The smooth rounded wall of the Van Gogh Museum glowed, its glass wall illuminating the walkway between it and the other museums. Sidewalks crisscrossed the wet grassy area, and people were ambling along while children kicked soccer balls, sending up sprays of water from the damp lawn. Beyond the gift shop, food stalls lined one side of the open area. Some of the stalls were closed, but several had remained open to serve the late museum crowd. Zoe scanned the people milling around the stalls. She reached for Jack to pull him in the direction she was looking. "By the herring stand. That's Farina."

They dashed forward, but a large group of tourists following a tour guide cut between them and the food stalls. By the time they worked through the crowd, Farina was gone.

Zoe's phone buzzed, and she dug in her messenger bag. The number was familiar. "It's Pieter."

Quick, rough breaths came across the line when she answered, then Pieter said, "You didn't say that Vokos was involved in this." The sounds of wind and the distant laughter of kids came through the phone.

He couldn't have gone far. He was obviously still outdoors. "Vokos?" Zoe asked, playing for time as she turned in a slow circle, skimming the crowd for Pieter's ginger hair.

"Yeah, Vokos. I'm not messing with him."

"What do you mean?"

"If he has anything to do with . . . what we discussed earlier today, then I'm not involved." His breath was choppy, and Zoe had to strain to hear his words over the sound of a tram bell.

Zoe whirled around to look for the nearest tram stop. As she moved, she mouthed the words to Jack, *he's near a tram.*

Jack jogged closer to the stop by the Van Gogh gift shop, then came back, shaking his head. "I don't see him."

Pieter was probably riding away on his bike and had been passing a tram as it slowed at a stop. Pieter's rough breathing drew her attention back to the phone conversation. "So I'm not involved. Do you understand that? I had nothing to do with anything. As far as you're concerned, you never talked to me."

Zoe opened her mouth to tell him she couldn't make any promises, but Pieter didn't pause. "I'm out. Done. Go to the Museumplein, to the stall selling herring. It's the first one you come to when you walk from the Rijks down to the Van Gogh. Go to the middle table and have a look around."

He cut the connection.

Zoe put her phone away, already walking toward the food stalls as she told Jack what Pieter had said. Zoe kept looking around for Farina but didn't see her either. "How could we lose them both?"

"It's a big area full of people—perfect for losing a tail."

The herring stall was closed. A man was lowering the last big panel and locking it into place, covering the service counter. He moved off down the sidewalk, avoiding eye contact with them, which was just fine with Zoe.

A couple of trestle tables stood to the side of the food stand under an awning. Zoe and Jack went to opposite ends of the middle table and ducked down. A tube was taped to the underside of the table. They shared a grin as Zoe pulled it free. Heart beating fast, she unscrewed the lid and edged the rolled contents out a few inches. "It's canvas, not paper."

"Zoe." Jack's voice was low and soft, the tone one would use when they didn't want to frighten off a scared animal. He was looking beyond her shoulder. Zoe spun around, the tube still firmly gripped in her hands.

Farina stood holding a bike by the handlebars. All her concentration was fixed on the tube. Farina walked forward, rolling the bike along with her. "Did Pieter leave that?"

"Apparently." Zoe tipped the contents fully onto the table, and the roll unfurled.

The painting on the top was one of Farina's, the black dot on the white background. Zoe lifted the edge of it, revealing the inverse painting, the one with a white dot on a black background. Zoe blew out a breath and inched that painting aside. Rich tones of purple and a shimmering, luminescent white showed up sharp and clear even in the dimness under the awning with sunset fast approaching.

Farina muttered something in Dutch, and the bike clattered to the ground. She collapsed onto the bench of the picnic table. She leaned forward, her hands over her face, and let out a shaky gulp.

The tube began to roll away across the table. Zoe caught it as she asked, "Are you okay, Farina?"

Farina sat up and ran her fingers under her eyes. "I'm fine. It was just the stress and worry. How did you get him to give them up?"

"I didn't. It was something he saw on television—the news story about Vokos. Did you see that?"

"Yes. But I don't understand. Why would that cause Pieter to give them up? Vokos' painting has to be a copy. This is the real one—it has to be. It was in Sebastian Blakely's estate and has been for decades."

"Apparently Vokos has a shady reputation, which Pieter

must have known about. Pieter said he didn't want to be associated with anything to do with Vokos."

"Well, I don't care why Pieter gave them up. I'm just glad he did." Farina wiped her eyes again and blinked a couple of times. "Well, this is wonderful."

Zoe took out her phone and scrolled, looking for the name Harrington had given her. "I'll call a contact I have in the Amsterdam police and let them know we've recovered the paintings."

"Now? You're going to call them now?"

Zoe zipped through the contact list. "We have to. We don't want to be on the hook for them."

Farina stood and leaned toward the paintings. "Let's wait. I can take them directly back to London first thing in the morning."

Jack deftly slipped the paintings out of her reach and began to roll them up. "You want to transport stolen goods?"

Farina turned her attention away from Jack to Zoe. "You don't have to call the police. Just call the Janus Gallery. Tell them you've located the paintings, and I'll bring them in tomorrow."

Zoe found the name, dialed, and put the phone to her ear. "Farina, we have to call the police. We need to lay everything out and let them know what happened. This is an international police matter. You can't just cart stolen art across borders."

Farina flexed her hands into fists as Jack fed the paintings back into the tube. "No. There's got to be a different way."

"I'm afraid not." A voice came through the phone, and Zoe turned away slightly from Farina's pleading gaze. "May I speak with Superintendent Visser? This is Zoe Andrews. I'm an associate of Harrington Throckmorton."

Metal rattled, and when Zoe looked up, Farina was nearly to the street, her coat flapping out around her as she pedaled away.

A voice came on the line. "This is Visser."

"I'm sorry to interrupt your evening, Superintendent, but I have some good news for you about some missing artwork . . ."

33

Zoe contemplated the enormous pancake the waiter placed in front of her. "After running away from us last night, I still can't believe Farina was on the news this morning."

Jack leaned back as the waiter set a plate in front of him. "She couldn't resist the spotlight."

After spending most of the previous night answering the police's questions and coordinating the return of the painting, Zoe and Jack were in a pancake restaurant. They'd ordered pannenkoeken, or Dutch pancakes, which were dinner-plate sized. They'd had their choice of sweet or savory accents. Zoe had opted for strawberries while Jack had gone for basically the fruit salad pancake. Bananas, strawberries, blueberries, and raspberries topped his.

Zoe spread her paper napkin in her lap. "Well, Farina's certainly spun her story to wring every drop of publicity out of the situation." The news story they'd seen that morning as they walked through the hotel lobby had English captions, and they'd stopped to watch it, amazed to see Farina smiling at the camera.

Jack drizzled syrup over his pancake. "And she told the whole story too. That was surprising."

"Yes. I didn't expect that either." Farina had held nothing back. Without mentioning names, she'd told how she'd hired someone to steal the three paintings, and of her dismay when the thief hadn't followed her instructions to give them up the next day. Zoe took the syrup bottle Jack held out. "But I think I understand what she did. Just like Vokos, she wanted to get ahead of the story and set the narrative for the media. She played up her role as an underdog. Her story is that she couldn't get any traction with the snobby art community, so she had to subvert the establishment. Public sentiment will be on her side, and the police will look bad if they want to charge her with anything. She's the new Banksy—well, except she's far from anonymous."

"Who?"

"The graffiti artist whose painting was shredded when it sold at auction, remember that?"

"Vaguely."

"There was a paper shredder built into the frame. When the gavel came down, the shredder was switched on and cut the painting into strips, but it malfunctioned. Only half of the painting was shredded. The media ate it up, of course. I bet that's what Farina hopes happens to her too."

Jack tilted his head at the television mounted in the corner of the room behind Zoe. "Looks like she's succeeding. They're running the story again."

Zoe twisted around. Farina, looking spectacular with full makeup and a snazzy black jacket, stood in front of the Rijksmuseum, a light breeze teasing her freshly styled white bangs. Captions scrolled across the bottom of the screen. *Never meant*

*for it to turn out the way it did ... horrified when they didn't turn up .
.. sort of a joke that got out of hand ...*

Zoe turned back around and picked up her fork as Jack said,
"Now, Pieter, he's different. I think he'll lay low for a long time.
He's probably halfway across Europe now."

The police had gone to Pieter's apartment, but he'd cleared
out. He'd used his metro card to get to the train station, but the
police hadn't been able to trace him from that point.

Zoe forked up a bite of the pancake. "I agree. Pieter wanted
zero attention from the media or the police."

Jack sipped his coffee. "So now that the paintings are recovered, what do you want to do? We have several days left, and our
return flight is open."

"Well, Harrington's paying for wherever we go next. He said
he'd underwrite the rest of our vacation. We should pick somewhere good."

"Tahiti," Jack said instantly.

"That could be fun, but I do think there might be a teensy
issue on the reimbursement for that."

"I suppose so. Harrington is generous, but you're right. Even
he might balk at an overwater bungalow."

"We could go back to Greece. We only saw a little bit of the city.
We didn't even get to explore the Agora or the Acropolis Museum."

Jack nodded. "I could do with another gyro."

"And the temple of Poseidon isn't that far away. It's supposed
to be amazing, not to mention Santorini."

"I'm sold." Jack put down his coffee and took out his phone.
"There might be an evening flight we could get on."

Zoe concentrated on eating while Jack scrolled, her thoughts
clicking away over everything that had happened over the last
few days until she realized Jack was speaking.

"I'm sorry, what did you say?"

Jack slipped his phone into his pocket. "I said there's a flight at seven."

"That'll be perfect."

"You're preoccupied."

Zoe put down her fork. "I think I know what happened in nineteen twenty-three."

Jack speared a blueberry. "We already know what happened in the twenties. Carter painted a copy of *Woman in a White Fur*, took it to Greece, and sold it to Vokos' grandmother."

"Yes, but I think I know what happened with the provenance documents." She inched forward on her chair. "I've been thinking about it ever since we left the police last night. Did I tell you that the original bill of sale for *Woman in a White Fur* was missing from the Blakely estate's paperwork? We had to get a copy from the artist's estate."

"No, I don't remember you mentioning that."

"The information Harrington was given was that it had been destroyed in a fire in London during World War I. But what if the bill of sale was stolen?"

The waiter refilled their coffee cups. Once he moved away, Zoe moved the salt and pepper shakers to the center of the table. She lifted the salt. "Let's say this is the original painting." She put it to one side. "It stays in Hawthorne Hall." She picked up the pepper. "Let's say this is the copy. What if Carter took the copy of *Woman in a White Fur* along with the original bill of sale?" Zoe put her napkin beside the pepper. "If he had the paperwork"—she set the pepper on the napkin and dragged them to the opposite side of the table—"to prove it was an original de Lempicka painting, it would be so much easier to sell it."

Zoe sat back and crossed her arms. "In the early twenties it would have been much easier for Carter to sell his copy as an original than it would be today. Communication wasn't like it is now—for people or for the police forces. It seems Blakely was content to enjoy his painting and not make it known that a copy had been made, which isn't uncommon when someone's been swindled. They don't want the world to know about it. Later, the Blakely family must have assumed that the documentation had been lost—destroyed in the firebombing during World War I in London."

Jack said, "Clever—on Carter's part."

"And no one ever did an inventory of the paperwork. Olive's inventory focused on the physical paintings. She didn't check any of the provenance records. Nobody looked for the original documentation until now."

Zoe picked up her fork and swirled a bite of pancake through the strawberry-flavored syrup. "I don't think there's any way to prove it beyond a shadow of a doubt. But if the paperwork that Vokos showed me checks out as being from the early 20th century, then . . ."

The waiter removed Jack's empty plate. "That's probably what happened."

"I do like it when all the questions are answered—all the wrinkles ironed out." Zoe sipped her coffee. "Poor Olive. She figured out the painting had been copied and that Carter had taken it, but she never knew what became of it after that."

"Sometimes it takes years to find a good solution to a problem. Speaking of that . . ." Jack reached into his jacket pocket and pulled out a sheaf of papers stapled together. "Take a look at that."

Zoe retrieved her napkins and wiped her fingers before reaching for the papers. "Is this what you were doing in the business center this morning?" Jack had received an early phone call. He'd showered, kissed her while she was still groggy, told her he'd be downstairs, and gone out the door humming an upbeat tune.

"Yep."

There was something—a hint of excitement—in Jack's tone that made Zoe give him a long look before she flipped back the blank cover page. She read the title aloud. "Partnership proposal?" She skimmed down the page, then nearly dropped the paper on her syrupy plate. "You want to go into partnership with me?"

"You've been talking about taking on a partner, haven't you? You're swamped with business. You need someone."

"I do. But what about your business?"

"That meeting I had last week in London took an interesting turn. One of the executives from Fulsen offered to buy me out."

"But you've worked so hard. You're finally established, and the business is going great."

Jack fiddled with a spoon from an unused place setting. "Maybe a little too great." He put down the spoon and held Zoe's gaze. "That's what I've been thinking about lately. We're both run off our feet. We don't have time to spend with each other. We had issues with my work pulling us apart last time. I don't want that to happen again."

He reached across the table. Zoe slid her hand into his. "You'd give up your job for me?"

"It's not quite the noble self-sacrificing move you make it sound like. The work's not quite what I thought it would be." He stroked his thumb over the back of her hand. "I love the security aspect of it, but"—Jack wrinkled his nose—"chasing down clients and finding new client leads wears me out. If I'm honest, I really dislike that part, and I have to do it to keep the business going." Jack squeezed her hand. "Your business, however, is different. People are coming to you. You're overwhelmed. You need someone to help you. And Fulsen wants to keep me on as a paid part-time consultant for a year to ease the transition and troubleshoot any issues. While I'm doing that, you can be training me in art recovery."

"Now that sounds like a very interesting proposal. I like it."

"Good. You can think it over—"

"Jack, when have you ever known me to think anything over? I like the idea. Let's do it."

"Okay, then." Jack unlinked their hands and extended his. "Should we shake on it?"

"I have a better idea." Zoe leaned across the table and kissed him on the mouth. "Partners in love and work. Sounds ideal."

EPILOGUE

Retired Greek businessman and art connoisseur Darias Vokos was astounded to discover a painting, *Woman in a White Fur*, owned by his family for decades was actually a forgery, not the original oil painting by the famous Art Deco artist Tamara de Lempicka. "I was shocked to learn it was a copy. Shocked!" Vokos said. "We had no idea."

Vokos' painting had hung in his grandparents' home, which he inherited, since the nineteen twenties. The original painting of *Woman in a White Fur,* which was in London, hadn't been on display "for decades" according to the owner, Rosalind Kingwood, because of concerns over theft.

"It was too valuable to leave it hanging on the wall in Hawthorne House. We had to put it in secure storage."
The de Lempicka painting was first seen in public only recently when Kingwood decided to sell it, and it went on display at Janus Gallery in London.

In a strange twist, the painting was stolen from the London gallery along with Farina Vee's *Titled* and *Untitled* in a now-famous publicity ploy. The three paintings were later recovered in Amsterdam.

Both paintings of *Woman in a White Fur* were examined by experts. "After extensive testing, the painting owned by Rosalind Kingwood was determined to be an original de Lempicka, while Vokos' painting was determined to be a copy," said Daniel Janus, owner of the London gallery that handled the sale of the original painting. "Mr. Vokos owned a very good copy, but it is a copy nonetheless," said Janus.

Vokos was saddened to learn that his grandmother had been defrauded when she bought the painting, but he's purchased the original *Woman in a White Fur* and plans to hang it and the forgery side-by-side in his new gallery, which will open to the public next year.

THE STORY BEHIND THE STORY

T hank you for joining me for Zoe's final adventure. Yes, I'm sad to say that this is the final planned *On the Run* novel. You'll notice I said "planned." Life has a way of taking interesting turns, so I never say never, especially when it comes to books and writing. There might be another Zoe book in the future, but for now, Zoe and Jack are in a good place, and I'm setting the series aside.

The idea for *Duplicity* had been percolating for a while, but it didn't fully come together until a writer friend and I talked about crossover books. I thought about how much fun it would be for one of Zoe's investigations to revolve around one of Olive's cases. I enjoyed interweaving the storylines of two favorite characters, but juggling two timelines was a challenge!

For a refresher on art theft investigation, I again dipped into Robert K. Wittman's book *Priceless: How I Went Undercover to Rescue the World's Stolen Treasures*. On the flip side, I read Anthony M. Amore's book *The Art of the Con: The Most Notorious Fakes, Frauds, and Forgeries in the Art World* to get the inside story on how con artists work in the art world. While the story of

Carter's con is completely fictional, Amore's book documents many recent cases of fakes and forgeries that fooled art collectors, brokers, galleries, and auction houses.

While *Woman in a White Fur* is a fictional painting, the artist Tamara de Lempicka is a well-known Art Deco artist. Her paintings capture the vibrant, sophisticated atmosphere of the twenties and thirties.

If you're a reader of the *High Society Lady Detective* series, you'll recognize Sebastian Blakely, who appeared in the first book, *Murder at Archly Manor*. When I thought about the character who would own *Woman in a White Fur,* I knew Sebastian was just the sort of person who'd collect that painting. It was fun to explore Sebastian's legacy as a famous photographer and link the two storylines through him.

The Dada art exhibit described in the book is a creation of my imagination. I also made up most of the art pieces. However, the postcard of the *Mona Lisa* is an actual piece of Dada art. I took the liberty of adding it to my fictional exhibit in London for this book.

As I read books and research, I'm always collecting interesting facts, storing them up for future stories. I found it fascinating that during World War I, valuable artwork from the National Portrait Gallery had been shipped to country houses to get the paintings out of London. Hawthorne House, with its remote location, seemed a perfect spot to send valuable canvases to keep them safe from Zeppelin raids. As an interesting side note, paintings from the National Portrait Gallery as well as artifacts from the British Museum were moved to London tube stations and tunnels to keep them safe.

I traveled to both Amsterdam and Athens recently and thoroughly enjoyed both cities. Thanks to Kathy for her helpful tips on what to see and do in Athens. I didn't make it to all the places she suggested, so I'll just have to go back. Also, thanks to my readers who suggested travel destinations for Zoe, and to Leslie for sharing her travel suggestions for the Netherlands. Again, I couldn't see it all, so a return trip is in order. Check out the *Duplicity* Pinterest board to see my travel photos as well as images of Tamara de Lempicka's artwork and links to ideas and inspiration for the modern and historical storylines.

I hope *Duplicity* gave you a fun and interesting armchair travel experience as well as an inside look at art heists and recovery. If you'd like to keep up with me and my books, you can sign up for my updates at SaraRosett.com/signup. I'd love to stay in touch!

ABOUT THE AUTHOR

USA Today bestselling author Sara Rosett writes lighthearted mysteries for readers who enjoy atmospheric settings, fun characters, and puzzling whodunits.

She is the author of the High Society Lady Detective historical mystery series as well as three contemporary cozy series: the Murder on Location series, the On the Run series, and the Ellie Avery series. Sara also teaches an online course, How to Outline A Cozy Mystery, and is the author of How to Write a Series.

Publishers Weekly called Sara's books "enchanting," "well-executed," and "sparkling." Sara loves to get new stamps in her passport and considers dark chocolate a daily requirement. Find out more at SaraRosett.com.

Connect with Sara
www.SaraRosett.com

ALSO BY SARA ROSETT

This is Sara's complete catalogue at the time of publication, but new books are in the works. To be the first to find out when Sara has a new book, sign up for her updates.

On the Run series

Elusive

Secretive

Deceptive

Suspicious

Devious

Treacherous

Duplicity

Murder on Location series

Death in the English Countryside

Death in an English Cottage

Death in a Stately Home

Death in an Elegant City

Menace at the Christmas Market (novella)

Death in an English Garden

Death at an English Wedding

CPSIA information can be obtained
at www.ICGtesting.com
Printed in the USA
BVHW031950181021
619254BV00013B/81